HONOLULU NOIR

Honoré Noir

HONOLULU NOIR

EDITED BY
CHRIS MCKINNEY

BROOKLYN, NEW YORK

Published by Akashic Books
©2024 Akashic Books
Copyright to the individual stories is retained by the authors.

Series concept by Tim McLoughlin and Johnny Temple
Map of Honolulu by Sohrab Habibion

Paperback ISBN: 978-1-63614-198-5
Library of Congress Control Number: 2024936194

Akashic Books
Brooklyn, New York
Instagram, X, Facebook: AkashicBooks
E-mail: info@akashicbooks.com
Website: www.akashicbooks.com

To Susie Bright, a champion for Hawaii writers

ALSO IN THE AKASHIC NOIR SERIES

FORTHCOMING

NI'IHAU

KAUA'I

NORTH PACIFIC OCEAN

OAHU

SEE INSET MAP

HONOLULU

61

KAPALAMA

KALIHI

CHINATOWN

DOWNTOWN

KAKA'AKO

ALA MOANA

TANTALUS

PUNAHOU

ALA WAI

WAIKIKI

MANOA

HONOLULU
WATERSHED
FOREST
RESERVE

72

H1

KOKO
HEAD

DIAMOND
HEAD

HAWAII

MOLOKA'I

LANA'I

MAUI

KAHO'OLAWE

ISLAND OF HAWAII

TABLE OF CONTENTS

INTRODUCTION
A Tsunami of Colonization

When one thinks of Honolulu, I'm sure "noir" is not the first word to pop into one's mind. Instead, one thinks surfing and hula—white sandy beaches and crystal-blue waters. Honolulu is a vacation destination. It's a sanctuary for those seeking warmth during winter, sunny solace for the overworked and landlocked worldwide. Tourists want Honolulu and Hawaii in general to be what they imagine. They want their money's worth. The powers that be in the state also want to preserve and promote this image for obvious financial reasons. Tourism is the state's biggest industry.

However, when I think of Honolulu, where I was born and still live, my mind often harkens back to the Europeans who made earliest contact with the indigenous people of these islands. Famously, Captain James Cook was the first European to find the island chain in 1778. About a year later, he was stabbed to death by Native Hawaiians. The European sailor who was the first to lay eyes on Honolulu specifically, merchant ship captain William Brown, didn't make it out alive either. He was also killed by Native Hawaiians. Of course, eventually, the tsunami of colonization washed over the islands. The killing of white explorers for breaking *kapu*—the code of conduct of the Native Hawaiians—stopped, and the wiping out of the Native people, mostly through disease, began. And the deliberate eradication of Hawaiian culture, perpetrated by Christian missionaries, soon followed. Between the time of Cook's discovery in 1778 and the year 1900, 90 percent of the Native Hawaiian population perished.

After Captain William Brown's misfortune, Honolulu was first established as a whaling port. And from there, the town grew. In 1850, it was declared the capital of the Hawaiian Kingdom by King Kamehameha III. It transformed into a city that exported sugar and pineapple to the United States. In the 1800s, Melville, Twain, and Robert Louis Stevenson visited and found it a "worthy" place to write about. And while Native Hawaiians died in droves, business was booming. Labor was imported from Japan, China, Portugal, and later, the Philippines and Korea, among other places. A new dialect, an English-based creole, was born so that all these plantation workers could communicate with each other in the sugarcane fields. We call it pidgin, and it still thrives today. By 1893, the monarchy was overthrown by the plantation owners, and in 1898, Hawaii was annexed by the United States. In 1899, the first car came to Honolulu. In 1900, the first auto theft followed (I credit historian Gavan Daws for this tidbit). I'm not even into the twentieth century, and I'm telling you that, tragically, Honolulu is a great place for noir fiction.

The sugar and pineapple fields are now gone, and tourism is king, the hotels and resorts the new plantations for those who live here. And we have our problems. To this day, Native Hawaiians and other Pacific Islanders are disproportionately incarcerated and victims of poverty in a place where the average cost of a single-family home has skyrocketed to a million dollars. It's not uncommon for four generations of a family to live in the same house. Drugs, homelessness, child abuse, and sex trafficking are pervasive. Development on sacred land still persists with impunity. There's also a tough-guy, testosterone-fueled feel to this city. Outside the handful of affluent neighborhoods, one can't drive more than several blocks without seeing a tattoo parlor or mixed martial arts gym. Among our present heroes are MMA champions Max Holloway and B.J. Penn. Before them, there was Akebono, the first grand sumo champion born outside of Japan, and Super Bowl champions Russ Francis, Jesse Sapolu, Mark Tuinei, and a prolific list of pro boxers and wrestlers. That attitude that led to the demise of the first explorers who arrived over two hundred years ago—it still exists. *Kapu* may no longer be enforced, but there's still a code here. A proper way to act. And it's honored with fists. I'm not just talking about males either. We have *titas* and *mahus* who can scrap.

Unlike most American cities, Honolulu (and Hawaii in general) is also a place teeming with myth. Pele, the goddess of fire; Kanaloa, the god of the ocean; Laka, the goddess of hula; and Kane, the god of creation and sky—Native Hawaiians have always had their own gods, and the supernatural continues to endure in the consciousness of this place today. From *mo'o* (shape-shifting lizard spirits) to *'aumakua* (ancestral spirits transformed into creatures like sharks and owls)—nature and myth are still often intertwined in just about every art practiced here. The Japanese, Chinese, and others brought along their spiritual beliefs well over a century ago and added to the vibe. To this day, there are places considered haunted, and practices to avoid (for example, don't take pork from one side of the Pali Mountain to the other or bad shit will happen to you). I challenge anyone to find me an American city with more believers in ghosts per capita.

Honolulu is also the great bridge of the Pacific. And

when it comes to noir, this makes it a setting with unique potential. There has been a yakuza presence here as far back as I can remember. Cocaine distribution is rumored to be run by the Mexican cartels along with Samoan gangs on the West Coast with connections to Hawaii. It's been said that much of the crystal meth was originally imported from South Korea. We used to know who ran organized crime in Honolulu, or at least some of its major players. Back in the day (in the 1970s and 1980s), there were Charlie Stevens, Henry Huihui, and Ronnie Ching. They bribed judges. Their body count included informants, a labor leader, the son of a prosecutor, and a state senator. When I was a young child, names like these were spoken with fear and reverence. Now, it's a mystery who runs the show. The feds come here and clean house every handful of years. The names of the corrupt quickly come and go. Today, most likely, no one entity or group lords over crime in Honolulu. Like just about everything else, whether it be land or the rackets, it's being gobbled up by outside forces from both East and West. Outside forces so powerful and scary that the few in the know don't want to talk about them, and most don't want to ask. This leaves a lot of room for fictional speculation. When you're a small island chain that's part of an empire, it's hard not to feel like you're just being slowly digested.

I was excited to be tasked with editing this anthology because the setting of Honolulu for the purposes of noir is and always has been full of possibility. Wherever crime, poverty, and corruption exist, noir is easy, and despite its glossy reputation, Honolulu has all these things. On top of that, I'm betting this will be one of the most diverse anthologies in Akashic Books's impressively popular and abundant collection.

Native Hawaiian writers like the great Kiana Davenport, Lono Waiwai'ole, and Christy Passion have contributed. Writing vets Mindy Eun Soo Pennybacker and Stephanie Han are Korean Americans, one born and raised here, and the other, who has roots here, has made Honolulu her home. Michelle Cruz Skinner is a well-known Philippine American writer. Scott Kikkawa, our resident historical noir novelist, is of Japanese descent. Then there's the mutts (part Japanese and part other stuff) like me, B.A. Kobayashi, and Morgan Miryung McKinney. Hawaii is the only state where Asian Americans and mixed-race Americans outnumber white residents. That's reflected in this collection. The prolific Alan Brennert, Don Wallace, and Tom Gammarino generously round out the list of authors. I'm deeply grateful to all of these contributors.

We all mostly get along in this city in the middle of the Pacific Ocean, about 2,500 miles from the closest continent. And when we don't? Well, you can read all about it here in *Honolulu Noir*.

Chris McKinney
Honolulu, Hawaii
July 2024

PART I

ONE-WAY TICKET

THE SWIMMERS

BY STEPHANIE HAN

Waikiki

There is always an hour of light after people decide to go home. The desire to remain in the moment, to linger on, those few minutes before memory crystallizes, yields a melancholy before anything has passed. Kevin wanted everything to be over. He stood on the curb, towel in hand, ready to swim before heading back to his hotel room. He had walked to the end of the beach after working all day, tracking the financial markets, occasionally glancing out the window to take in the view of the shallow end of a kidney-shaped pool and a row of trash cans. He had flown in from Hong Kong for divorce mediation at the end of the week and had paid for a lousy hotel. Trixie wouldn't allow him to stay in the condo. *Burning money*, thought Kevin angrily. All the more reason to split.

By the time Trixie pulled up to the beach to drop off Connie, the sun had begun its slow descent, a cool evening breeze blowing through the trees. Drops of rain? Wind? Kevin looked out at the blue and the people sprawled on the sand. A lifeguard tower in the middle. Beyond the orange wind sock, the flag on a pole that marked the reef. Everyone in paradise having the time of their lives.

Kaimana. Or what did people call it? Sans Souci? *Without worry, my ass*, thought Kevin. *What a bullshit name*. To the right, the crumbling War Memorial Natatorium, an abandoned salute to swimming exhibitions; to the left, a single hau tree in the middle of the lanai at a hotel restaurant. Strangled. Green and concrete. Waikiki.

He and Trixie had stayed at that hotel for their wedding, days before they moved to Hong Kong. He played a few pickup games across the street. Soccer, not football. Back then, Trixie had been excited to move overseas, but a few years later on that very beach, she'd announced, "I don't fit in there. It's a former British colony. And don't tell me there's more to it."

"There's more to it. And a short history lesson my little American: Hawaii's a former colony. Briefly a British one. And you married a Brit."

"It's polluted."

"Run the air purifier. You sound like a pathetic flag-waving jingoist. *America—America*—what's that song?" he laughed.

"You sound like a British colonizing asshole."

"That's right. FILTH: Failed in Life, Try Hong Kong."

"Is that a brag?"

"Where else can a white guy jump four social classes when he steps off a plane?" he joked.

"Anywhere in Asia. Well, frankly, here too. But I want to come back home."

Hawaii: who didn't like the place? Kevin gazed at the ocean. It was beautiful. But there was no work. Tourism. Military. What else? Trixie's family. For fuck's sake, that made it all the worse. Stuck on an island in the middle of the ocean with goddamn in-laws? Hong Kong wasn't ideal, but at least there wasn't anyone Trixie was related to, or even knew for that matter, which made life a lot easier.

Clouds inched across the sky, the bright blue giving way to

a quiet gray wash. Brisk wind skipped off the water; a white foam rimming long strips of turquoise, receding into the horizon, air and water melding into the possibility of time until it all disappeared with a green dot. They packed up: Tourists with matching hotel towels, locals with thin rubber slippers and aluminum tins of leftover macaroni salad. Adults shoved snorkels and masks in plastic bags, tossed coolers and grills in the back of cars and trucks. Children ran back and forth, squealing when they stepped on the blankets of scattered pricklies and pine needles that fell from the sway of the casuarina trees edging the sidewalks of Kapiolani. The water was choppy, crisscrossing waves breaking one after another in staccato rhythms.

"The water looks rough. The tide. It's after six," said Trixie, barely glancing at Kevin. She peered out the front window of her car and pointed. "Look at the flag. The wind is strong. It's nearly straight."

A small orange wind sock confidently flew. Just 250 meters out, the flag lightly fluttered back and forth but was held in position by a steady wind. Fifteen knots? Twenty? Kevin studied the water. Sure, there were waves, the ocean wasn't flat, but he had planned swimming for the day's workout. He never missed his routine. Connie could do it—he better after all of those swimming lessons. Instruction cost a small fortune. They would swim together. Kevin's back had been bothering him, but swimming would be good for it. What other upside was there to this miserable trip? He wasn't getting any sun, and who the fuck goes to Hawaii and comes back to the office with no tan? The water was fine. Trixie worried about everything. When they first met, he had teased her, thought her worries endearing. *Everything will be fine.* Now she pissed him off.

"Pick up Conrad in an hour," he ordered.

Trixie held up Connie's bag and gestured for him to grab it. "He's spending the night with you at the hotel."

Kevin leaned into the car window and whispered, "Trixie, give me a break. Please, for fuck's sake. I have a full day tomorrow."

"You haven't seen him for three months. You could eat dinner together."

"No, I can't. I don't have time." He was exhausted. He needed to unwind, hit the gym, get room service, catch up with Becky about their holiday plans. Trixie didn't get how tired he was, of course. What did a sixth-grade teacher know about an eighteen-hour time difference?

"I'll pick you up in an hour," she told Connie.

"I thought I was staying with Daddy."

"Listen, mate, we'll do it at the end of the week, okay? And we can have burgers and watch movies—the kind Mommy says you can't watch," said Kevin with a wink.

"Bye, Mom!" said Connie, laughing, trying to climb on his father's back.

"You and Daddy stay on the inside. The water's choppy now, sweetheart," she said to the boy, looking at Kevin.

"Tell Mommy you're a big kid, Connie. You're ten. She shouldn't treat you like a baby."

Connie shouted to Trixie, "I'm not a baby, Mom!"

"I know, Connie, but the ocean is always the boss. Not you. Not Daddy, right? Okay?"

Kevin pulled on his goggles and looked at Connie through the blue tint. The boy was a slender frame of skin and muscle, lanky, his hair splashed light by sun. As a baby, he had been blond. Now and then Trixie had mentioned how some people didn't know she was Connie's mother, but they always knew he was Kevin's son. Back then, he enjoyed being seen as a father and had proudly showed off his son. A beautiful baby parted crowds. It had been hard getting used to coming in second to his son. Trixie once declared he was jealous of Connie, but that wasn't true. He had adjusted. Parenting just wasn't something he had envisioned unfolding as it did—it never stopped. There were moments: watching him run through the playground, scooping him up and carrying him to bed. He knew it was like that for all parents, but somehow he still resented the small infringements of time, how, in short, he couldn't do whatever the fuck he felt like doing. In the end, he still did whatever he wanted—but the extra weight bothered him.

Divorce, at least, was a way to get rid of the lies. He had written in his journal: *No one understands the misery of the liar. We're misunderstood, dismissed, but the burden is so very real. We who lie are the only ones who see the truth, and we're blamed by all for seeing it.* He felt the slightest twinge of discomfort that Connie wouldn't spend the night in the hotel, but no kid was a path to relaxation, and he was looking forward to talking to Becky about the trip. They'd started planning it right after Trixie served him papers. The perfect divorce bonus: a proper kid-free holiday. What would he do with Connie anyway? Thinking about how to manage him over Christmas had annoyed him. He would absolutely *not* use his days off for babysitting. He would work that out later. This December, at least, Trixie had Connie. He played it up a bit, how it was best for the kid to be near grandparents, how he would miss him, but how he was willing to sacrifice this first Christmas and let Trixie have him. He had sealed it with a few tears.

The next day she told her lawyer she didn't want alimony. His lawyer told him whatever he'd said must have worked—since they'd been married for twenty years, she was entitled to it. Kevin hadn't expected that from her, but even so, child support—which he did believe in, after all, he was the father—was going to kill him. He'd grown up with nothing back in the England. Trixie was wrong. He wanted to give Connie what he hadn't had. But the boy needed perspective, they all did. Money brought freedom, but this didn't mean that *he* should be paying for everything Conrad wanted, or needed for that matter. Success was the ability to delay gratification. He had been a sociology major—basic shit to understand. You don't let a child run the fucking show, and real life is real life.

"Stop telling Connie to try his best," he had told Trixie. "Trying is for losers. You make it or you don't. Quit making him fucking soft."

"He's only six years old."

"At this rate, he'll never work."

"What? You want your son to be a goddamn Victorian chimney sweep?"

"Some of us had to work for things, Trixie. Not all of us were given everything."

"He's your son. Why wouldn't you want him to have opportunities you didn't have?"

The more money he made, the angrier he felt. He was the only one in his family to attend college, to leave that fucking hellhole behind, that town, that country. What did she know about it? Look how she grew up: Private school. Tutors. He would have liked to have had music lessons, gone to France to learn French. Such bullshit. She had turned away from it—rebelled by marrying him, some might say. He wouldn't have burned away what she did, like her father did. Her old man was now broke. All the more reason to split.

"Dad—Mom told me not to swim to the flag," said Connie, looking out at the water, tapping Kevin's shoulder.

"We all know that Mom doesn't like to have fun," said Kevin. Connie laughed. "Think you can swim to the flag?"

"Sure."

"You're probably faster than I am," said Kevin.

"Yeah, probably! You're old and slow."

"Old?"

"You have white hair."

"So will you one day."

"You're ancient. And you have wrinkles. Mom said haoles get them faster."

"That's nice of Mommy to say. So I guess half of you will wrinkle faster."

"That will be so weird. Half my face. Like this," said Connie, contorting one side of his face.

They waded out and then Connie jumped on his father. "Hey, knock it off," said Kevin, sharply. "My back, you're gonna fuck it up!"

Startled, Connie nervously paddled a few feet away.

"Hey, I mean, watch your dad's back. Right? You're heavy now. We're going to do this. Then burgers and movies on Friday, right?"

"Yeah," said Connie tentatively. He submerged his head underwater and then came up for air, keeping his distance.

The waves were breaking. But it was only 250 meters out. Lifeguards had gone home for the day. The tower was empty. They would be fine. It was about pacing. Everything was timing.

"When you get tired, just tell me. Dad's got you . . . Okay,

Conrad, show me how you swim." *Focus on the swim*, thought Kevin. Connie was a good kid. At least the boy liked sports. He was fast. And he kept up, more or less. It was easier now that he was older.

The crawl. Reaching and extending, Connie a few paces behind at Kevin's feet, and Kevin slowing down to let his son shoot ahead. Even kicks. Hands pulling through water. Freestyle. Ripples and breathing. Connie angled his head and grabbed air on his right side; Kevin on his left. Cinder blocks. Fish darting about. A pipe. Rocks. Within a few minutes they were out ten, fifteen, twenty feet. They cut through a small school of silver that caught the light. Man and boy. Swimmers, the two of them.

Kevin had hired a swimming coach only a year ago to perfect his stroke. It had bothered him that Trixie swam so well. Now, after a few sessions, he was a superior swimmer. It didn't take much to beat her. He had wryly reminded Trixie that he'd learned from his father, a self-taught swimmer, unlike her, who had taken years of private lessons. It was important to point this out, he thought. Looking at Connie's technique, Kevin could see that in a few years his son would surpass him. No need to compete with his own kid about swimming. A skill one must have, but of relatively minor importance.

Connie reached out to touch Kevin's leg and paused to tread water. "Trumpet fish!"

"Cool," said Kevin. "Let's keep going, mate."

Connie kicked ahead and Kevin followed.

The water turned cooler. Swimming was easy, they were pulled straight to the pole with the orange flag on top. Moving with the current. The water held them. Swimming was good to clear the mind, except when it couldn't.

Fuck Trixie. He loved Connie, but damn it, he did everything for the boy, and what was he, Kevin, getting out of it exactly? Why was it all so difficult? Connie's tuition, activities—what the hell, it cost him a fortune. Trixie made everything worse. No, he didn't want to play with Connie. Did it look like he had time to kick a ball? No, he couldn't watch Connie for the afternoon. Isn't that why they had a nanny? Didn't Trixie see how exhausted he was, providing for the family? No, he didn't want to bring Connie to school on his way into work—that would mean he would have to take the ferry that left fifteen minutes earlier—he needed those minutes in the morning, damn it. No. No. No. And now she was getting a PhD? *Who has time for that? I would do it too, but I am very, very busy. I am forced to do this because you are incompetent,* he would rage. Bitterness. Indifference. All of it.

He needed his life back, away from both of them. They'd been apart a year now, commuting back and forth, but now he could face the truth: he had never wanted to join them. What a relief that it was all out in the open. Sure, he had missed them at first, who wouldn't? He did feel something. But it was a new chance! Now he was reframing everything. He could be someone different. He felt sorry for himself. They were the reason he was doing this fucking job. And what for? Finance had bored him. Yet here he was. Did he ever want a family? He had left one back in England. Here he was, divorcing, and nothing was right. It was a huge mess, and this was not how he'd planned his life at all. *Fuck Trixie.* She had ruined his life. Well, it was now going to be his turn to ruin hers.

Divorce was a good start. He took some smug satisfaction in knowing that however bad he felt, she would feel worse. His own parents had split. So yes, divorce happened. He was filled with loathing. He wanted her to feel miserable. The desire was intense. He would bankrupt her. Ruin her. Do whatever he could. He'd already started posting about it. She had blocked him. Public opinion was important. She never understood that, ever. He would win that. He had to win. He kicked harder and pulled his arm tighter to his body.

He hit his foot and felt the hard rock on his instep. He twisted to look—a little blood, but he'd live. So much for swimming to forget it all. Where was Connie? He turned to the side and saw the kid lagging behind, steady but faltering. He swam over and held the boy up while they both treaded water.

"Connie, I got you, we're almost there. Ten feet."

Connie coughed and snorted. He looked up at his father. "I swallowed water."

"We're almost there. Hold your breath. Get to the pole," he directed. A wave came forward, and they went underwater. The boy clung to him. Kevin pushed Connie forward. The boy kicked away from his father and grabbed the pole. There, under the orange flag, with one hand held on to a jagged outcrop of rock. Connie tried to position himself to stand, but the waves were too strong, and he sank into the water, letting his legs float out and holding on with his hands. He wore a steely expression, pushing down the anxiety, refusing to give in to his fear. Kevin held Connie's arm with one hand and grabbed the pole with the other. Next to each other. Floating.

Tossed by the waves. Holding on.

"I got you, mate."

Connie breathed and shook. The sky had quickly darkened. Farther out, the waves were breaking. Bigger. It had taken ten minutes at the most to get to the pole. Why did it seem so far? Connie held on. As the waves broke across the reef, he held his breath. Kevin placed his arms around Connie.

"Rest here a bit. Fun, eh? An adventure. Just you and me, Connie. Hold your breath!"

The boy released one hand from the pole and clung to his father instead. "Daddy, I'm tired."

"No problem, dude. We got this." Kevin looked back to shore. No one at the lifeguard tower, as far as he could see. All the equipment in for the evening. Not a big deal. Had the waves gotten bigger since they swam out? Nothing to really worry about, just had to catch a breath for a few minutes, and then they would head back to shore, ride some waves in. Connie first, push him off. Then he'd follow. They'd do it together. Trixie was right, thought Kevin begrudgingly. It was late in the day.

Connie stared resolutely at the waves, and when they came, he held his breath, went under, and then surfaced. He looked at Kevin with an expression Kevin understood. Fear. Connie was afraid of him.

How long had they been at the pole? His son had pushed his goggles up on his forehead. "It's not so far back, Connie. We only swam, what, ten minutes."

"We'll be okay," said Connie, coughing.

"That's right, mate."

"Beach looks far away. The people look small."

"And they get smaller the farther away you are," said Kevin, admiring his own joke. He smiled, a little too wide, at Connie, who stared back, glassy-eyed. He had to reassure his son. This was his job. "Connie. Awesome swimming. We go back against the current. So swim parallel to the shore, right?" He pointed. "Mommy told you, didn't she, about that? Then we'll head straight back in."

"Wave," said Connie, looking ahead. He pulled his goggles down and clutched the pole with both hands. The two went underwater and held their breath as the water swirled and lapped their bodies, and then surfaced. Kevin spit water out.

"Easy-peasy. Goggles, okay?" said Kevin. Connie nodded. "Push off of my thighs. Get this wave. I'll follow you."

They were off. Connie's body neatly moved into the wave. Kevin followed. It dropped them ahead, and then the boy started swimming against the current. Pushing too hard, not moving with the water. Kevin saw and could feel the water. They had to swim parallel now and move out of it. Diagonal to the shore. Parallel to the shore. What the fuck was it? Just not against it. Kevin felt himself tense up and then reminded himself to relax. He swam next to Connie. *Don't fight the water. Don't fight anything.* Fight. Fight. Fight. He was sick of it.

It wasn't who he was. This was all Trixie's fault. She had made it impossible for him to be himself. He felt foolish for even thinking this, but Connie had changed everything. Or was it Trixie all along? It was a mess, the two of them, the three of them. No, not him: *them.* It didn't feel great letting Connie know about the divorce, but afterward, he told Trixie it was time they started living their own lives, not just for Connie. She had stared back at him and said nothing. This was not his fault! It was everyone's fault! Connie's! Trixie's! Everyone, not just him, needed to take responsibility for the years he had lost! He was so done. He wanted Trixie out of his life. He was over it all.

Dead, he thought coolly. He wanted her dead.

During his last visit, he had taken Connie down to the gym with his boxing gloves. He had been complaining to Trixie that Connie was becoming one of those kids who only pretended to be tough, the kind who showed off but got knocked down in a second. The kind of kid who got beat up for mouthing off to the wrong person. If he didn't watch it, he was going to get it from someone who was the real thing, Kevin told Trixie.

"What's your problem? He's ten. What do you want from him?"

"Trixie, you don't understand how it works."

"Kevin, Connie lives in a different world than you did."

Connie had put on the boxing gloves and started bouncing up and down, dancing on his toes. He jabbed and missed. He laughed, ran in a circle around Kevin, shuffled in, and smacked Kevin on the back. Hard. Kevin stepped back, surprised, and shouted. *The punk behavior of a loser*. Just looking at his boy stoked his anger. He didn't know why. No rational reason.

He's Trixie's son, thought Kevin, enraged. *Weak*.

Connie had dropped the gloves in front of his face and stepped back in fear. His eyes had met Kevin's and just then the boy twisted his face into a tight grimace, leaned in, and swung hard, a right hook. Kevin reached—a sharp jab straight to Connie's nose. The shock had stunned them both. Connie began crying hysterically. He backed away from Kevin in terror. He had done this to his son. Why? He didn't mean it. He didn't. He had it coming to him, but still, he didn't mean it. Blood poured from Connie's nose. It was an accident. How else was he going to learn the lesson? There were assholes out there and Connie knew nothing, thought Kevin. Right? Right? What had he done? Okay, the nose wasn't broken. He hastily cleaned up Connie's nose. *You're good, mate. Great fighter. Daddy is so sorry, but you're okay, you handled it! Excellent. You don't want us to get in trouble with Mom.*

He now felt a body on his elbow. Connie. The boy was dog-paddling next to him through the waves, barely keeping up. Why were they so high? He could feel the current. He grabbed the boy's shirt to drag him in. Connie was tired. It had started to rain. Kevin felt like they had barely moved. The top of his foot throbbed. Hard to see, but they were getting closer. He grabbed Connie's shirt, pulling him. The boy was helping; he kept swimming. Kevin felt the urgency. He stopped for a second. "I have you. I won't let go."

The plan had been to bankrupt Trixie. Let her experience what he had lived. Maybe then she would understand. The plan was unfolding. Becky was taking over part of the mortgage, and together they had kicked off the real estate agent who Trixie knew, and cut a deal with another. Trixie had hired a lawyer in the US, two in Hong Kong. She was slowing it down. He had warned her before that they didn't need a lawyer, they could work it out between themselves, they didn't have to follow the law. Who followed it anyway? But no, she had refused to believe him, and now money was burned on legal fees. Her death would make it a lot easier. Bankrupting her alone would not kill her. He had to win. Trixie was a fucking cockroach. They survive nuclear war—if she were there right now, he would throttle her.

She didn't care about anything but Connie. She had easily capitulated when he'd threatened her. *If you do that one more time, I will take Connie away from you so fast, you will never see him again.* Why had he said that? He only knew that he had scared her, and he hated her for that. He despised her for her compliance. She surrendered and did whatever he demanded because of Connie. He bought a fucking house. He worked to stick Connie in private school and the little shit was flunking. He was angry at the entire mess. He didn't want to pay her a cent. He would fucking kill her if he could. But then, he'd be stuck with Connie!

He wanted out.

It would kill her to lose Connie. She would never recover. Ever. The funeral. Yes, that would be where they would come together. Trixie would forgive him, and they would cry together, and he would be able to enjoy her mourning and misery, and at the same time, comfort her. To relish guilt, he had once explained to Trixie, was one of his intimate pleasures. He wasn't Catholic anymore, at all. The nonsense was nonsense; but that feeling of knowing something was wrong, yet staying, almost willingly, in that moment of misery. The longing for it to go away, while understanding the impossibility of it ever leaving. He never thought about why, exactly, he enjoyed the feeling, but he did.

The entire drama would be a performance, and yet would absolve him of any potential accusation of ill intent with anything divorce-related. She would comply, sign the paperwork to the house, the condo, sign off on whatever money she had, thought Kevin. He would generously give her some, of course. Encourage her to get her life together. People would go on about the death of a child, and unpleasantly sniffle or sob, but the divorce itself would fade to the background. Trixie would never want to get back together with him, and he didn't want that either, but at least there would be a kind of public dignity to the whole thing and the money could be sorted. Everyone would say that the parents would suffer. No mention of Becky. He imagined the kind words. He and

Trixie, mourning the loss of their son. Thinking about it was touching, really. They hadn't always argued.

The morning of their wedding, Trixie had flung open the curtains of the hotel room and asked him if he wanted to go down for a quick swim. He had declined. When she came back, she burst into the room upset, shaken. She had been pulled out by a rip, hours before their wedding.

"I almost drowned. I could have drowned," she said, breathing heavily.

"Don't swim without me. Don't ever swim without me," he had responded softly. He'd hugged her tightly, and she began to cry with relief.

"I could have drowned. I could have drowned."

"I'm here. Don't worry, Trixie. I'm always here."

The feeling. What would he have done without her? What would be the point of anything?

He couldn't imagine. She had to be there always. He would never let her drown.

Life without Connie would kill her. She deserved the worst. She ruined everything. *Connie's getting heavy*, thought Kevin. The boy continued to kick, his arms reaching out, pulling the water in his gently cupped hands. Connie's shirt was in his fist. He tried to guide the boy out of the current. The kid was tiring, but he had him. They were attached.

Kevin's grip loosened and his fingers butterflied open, releasing the fabric of Connie's shirt. Kevin had felt the boy's back bounce against his fist while the ocean churned up and down, the stretch of the material playing Connie like an accordion between his knuckles and the water's pull.

Life hadn't started that way. There was the day when they'd dug a hole together on the beach in Hong Kong. Con-

nie was small, four years old? The two of them had begun
with their hands, and then there was the small garden shovel,
a real one that the boy had insisted on taking to the beach.
Connie had run into the water and then back, excitedly
helping Kevin dig. The hole got bigger and bigger.

"It's very deep. We're digging a hole to China," said
Kevin. "Except we're already there."

"Can this hole be my house?"

"Your house?"

"We can both live in it, Daddy. See, I fit. Let's live here
forever. I love you, Daddy."

"Yes, forever," said Kevin. "I love you too."

Now he had let go. Weight gone. Lost in a wave. Kevin
extended his arm forward and the water pushed him downward. He didn't, he couldn't, turn back or surface. He gave a
hapless kick; the rush and twist of the ocean cradled his body.
Connie. He reached . . . he didn't—a mistake. Nothing. The
white water called from above, a shuddering escape, a beat
and years in the making.

Trixie had parked at the end of the narrow drive by the
banyan tree. She turned her head when she heard the siren
and began running down the beach. "Connie! Connie!" she
called, sprinting to the water's edge.

There on the shore, a body was sprawled on a surfboard.
A medic stood up to speak with a few people rushing forward
with a cot.

Trixie walked up as Connie stumbled toward her and began crying. "Dad. He let go."

MELELANI'S MANA

BY LONO WAIWAI'OLE

Kalihi

1

Melelani looked up from the book she was reading and shook her head slowly. "Beats me why you guys still bring all that cash to these games," she said. "World finance has pretty much gone electronic, yeah?"

"Pretty much," Wiley said, his eyes still focused on the pictures of Ulysses Simpson Grant he was stacking on the table in front of him.

"But not you guys?"

"Some of us would rather our cash didn't leave a trail."

"In that case, who's providing security?"

Wiley looked up with a question on his lean brown face, and Mele knew what it was without hearing it put into words. "I keep forgetting you're one of those mainland *kanakas*," she said.

"Something else I missed before I got here?" Wiley said, referring to his relatively recent arrival to the islands after a lifetime on the West Coast of North America.

"There was a firefight a few years ago outside an illegal gambling spot. Apparently a certified clown show between two groups who wanted to provide security."

"I wonder how you get something like that certified," said Wiley, the beginning of a grin playing across his face.

"Do you ever pass on a chance to say shit like that?" Mele responded, her own grin dangerously close to a grimace.

"Not intentionally, no."

"You know what the fock I mean, right?"

"Well, this isn't actually an illegal gambling spot. It's just a private-home game."

"With a $10,000 buy-in! Multiply that by six or seven players, and you better hope it's a *very* private game."

"Yeah," Wiley said as soon as the point she was making slapped the grin off his face. "Plus, I doubt anyone comes without an extra bullet or two."

"Bullet?"

"Buy-in."

"Awkward word choice, all things considered."

"It's never the words that are awkward, it's the people doing the talking."

"Whatever. How many of these bullets are you taking?"

"Two or three."

"Make it two, and give me the third."

"You don't really play at this level, Mele."

"I don't fockin' play at all. That's why I wanna be there."

"No shit." Wiley focused his gaze on the long scar that ran from Mele's right ear to the tip of her chin—a stark reminder of a confrontation with a knife-wielding assailant who ultimately had not survived the encounter. "You still have that savior complex going on, girl. You shouldn't have to save my life more than once."

"Who gives a fock about your life?" she said with a laugh that lit up the unscarred side of her gorgeous face. "It's the cash I wanna save."

2

Isoroku Yamamoto had the same name as the architect of the attack at Pearl Harbor during the war in the Pacific, and he cursed it. He was not related to that man and had almost nothing in common with him, but was nonetheless stuck with a very strong name that he carried like a weight around his neck.

Not that he gave the celebrated admiral more credit than was due. "Didn't exactly finish the fucking job, did he?" he said softly as his Lexus wound through a Honolulu still overwhelmed by the American military presence in spite of the great man's best effort back in 1941.

"Say what?" Kenji said from the driver's seat.

"It was nothing," Yamamoto said, softly again. "Just the mumbling of an old man."

"You're not an old man. Not even close."

"I suppose you don't think I'm a fat man, either."

"Oh, hell no! You are most definitely a fat man."

"Maybe all is not lost. Just remind me to never put you in charge of counting anything."

"Noted."

"So everything is set?" Yamamoto said, not anywhere near as softly as before.

"That's the second time you've asked me that."

"*Almost* pulling this off won't cut it," Yamamoto countered with a cold edge.

"Yes, Boss, everything is set. All you gotta do now is play the fucking game."

Yamamoto leaned back with his eyes closed while he reflected on how he had worked himself into such a precarious position. Money had never been a problem before—his take from the massage parlors plus what he claimed from several high-stakes poker games funded his lavish lifestyle quite easily. Until the poker suddenly went sideways and turned his cash flow inside out, leaving him where he was at that moment—many thousands of dollars short of what he owed the motherfuckers in Tokyo.

Yeah, he said to himself, *all I gotta do now is play the fucking game.*

3

What the fuck is this? Yamamoto thought when Wiley walked in with a Polynesian princess at his side. She immediately turned every head in the room, and she did it twice—first because she could have stepped straight out of a picture post-card, and second because of the long scar across one side of her face.

She was wearing slacks and a sleeveless blouse that exposed very little of her body but suggested quite a lot. *You could generate some serious money in my world*, Yamamoto thought, *even with the fucking scar.*

"This is Melelani," Swanson said. "Anyone object to letting her play?"

"I take it she's with him." Yamamoto nodded toward Wiley.

"Yes."

"Makes her judgment highly questionable, doesn't it?"

"Your point being?"

"My point being most definitely let her play," Yamamoto replied, which drew a short laugh from the guy wearing mirrored sunglasses seated to his left.

"The rest of you guys?" Swanson said as he surveyed the other three players already at the table.

"It's *your* game," the guy with the sunglasses said after no one else responded. "Sit her the fuck down if you want to."

By this time, a woman at the table with a deck in her hands had eight cards spread facedown on the felt. Swanson nodded in that direction. "Draw for seats, then!" he said.

Yamamoto drew the four, which corresponded to the seat he was already in, but the guy with the sunglasses drew the eight and had to vacate his spot. That seat remained empty until everyone had settled down except for Wiley, who eventually tossed the five on the table.

"Might not be your lucky day," Wiley said, a reference to the fact that he was in position to act *after* Yamamoto all night—a significant advantage in poker.

"Might be a little too early to tell," Yamamoto replied, a reference to a fact of his own—that Wiley's position at the table was going to make no fucking difference at all on this particular night.

4

Wiley had nothing against the Japanese in general, even though they had sneak-attacked his father's native land. That was a first-class fuck-you move and he had nothing but respect for people with balls enough to do it. On the other hand, Yamamoto's inclination to look down on everyone had rubbed Wiley the wrong way from day one.

He did like two things about the guy, however—Yamamoto seemed to have a connection to every high-stakes Texas Hold'em game on the islands, and he couldn't play Texas Hold'em worth a damn. Considering the absence of legal card rooms in Hawaii, this was a very big deal—Yamamoto was a major reason Wiley didn't have to fly to the mainland constantly to make a living.

5

"This is Stephanie," Swanson said, nodding toward the woman with the cards in her hands. "She's got first shift."

Another Korean, Yamamoto thought as he watched Mele

cut some chips out of the stack in front of her. *What is it with Swanson and all these fucking Korean dealers?*

"These are for both of you," Mele said as she slid the chips toward the dealer.

"Wow!" Stephanie said, her dark eyes sparkling for a moment. "People generally have to win *very* big before we get a tip like this!"

"I think it sucks that we don't support the dealers unless we win. I want to thank you guys for working this game no matter what happens."

"That is very much appreciated, believe me."

"That shit won't work, you know," Yamamoto interjected.

"Sure it will," Mele replied. "What goes around always eventually comes around."

You don't even know that makes no fucking sense, do you? Yamamoto said where only he could hear it. "How about actually dealing the fucking cards?" he said aloud, and that's exactly what Stephanie did.

6

"I'd love to see the cards you're waiting for," Yamamoto said about an hour later, when Mele had yet to play a hand all the way through by the time a new dealer stepped in.

"If you're here long enough, you will," Mele said, "but I doubt that you'll like them when that happens."

"Oh, I'll be here as long as you are, I can assure you of that, and I'll like whatever happens a lot more than you will."

"Pay him no mind, Mele," Swanson said, chuckling. "No one can make him happy, I promise."

"Not true," Yamamoto said. "When I'm not around you fucking fools, I'm happy all the time."

"Maybe," Swanson said, his chuckle graduating to a

laugh, "but you are literally *always* around us fucking fools."

No shit, Yamamoto thought as he threw another hand in the muck.

7

The worm appeared to turn as soon as Stephanie was back in the dealer's chair, which was when Yamamoto woke up with the best starting hand in Texas Hold'em—a pair of aces. Mele was in the big blind, so she had fifty dollars in the pot *before* she got her cards, and everyone had matched that bet until the action got around to Yamamoto. *Some of you fools need to get out of this hand,* he thought, and he bet three hundred in an effort to make that happen.

Wiley and the player next to him tossed their cards toward the middle of the table almost immediately, making Mele the next to act. But she didn't do it—instead, she stared at Yamamoto like a mongoose face-to-face with a cobra for what seemed like a very long time.

Yamamoto didn't mind the pause in the flow of the game at all. "Don't tell me the little lady might finally get off some of those chips," he said, hoping she'd decide to do exactly that.

"Little lady?" she repeated, the words cold enough to cause frostbite if handled with bare hands for too long.

"Pardon me, I guess," Yamamoto replied with ice of his own. "Is it you're not little, or not a lady?"

"I don't know. That's kind of relative, yeah?"

"Is it?"

"Of course. I'm little compared to you, obviously, but compared to you, am I a lady?"

Those words provoked a flash of anger in Yamamoto, but he let it pass before he spoke again. "Maybe you should make a decision here. You're kind of holding up the game."

"My apologies," she said as she counted out some chips. "I'm going to call that obvious bluff." The move raised a few eyebrows around the table and a wisecrack or two, but no one else made the same bet.

"Things aren't always what they seem," Yamamoto said. He was left with exactly what he wanted—a monster starting hand and a single opponent.

"Ain't dat the fockin' trut'," Mele said, slipping into a lot more pidgin than usual. "You about to find da kine cards I been waitin' fo', fat man."

Yamamoto felt his anger return, but Stephanie washed it away by flopping an ace and two threes face up on the table—cards that turned his pair of aces into a full house.

"You da man," Mele said. "I check to you."

This time, Yamamoto was the one who paused. He could think of two ways to proceed—try to extract some chips from the fucking *baishunpu* now or give her a chance to improve her hand first. *How about we let you dig your own grave, you fucking whore?* he thought. "I can wait just as long as you can," he said, at which point Stephanie added a ten to the common cards on the table.

"I check," Mele said again, without a second glance at the ten.

So that one doesn't help you, Yamamoto guessed as he switched his focus from Mele to Stephanie. "Go ahead and deal."

This time Stephanie turned over a king, and Mele lit up like New Year's Eve. *Oh, that one you like*, Yamamoto said to himself. *You've had a pair of kings in your hand all this time, so it's kings full of threes now? Almost good enough to win this pot, little lady!*

Mele studied the cards on the table for another moment,

looked at the cards in her hand again, then turned her attention back to Yamamoto. "I check," she said.

Oh, so now I bet and you raise, right? Kind of a tricky, little lady, aren't you? "How about I let you off easy?" Yamamoto said in a tone he hoped she would find unbearably irritating. "I'll only make it a thousand more for you."

Mele closed her eyes and drummed her fingers on the table for a moment while she appeared to weigh her options, then leaned forward and locked eyes with Yamamoto again. "Oh, why don't you just take it all?" She edged all of her chips toward the middle of the table. "I'm all in."

"Call," Yamamoto said immediately as he flipped over his aces. "Those kings aren't worth shit, sweetie."

"True dat," Mele said as she revealed a pair of threes, giving her four of a kind and reducing Yamamoto's full house to rubble.

The table erupted as soon as everyone saw Mele's cards. "Motherfucker!" Yamamoto spat into the din. "I can't believe you played a fucking pair of threes after sitting on your ass all night!"

"Do you know what they called the bomb they dropped on Hiroshima back in the day?" Mele asked.

"Motherfucker!" Yamamoto said again, more in response to the threes than the question.

"A'ole," Mele said, shaking her head while she started dragging all of Yamamoto's chips in her direction.

"Those fucking threes should have been in the muck as soon as I raised!" he snapped.

"Maybe it's just karma," Mele said. "What goes around always comes around, yeah?"

Yamamoto shook his head as he reached below the table and came up with a canvas bag. "Give me another stack," he said, sliding the bag toward Swanson.

Swanson got up, grabbed the bag, and headed for more chips, but he didn't leave Mele's question behind. "What *did* they call that bomb?" he asked.

"Fat Man," Mele said, her eyes trained on Yamamoto again. "How sweet is that?"

8

The game was about five hours old when it blew the fuck up again, this time even more profoundly than it had in response to Mele's quad threes. Four armed men wearing ski masks burst into the room behind a slim, middle-aged Japanese man bleeding slightly from a cut on the left side of his head.

"What the fuck, Kenji?" Yamamoto said.

"Sorry, Boss. They were on me before I knew they were there."

Mele heard the exchange but ignored it. She focused instead on the other new arrivals, to which she had a strangely mixed reaction. *Do I know any of these fools?* she wondered. Then she caught Wiley shaking his head slowly with another hint of a grin on his face. *Here comes another fucking wisecrack,* she said to herself.

"You t'ink da kine is funny, brah?" the smallest of the intruders said, pointing a cut-down shotgun directly at Wiley while his companions fanned out around the table.

"The ski masks are fucking hilarious," Wiley said. "Is there any use for them on this island other than the way you fools are using them?"

The guy with the shotgun ignored Wiley. "The buy-ins and all the extra cash, on the fockin' table!" he yelled. "And we're gonna hurt people if we gotta dig for it, I promise."

"Not too fucking likely," Mele said quietly, in a tone that immediately commanded the attention of everyone in the room.

"What da fock?" the guy with the shotgun said.

"You need to look at me a little closer, *brah*," Mele said, turning her face slightly to make her scar unmistakably evident.

"Muddafockah!" the guy with the shotgun said. "What da fock you doing here?"

"The question is what are *you* doing here?"

"I nevah know you in dis fockin' game!"

"You know it now."

"Look! No harm, no foul, yeah?"

"Jury's still out on that."

The guy with the shotgun nodded vaguely toward the door and began to back away in that direction. "Remembah, sistah," he said right before all four of the men moved out of sight, "not'ing really happened, yeah?"

9

Un-fucking-believable! Yamamoto thought as he watched the local thugs Kenji had recruited dry up and blow away, his financial rescue plan disappearing with them. *Talk about running cold—not only can I not win the money I need in this game, I apparently can't even fucking steal it.*

Swanson was the first person to say something as soon as the intruders were gone, and it was the same question burning in Yamamoto's head: "Would you mind telling me who the fuck you are?"

The words didn't stick—Mele ignored the question and fixed her attention on Kenji instead. "You're bleeding a little."

Kenji produced a handkerchief and applied it to his head. "Could have been a lot worse," he said.

"Watch out for concussion, though. The symptoms can sneak up on you."

Yamamoto saw his driver nod without another word.

How fucking sweet, he thought. *Maybe we can have a big group hug now.* "I'd also like to know what just happened here and who the fuck you are," he said.

"What just happened here is pretty fucking obvious," Swanson cut in, the shock of the moment wearing off. "Someone just tried to hijack my game!"

"And she stopped them without raising a finger," the guy with the sunglasses said.

"It wasn't me, actually," Mele said. "I couldn't have stopped those fools from walking out of here with every dollar in the room."

"What, then?" Swanson said.

"Are we playing cards here or not?" Mele asked.

"Fuck the game," Swanson said. "Who are you?"

"I don't see what difference that makes. You're still the one hosting this game without sufficient security."

That observation threw a blanket on the conversation for a moment, but when the moment was over, the guy with the sunglasses made an observation of his own: "Actually, I'd have to say the security turned out to be sufficient after all."

Neither of these observations appeared to mollify Swanson. "Wiley, you brought her here? I need an answer."

Wiley took the time to make eye contact with everyone at the table before he responded. "You could say she's the recognizable face of a family that few of the lowlifes on this island want to fuck with," he eventually said.

"Is that it?" Swanson pointed the words at Mele again.

"Whatever," she responded. "That's not really the most appropriate question at the moment."

"That being *what?*"

"That being, how did those fools find out about this game in the first place?"

10

Yamamoto closed his eyes and let the talk flow around him. He could feel a cold fist forming in his gut, and he tried to ignore it. *Job one,* he thought, *is get the fuck out of this conversation as subayaku as possible.* His next thought trumped that one, however: *On the other hand, I still need that motherfucking money.*

"What fucking difference does *how* even make?" Swanson asked.

"Might help us figure out *who,*" Mele replied.

"It wasn't in the *Advertiser,* if that's what you're asking."

"Who'd you reach out to that isn't in the room?"

"No one."

"Not too fucking likely," she said for the second time that night.

"These are the people I invited, plus you. Period."

"These the only two dealers you spoke to?"

"Fuck," Swanson said, taking more time than usually required to utter a single word.

"Household staff, catering companies, random playmates?"

"I get it. There could be dozens of ways the word got around, all coming from me."

"The number might not be anywhere near that big," Mele said. "Are any of your contacts people you don't usually work or mingle with?"

"No."

"Not really likely to suddenly go rogue, then."

"Probably not, but this shit is not in the 'likely' range or it would've happened before."

"What about the rest of us?" Mele said, turning toward Wiley.

"I told *you*," Wiley answered, "and nobody else."

"And I told no one," Mele said. "How 'bout you, fat man?"

Yamamoto opened his eyes and leaned forward until he was able to rest his forearms on the felt in front of him. *I'm going to respond to your smart mouth, you fucking* baishunpu, he said to himself, *but I will pick and choose the time.* "I told my driver, obviously," he said where everyone could hear it, "and my driver *saredake.*"

"*Saredake?*"

"Only."

"And you?" Mele said, turning toward Kenji.

"I told a few people what I had to do tonight," he said after a moment of reflection. "I didn't give it a second thought."

"I doubt that many of us did," Mele said, an assertion she proceeded to confirm by walking the question all the way around the table.

"Now what?" Swanson asked.

"Why the fuck are you asking *her?*" Yamamoto said. "It's still *your* game, right?" He was down his first bullet and more than half of his second, which hadn't bothered him at all while he thought he was picking up all the cash in the room anyway. At this point, the opposite was true—and the losses were likely to bother the motherfuckers in Tokyo even more.

11

"The next step is obvious," Mele said.

"Humor me," Swanson replied.

"We need to look at this thing the other way around for a minute."

"Which is what?"

"What if the person responsible is someone in the room right now?"

Yamamoto took that comment in without a visible re-action, but his mind immediately kicked into overdrive: *If I can't spin the shit that's coming now, what's my next move?*

"I suppose that *is* one of the possibilities," Swanson said. "Has to be someone who isn't here, or someone who is."

"And is there someone who seems to be setting his money on fire lately?" Mele said, her gaze shifting slowly in Yamamo-to's direction and sticking when it got to him.

"I get aces cracked by fucking threes, and I'm a suspect?" Yamamoto said. "That's fucking brilliant!"

"No one's calling you a suspect," Swanson said.

"Actually, someone is," Mele said quietly, eyeing Yama-moto like she had never seen him before. "How often do you bleed money like you are tonight?"

You know, little lady, I really don't like you. "That's one question," Yamamoto said aloud. "Another one is: how much money do I get paid for every happy ending on this fucking island—as compared to the guy you walked in with, who has no other income at all?"

"Good point," Mele said. "Of course, if tonight was his hit, he probably wouldn't have brought *me* along. Plus the fact that he doesn't need a shotgun to take your money, does he?"

"Can you prove any of this shit?" Swanson asked.

"Not exactly a relevant question."

"What the fuck does that mean?" Yamamoto said.

"It just means that proof won't be required to adjudicate what happened here tonight."

"*Nothing* happened here tonight!" Yamamoto shot back.

"Not according to Kenji," Mele said, shifting her focus from the boss to the driver. "How'd you get that cut on your head?"

"The motherfucker with the shotgun," Kenji said after a moment.

"That's more *who* than *how*," she said, watching the comment rub him the wrong way as soon as it was out of her mouth.

"What the fuck's it to you?" Kenji said, heat pouring off his words for the first time.

"What it is to me is someone just stuck a gun in my face and tried to rob me."

"Sorry," Kenji said, once again without heat in his voice. "Not exactly my night."

"Why were you out there, anyway?"

"I get paid to wait around so the boss doesn't have to," he said with a shrug. "Not a unique experience tonight, believe me."

"Well, up to the point when clowns with guns showed up."

"Up to then, yeah."

"So what caused the cut on your head?" she asked again.

"Motherfucker tapped me with the fucking shotgun."

"Hmm."

"What?"

"I'm wondering why."

"Maybe you should have asked him that before you ran him out of here," Kenji said, starting to warm up again. "I don't have a fucking clue."

"Lucky I don't need one of those, huh? All I need is the good guess that I *do* have."

"Which is what?" Swanson interjected.

"Now we're all the way down to wild fucking guesses?" Yamamoto said.

"It's not that wild," Mele said. "Maybe the little owie was supposed to convince us that Kenji was not part of the plan—and by extension, neither was his boss."

"You sound unconvinced," Swanson said, "but I don't really get why."

"Did you at least lock the front door?"

"Of course I did."

"Well, these clowns either knocked it down without making a sound or it was open when they got here. So I'm a little underwhelmed so far, yeah."

"I don't really give a fuck what you are," Yamamoto said, rising from his seat. "I've heard enough of this shit for one night."

"It's not like there's anywhere you can go, fat man!" Mele said.

"Don't confuse me with these fucking locals you have pissing all over themselves. You don't want to be anywhere I'm at going forward from here."

Mele responded to that statement with a laugh that lasted a lot longer than Yamamoto found tolerable. "What's so funny?" he said when he could no longer keep the words from barging out of his mouth.

"Your threat would mean a lot more except for one thing, fat man."

"What's that?" Yamamoto said, in spite of the fact that he was trying to say nothing at all.

"If we come for you," Mele said after she shut the laugh down, "you won't even see us coming."

12

"Fucking brilliant hiring job!" Yamamoto barked as soon as he was settled into the Lexus.

"You're the one who didn't want to use any of our own people," Kenji replied.

"For obvious reasons."

"Just saying. Was there a way we could have seen this coming?"

No, Yamamoto conceded silently. *The question is, what now?*

Kenji was the next to say something out loud: "We could probably rip off the two of them ourselves."

"We'd have to kill them both to get away with it."

"You have a problem with that?"

"Something like that requires advance planning."

"We planned tonight in advance."

"Your point being?"

"Sometimes opportunities present themselves."

"Such as?"

"Those two are going to walk out of there with some serious money, right?"

No way they came in with less than thirty grand between them, Yamamoto thought, *and they were both up at the end.* "Probably fifty or sixty thousand, easy," he said. "But if you consider the fifteen grand I lost tonight, is that net enough to justify the risk?"

"That depends on what the risk is, doesn't it?"

"Yes, it does," Yamamoto said as the other players began to emerge from the house. "Let's follow those motherfuckers for a bit."

13

Wiley watched Mele hit her phone as soon as Yamamoto and Kenji left the room. "Who do we know on the high end of the massage parlors here?" she said. "Higher than that," she added after a pause. "The local clown just tried to rip us off, and the motherfuckers in Tokyo need to understand that actions like this one have consequences that will be administered very soon." After another pause, Mele lowered her phone.

"What?" Wiley asked.

"Chill until they get back to me."

"Actually, we kind of need the time."

"What do you mean?"

"You might be jumping to conclusions about our fat friend."

"Maybe, but it's not much of a jump."

"No question he's been bleeding money lately, though. I'd say he's lost at least a hundred grand so far this month."

"And if that money wasn't his, he has all the motive he would need to do something this fucking stupid."

14

Kenji took the call about fifteen minutes after leaving the house because it was from a number that had to be answered. The voice spoke Japanese, but for some reason Kenji always heard it in English now. "Are you with him?" the voice said.

That was fucking fast, Kenji thought. "Yes," he said.

"Is it true?"

What the fuck? Kenji asked himself, but it didn't take him long to come up with the answer. "Yes," he said again, the obvious choice because it fit every possible question Kenji could imagine coming from Tokyo at this particular moment.

"Do you know what you have to do now?"

"Yes."

"*Yoi,*" the voice said before it disappeared.

"What was that?" Yamamoto asked when Kenji dropped his phone into the cup holder next to his seat.

"Fucking woman."

"Nothing but 'yes' is no way to handle a woman."

"No shit." Kenji climbed out of the car, walked around to the back, and removed the Remington and Glock from the trunk. When he got back to his seat behind the wheel, he handed the shotgun to Yamamoto and slipped the pistol into the panel on his door. "Just in case the opportunity presents itself, right?"

"Almost sounds like the beginning of a plan," Yamamoto said as Scarface and her half-baked Hawaiian walked out of the house, climbed into a new Range Rover waiting half a block in front of the Lexus, and drove away.

15

"Pono," Wiley said to the burly Hawaiian driving the car, "do you mind swinging by the graveyard again?"

"Hook Chu?" Pono asked.

"Yeah."

"A'ole pilikia, brah."

"You won't be able to see much at night, you know," Mele said.

"I just want to drive by. Knowing I have family there helps me feel connected to this island even if I'm not."

"What brought this on?"

"You have to admit tonight was a little out of the ordinary."

"I do, indeed."

Wiley leaned back and watched Pono point them downhill toward the city, and after a moment or two Mele laced the fingers of her right hand with the fingers of his left. "You didn't even blink in there, did you?" he said.

"I have no idea."

"Take my word for it. Plus, I might have been wrong about you earlier."

"How so?"

"You cleared five grand tonight. Maybe you *do* play at this level."

"I was just lucky against those aces. I know the correct play was to muck my threes when he raised that much."

"Why didn't you?"

"The thing is, I knew I was going to win that hand."

"*What?*" Wiley shook his head like she had suddenly shifted from English to Hawaiian.

"I knew I was going to win—I could feel it in the air."

"Feelings like that are not very profitable, Mele, believe me."

"I don't think you're familiar with feelings like this. When I get one, I can bet the fucking house on it."

"We don't own our house, girl."

"If I can't lose, what fucking difference does that make?"

"Point taken," Wiley said, still shaking his head slowly. "Just let me know the next time it happens so I can get started on alternative living arrangements."

"I see you're back to normal again. I'd like to know who says you're funny."

"Actually, no one says that. I have never understood why not."

"Pono, can you explain it to him? I need a break at this point."

"Maybe," Pono said as he stopped at a red light. "Got one question first."

"What?"

"Why we got dis fockin' Lexus on our ass?"

16

"The driver makes three," Kenji said. "Does that make a difference?"

"Fuck no," Yamamoto said. "I'm saving the little lady for special treatment later, anyway."

What the fuck, Boss? Kenji thought, but he didn't let the absence of an answer slow him down. "There isn't anyone behind us at the moment," he said, "and there hasn't been much traffic all the way here. I'd say an opportunity is presenting itself."

"Agreed. Ram them as soon as they clear the intersection."

A moment later, that's exactly what Kenji did. As soon as the cars collided, Yamamoto spilled out of one door and Kenji exited the other while all three of the occupants of the car in front of them boiled into the street at the same time.

"What da fock?" the other driver said.

Awesome, Kenji said to himself as soon as a quick scan of the people in front of him did not reveal a weapon. *Couldn't really ask for much more.*

"You're coming with me, *little lady!*" Yamamoto said, raising the Remington in Mele's direction. "Won't that be fun!"

"Not too fucking likely," Mele responded, which turned out to be all the words she had time to squeeze out before Kenji used the Glock in his hand to put a permanent end to the dialogue.

The first shot hit Yamamoto in the left shoulder and knocked him off his feet. Kenji walked around the front of the Lexus, kicked the shotgun out of Yamamoto's hand, leaned down far enough to press the barrel against Yamamoto's forehead, and fired again.

"What the fuck, Kenji?" Mele said. "You were part of it!"

"They think this shit is over now," he replied as he picked up the Remington. "Do you think something else?"

"I guess I don't, but you'll be the first to know if I change my mind."

"Noted," Kenji said, then climbed back into the Lexus, drove around the body he'd left on the ground and the car he'd rammed, and disappeared into the darkness between the scene and the city below.

"Gotta fockin' call dis in, yeah?" Pono asked.

"Call *what* in?" Mele said as she headed for her seat in the car. "We were never here, Pono."

As soon as everyone was back in the vehicle, Pono started downhill in Kenji's wake.

"Are you sure about this?" Wiley asked.

"I'm sure this shit is over for *that* motherfucker," Mele said quietly, "whether I change my mind or not."

"Hook Chu still?" Pono asked.

"If you don't mind," Wiley said.

"And we might want to stop after all," Mele said as she reached up and tugged slightly on Wiley's left ear. "I'm pretty sure your *ohana* will be there for you tonight."

THE GAIJIN

BY Chris McKinney

Kaka'ako

"These motherfucking Americans appropriate everything," Fukuda-san, boss of the Takeda clan, sneers in Japanese.

It's 2022, New Year's Eve in Honolulu, and a pair of yakuza sit in a private karaoke room, watching a twenty-year-old local with a koi sleeve tattoo pour cheap champagne. Another hostess, a Korean American called Kate, is holding the mic and gazing up at the flat-screen mounted on the wall. She belts J-pop with gusto. A pink bubble bounces up and down above the lyrics that scrawl across the screen. The fireworks going off outside the bar are so loud, they sound like gunfire.

"To be fair," Masunaga-san, Fukuda's first lieutenant, says, "we always copy Americans. Baseball? Golf? 7-Eleven?" He points to the Japanese quartet gyrating on the television. "Pop music?"

"That is not appropriation. That is colonization," Fukuda responds. "We are in a *kyabakura*, listening to *kyabajo* sing karaoke while firecrackers pop outside. In America. This *hafu* girl serving us, probably some Asian, white, indigenous mutt, has more ink on her arm than some of our soldiers. Where is this business partner you spoke so highly about? He's fifteen minutes late."

Masunaga glances at his 14k gold Rolex Datejust. His left

sleeve is coiled up to the elbow so that everyone in the room can see the tattoos on his forearms. Thirty minutes till midnight. He doesn't like traveling to Hawaii with his boss. He thought this hostess bar's private room would make Fukuda feel more comfortable after a long flight, but the old man has been in a mood ever since they took off from Haneda in the gaijin's private jet. Sitting stiffly in a black suit too snug around his waistline and shoulders, Fukuda waves a girl away. He lights a cigarette and tosses the match on the musty carpet. Masunaga suspects the uptick in smoking is a personal health rebellion. The old man has COPD and is two heart attacks in, but if anything, these near-death experiences have pushed him beyond two packs a day. It's the criminal mentality, Masunaga supposes. When one cheats death, one does not horde life. One dares death to strike again. Masunaga bends down and picks up the smoldering match. He tosses it in the glass ashtray and looks at himself in one of the mirrored walls. His stubbled head. His clean-shaven, chiseled jaw. The scar that runs from his temple to his cheek. He has cheated death four times. He is no different as a result. He is here in an attempt to cheat it once more.

When the gaijin finally walks through the door, Masunaga cringes at the man's attire. Cargo shorts, a distressed T-shirt, and a worn denim jacket—Fukuda will interpret his casualness as disrespect. However, this is the new gaijin billionaire unform. Vintage stores. Eco-friendly. Comfort over style. Attempting desperately to *not* look like one's personal net worth is ten figures. The gaijin often deliberately talks about his young children to sound like a normal person. He speaks of soccer practice and his degrading eyesight as if he is a *bonjin*. Masunaga respects the deceit. They meet here in Honolulu at the end of every month for business—Hawaii, right between Tokyo and Silicon Valley: the perfect bridge of the Pacific.

"Sorry I'm late," the gaijin says, raising his voice over the blaring J-pop. "The kids refused to go to bed." He hands a credit card to the young woman with the koi sleeve tattoo. "This is on me," he says, smiling at her.

Masunaga's eyes narrow. That's *his* girl.

It's 11:37 p.m., and the three men walk out of the bar. Among the clan, only Fukuda and Masunaga know about this business trip. They felt it best to keep this possible investment away from family ears for now. If there is a leak and word gets out, another clan might compete for the opportunity. Heading to the curb, Fukuda-san almost trips over a sleeping woman. Her arms and calloused legs, covered with sores, are sprawled out like she's posing for a murder scene. Fukuda curses. "Americans," he hisses in Japanese. "These *homuresu* are all over the place."

It's true, Masunaga thinks to himself. Every time he comes to Honolulu, it feels like more and more homeless people pack the sidewalks. They walk around the woman toward the Sprinter waiting curbside. Masunaga, the last to enter the luxury van, looks up before stepping in. Fireworks bloom in the sky. Unlike most *real* Japanese back home, those of Japanese descent who have lived in Hawaii for generations still pound mochi every New Year's Eve. They make *ozoni* every New Year's Day. They are still obsessed with firecrackers despite all the regulations and permitting requirements instituted by the state government over the years. Masunaga knows. It's his organization that illegally imports most fireworks to Hawaii. He is pretty sure that Fukuda-san is unaware that the organization is also the majority owner of the hostess bar they just stepped out of. Masunaga grins to himself before stepping into the van while the pyrotechnics erupt overhead.

It's a short drive to their first destination, but Masunaga takes time to gaze out the window at the Kaka'ako skyline. Once a neighborhood saturated with industrial buildings and auto repair shops, Kaka'ako is now overrun by dozens of multiuse high rises that have sprouted over the last couple decades. The glass towers crowd Ala Moana Beach Park like concertgoers fighting to get closest to the stage. Most of the resident lights are off. Many of these units are the vacation homes of rich mainland Americans, Europeans, and Asians. Masunaga himself owns a unit in Pacifica. His girl here, the same one who was serving them back at the bar, the one who the gaijin smiled at, keeps it warm while Masunaga is back home. He's the one who paid for her sleeve tattoo, among other things.

"You wear too much fucking jewelry," Fukuda says.

Masunaga touches his gold chain. The old man doesn't get it. Masunaga likes being a gangster. He likes people knowing he's a gangster. Fukuda with his business suit and the gaijin with his thrift attire—Masunaga feels like the only honest man in the car. His shirt is buttoned down, and his sleeves are rolled up. The dragons coiling around his arms bulge when he flexes them, and the cherry blossoms beneath his clavicle almost glow under the van's neon light. More fireworks detonate in the sky. It's getting closer to midnight, when the entire night sky across the island will erupt with plumes of color.

They arrive at the gated construction site and pull in. The gaijin's driver, a nondescript local man wearing an aloha shirt, gets out first and opens the door for them. Fukuda steps out. The gaijin follows. Masunaga reaches between his legs and pulls a loaded VP9 from under the seat. It's a light 9mm with a short barrel, supposedly built for police work, but is really made for conceal-and-carry for gun-crazed Americans. Masunaga loves the freedoms of this country. He tucks the gun against the small of his back and exits the van. He gives the driver a double take. He doesn't trust islander males who wear aloha attire. From CEO to governor, in Hawaii, the humble aloha shirt is a costume that the powerful wear to camouflage their corruption.

"Have I seen you before?" Masunaga asks.

The driver shrugs. "Small island."

The locals like saying "small island" nauseatingly often. What it really means is that Honolulu is a place where everybody either knows or knows of everyone else. Everyone is a step or two removed from everybody else. An impossibility back home in Tokyo, a city of over thirteen million people.

"Hey!" Fukuda yells up ahead. "*Hyaku!*"

Masunaga turns away from the driver and marches toward Fukuda and the gaijin. The men stand at the edge of a huge, man-made crater—a cavity about to be filled with the foundational guts of a condominium. He steps next to gaijin so that the white man stands between the two criminals.

"This lot is about 45,000 square feet," the gaijin says. "That's smaller than a football field. When we build it, it'll be over forty stories high." He points to the sky. "Close to seven hundred units. Figure the average price for a unit is a million dollars. And that's a conservative estimate. This is a billion-dollar project. People buying vacant space in the sky. Isn't that fantastic? We turn a plot that could normally house nine families into something that can house seven hundred." The gaijin winks at Fukuda. "Capitalism isn't about adding wealth. It's about multiplying it."

"And you want my family to invest in it?" Fukuda-san asks.

"Absolutely," the gaijin says. "Maybe even get some of your friends to reserve units at a special price." Firecrackers explode a couple of blocks away. The man grins. "You know why they pop so many firecrackers every New Year's here?"

"Nostalgia?" Fukuda says, seeming to relax and warm to the gaijin and his potential investment opportunity.

"No," says the gaijin. "I thought so at first too. It's not nostalgia. It's protest. Protest that a way of life is dying. Protest that the locals and natives are being priced out of the place they were born and grew up in. Protest against this modern skyline being built. Yet, at the same time, do you know how many people vote in this city? Thirty percent." He shakes his head and takes a step back. Masunaga takes a step back too. "I can't muster sympathy for a people who don't organize and participate in democracy when democracy's given to them. They actually have the power to intelligently go about preserving their way of life. They could vote for politicians who could stop us from building this condo, but they don't. They could've voted for a legislature that could've stopped the construction of all these other condos that came before. I can't sympathize with a people who voice their malcontent by illegally popping nonlethal explosives every New Year's to snub the system."

Masunaga quietly pulls out the gun, careful so that his motions do not draw any attention. The darkness of night helps. He presses the gun into the gaijin's palm. The gaijin takes the pistol and points it at Fukuda, who is gazing up at the fireworks. More of them explode nearby. The gaijin shoots the old man in the temple.

Fukuda's body jolts, tips sideways, and tumbles into the crater. He hits the bottom, and his body is splayed out like the homeless woman's was earlier. The gaijin hands the gun back to Masunaga.

"Thanks," the gaijin says. "He was kind of a grouch, wasn't he? We still on for tomorrow?"

Masunaga blinks then slips the gun back against the small of his back. "Yes."

"Bring your girl. She'll love it. Nothing more majestic."

"The money?" Masunaga says.

"Check your phone."

Masunaga pulls his phone from his pocket and navigates to his offshore account. Two zeroes have been added to the amount. An engine suddenly rumbles behind him. Startled, he turns. It's the gaijin's driver. He's at the wheel, and the truck beeps while the cement mixer reverses toward the crater. Masunaga tries to relax by working up hatred for the man who plucked him from the fishing docks and eventually made him second in command of one of the most powerful organized crime organizations in Japan. *Fukuda*. The old man was never going to name Masunaga the new clan leader. His oldest son is the heir apparent. Back home, Masunaga has less value than a second son. The gaijin puts an arm around Masunaga's shoulder. Masunaga pockets his phone.

"Relax," the gaijin says. "You're the new boss, aren't you? Now, let's go out in my boat tomorrow and talk real estate. Or finance. Or tech if you want to. That's my original area of expertise. There's still investment opportunities there as well. I'm also thinking about producing a movie about your line of work. I want katanas in it. Lots and lots of katanas."

Masunaga watches cement plop onto the body of his boss. He thinks about how billionaires operate. How their money, in the public's eye, instantaneously makes them experts on everything from public health to space travel. How their money allows them their outrageous fetishes. The truth is, the gaijin didn't really get anything out of killing Fukuda, except for the perverse pleasure of satisfying a childhood fantasy that was probably born by watching anime as a child. *I want to kill an* oyabun, the gaijin had told him on their last meeting here. *Bring your boss, and I'll make you the new boss. I'll even pull the trigger and take care of the body. We can do business together for years.* Now he wants to make a movie with katanas in it. Maybe Fukuda was right. These motherfucking Americans appropriate everything.

When Masuanga gets to his apartment, he's desperate for a beer and a line. His girl, the hostess from the bar, thankfully has a beer and three lines of cocaine set up on the glass dining room table. Masunaga grabs the beer, takes a swig, then deftly pulls a C-note from his money clip. He rolls the bill tightly and rails a line. He takes another swig of beer and rails the next two. He's careful about his drug use. He only does cocaine when he's in America.

"Hey, one was for me," his girl says. She's standing behind him, arms crossed, wearing an oversized T-shirt of some American football team. "By the way, how do you say *cocaine* in Japanese?"

"Cocaine," Masunaga says, already exasperated. She talks to him like he's Siri on all things Japanese. These young Americans are too lazy to even google. But Masunaga only sees her about sixty days a year. He knows she probably hangs out with other men or women while he's gone. He doesn't care. He doesn't care that she's on OnlyFans trying to get famous by sticking things up her *chitsu*. She is American, and this apartment is under her name. Less paperwork that way.

Masunaga's eyes scan the living room. The calamity of digital camera equipment, makeup containers, and dirty clothes cluttered throughout indicates that the girl has definitely claimed the place as her own. She picks up her purse and pulls out a plastic baggie. She spills out a small pile of coke and chops it up with her driver's license. Its lamination is frayed at the ends from so much use.

Masunaga rerolls the C-note and snorts another line. For some reason, his mind keeps drifting back—not to Fukuda's shooting, but to the gaijin's local driver. He's seen him before. Maybe at a hotel in Waikiki, working as a valet or waiter, as many of the locals do. Maybe at another construction site. It doesn't matter. The clan thinks Fukuda is on vacation in Macau. They think Masunaga is still in Tokyo. They flew here on the gaijin's jet, and the gaijin assured Masunaga that there is no record of the flight, nor will there be a record of his flight back tomorrow night. He has other things to worry about right now. There is this excursion that the gaijin is taking him on in the morning. It would be impolite to miss that. And he might be doing too much coke to get it up to fuck his girl.

He glances at the wall behind the table and finds himself staring at an odd painting, framed. It's a map of the Hawaiian Islands, each textured with gunks of brown and green paint. From the north, a huge, cartoonish tidal wave crests, about to break over the entire chain. Under its fluffy whitewash, the wave appears to be smiling. Twister clouds form into arms that reach from east and west, about to envelop the islands in a cataclysmic embrace.

"Where did you get this piece of art?" Masunaga asks the girl.

"I painted it," she says.

"It's nice."

"It's kind of a portrait of someone I know."

The girl snuggles up to him and takes the C-note from his fingers. They begin to kiss.

When the gaijin's driver calls from downstairs, Masunaga curses to himself. It's seven, and he's only managed to sleep for an hour or two. He turns over and faces the girl's back. His eyes hungrily trace the hourglass curve of her naked body. He aches to wake her up and fuck her, but they need to hurry, get dressed, and go downstairs. Masunaga shakes the girl's shoulder. She stirs.

"We need to go," Masunaga says.

He stumbles out of bed, pours what remains of the coke onto the table, and cuts lines. The girl wakes and stretches like a cat. Half her back is covered with an orange koi swimming upstream and transforming into a dragon. Its body is more snake than fish, and wings bloom behind its gills. Maybe that's what Masunaga made himself last night. He went from one of countless fish to a dragon. When he returns to Tokyo tonight, he will resume his normal duties as first lieutenant of the clan and act as if nothing happened. Then *he* will be the one to sound the alarm when people begin to notice that Fukuda is missing. He will go to Macau and search for the boss. When Fukuda doesn't turn up, Masunaga will blame the triad. *He* will assume control over the organization, not Fukuda's son. And his first act as boss will be to report to the clan that he made a *legitimate* hundred-million-dollar deal with the gaijin tech giant. It will be the biggest investment in the clan's history. And the most lucrative.

After doing a line, Masunaga hurries and gets dressed. He's surprised that the girl has gotten ready more quickly than him. She's wearing an orange bikini, sarong, floppy hat, and oversized American influencer sunglasses. She looks natural in the attire, while Masunaga feels absolutely ridiculous wearing a T-shirt and board shorts. The girl points at his thick gold rope necklace.

"You should leave the chain," she says.

Masunaga takes the chain off and lays it on the table. He feels even more naked now. He glances down. His pale feet look absurd in flip-flops. He hopes the gaijin has an ample supply of sunscreen.

The drive from the south side of the island to the north is sleepy and quiet. It's as if the whole city is still slumbering and hungover from the New Year's Eve festivities. The roads are empty, and the landscape transforms from high rises to industrial, to suburban, to rural. They pass acres and acres of brush and red dirt. There's some kind of pineapple plantation museum to the right that they pass while rolling on the winding strip of two-way asphalt corralled by electrical poles and California grass. The girl sleeps the whole way there. Masunaga doesn't. The tinted partition that separates driver from passengers has been up the entire ride. He wonders where the driver's people were from. Were they Natives, here for centuries? Were some of them Japanese laborers tricked into indentured servitude over a hundred years ago? It's tough to peg down ethnicity in Honolulu. He doesn't even know what the girl is. All he knows is that she is not Japanese. At least not *real* Japanese.

When they finally get to the pier, Masunaga is exhausted. He just wants to get this over with. He shakes the girl awake and climbs out of the van. He stretches. It's an overcast day, gray. The water appears choppy and endless. The pier is quiet. The driver, wearing a faded aloha shirt and board shorts, leads Masunaga and the girl to the gaijin's boat. It's humbler than Masunaga expected. It's big, but the light-blue paint is peeling, the hull is covered with barnacles, and the cleats are somewhere between oxidized and rusted. The boat reminds Masunaga of the vessel his father worked all those years in Tokyo Bay. When Masunaga started working alongside his father as child, he hated the slippery feeling of the catch. The gas fumes that turned his stomach. The stench of fish. He chose Fukuda over his father. He chose crime over duty. If presented with the option, he would make the same choice again.

Masunaga and the girl step aboard. The gaijin emerges from below deck with a huge smile on his face. He's holding three wineglasses by their stems in one hand and a bottle of Caymus Special Selection in the other. He moves in to politely hug Masunaga, then the girl.

Masunaga eyes the bottle of wine. He has noticed that although ultra-wealthy Americans often dress humbly, often drive humble cars, and may even own humble boats such as this one, they are very particular in the way they travel, eat, and drink. The gaijin always flies private. He always stays in suites. The wine, like the bottle the gaijin is holding, doesn't have to be obscenely expensive, but it must be *good*. The gaijin uncorks the wine. The driver, who is now perched at the boat's console above, reverses the vessel out of its slip. Masunaga eyes the shark cage flipped and crammed against the boat's transom. Only Americans would call swimming with sharks recreational activity.

"The water will clear up once we get farther out," the gaijin says. He hands a glass of wine to the girl first, then Masunaga. "Hopefully we'll see a fifteen-footer today."

"I can't wait!" the girl chirps, drinking her wine too quickly.

She needs to learn to savor things. Masunaga, who plans to spend more time here once his leadership of the clan is solidified back home, will teach her. The boat skips over the chop. Masunaga slathers sunblock onto his body, making his pale skin even whiter. The gas fumes are starting to make him feel sick. Behind him, Oahu shrinks along the horizon.

When they are about ten miles out, and Masunaga finds himself floating inside the cage wearing full scuba regalia, he realizes that this is the most ridiculous he's ever felt in his entire life. He imagines himself as a caged penguin. He's so tired, he feels delirious. The sun has fully risen and the blue ocean is, of course, beautiful. It is one of the things that Masunaga appreciates about Hawaii. Whenever he returns home and sees the ocean, he is saddened. In fact, no matter where he goes—South Korea, China, Los Angeles, San Francisco, Thailand, Singapore—compared to Hawaii, it always feels like he is going back to an indifferent, weathered spouse, while Hawaii remains the ever-alluring mistress. The girl has already taken her turn in the cage. After twenty minutes underwater, she emerged bubbling with delight. He supposes there are worse things to be doing than shark watching.

The driver lowers the cage, and Masunaga looks up at the ripples of sunlight streaked across the water's surface. He turns and peers through the blue haze of the ocean. Already, there is a shark, a big one, its mouth cracked slightly open. Its jagged rows of teeth are visible, and its unmoving eyes seem to be looking not at Masunaga, but right through him. Silver fish dart to and fro behind the shark, nipping at the chum dumped into the water from the boat above.

Other sharks come. Some on the smaller side, one and a half meters maybe, while two others are three times that size. Masunaga thinks of a Hawaiian word the girl taught him when they first met: 'aumakua. Ancestral spirits that inhabit an animal, plant, or rock. The word reminds Masunaga of kami. His people, too, once believed that spirits could inhabit animals, as well as mountains, wind, and thunder. He is moved by the majesty of the shark that glides in front of him, sunlight from above dancing on its thick, gray skin. He respects its eyes—absent of emotion, just filled with single-minded forwardness. He doubts that the shark contains spirits. Incapable of self-pity, it is the most beautifully soulless thing he has ever seen.

The cage jolts, and Masunaga grabs the bars. He is being pulled up now. The driver leans down and extends his hand. Masunaga grabs it and is pulled up. Once onboard, he removes his mask, regulator, tank, and fins. He studies the driver's face then looks at the girl. He understands now. He hasn't actually seen the driver before. The man, with his hazel eyes, brown skin, plump lips, and narrow nose—he is clearly related to the girl.

"What d'you think?" the gaijin asks.

Masunaga pries his eyes from the girl and her . . . cousin? Brother? "It is as you said: majestic."

As if reading Masunaga's mind, the driver says, "Older brother. Small island."

When the driver sticks a knife into Masunaga's belly, his entire body jerks, then shudders. The pain is absolute. Blinding. Breathtaking. His mind attempts to sort out what has happened. My girl's brother stabbed me? his mind screams in alarm. My girl's brother stabbed me? It's the only thought he is able to process.

The driver puts a hand over Masunaga's mouth and shoves him overboard. Masunaga splashes into the ocean. He watches in horror as the water clouds red with his own blood. The sharks dart to him and tap his body with the sides of their heads, then twist and retreat. They do this over and over.

The gaijin leans over the transom, but he isn't looking down at Masunaga. Instead, his eyes are locked on the horizon with condescending benevolence. The girl appears next to him. The gaijin puts his arm around her. She glances down at Masunaga with a look that seems to shrug.

"God, I love this place," the gaijin says, smiling his golden smile. "I think I'm going to move here."

HAIRSTYLES OF THE JIHADI

BY KIANA DAVENPORT

Ala Wai

Honolulu, 2020

My nightmare has a face. A smell. It has body parts. It knows my name. On the worst nights, Emma holds me while my flying selves go off in all directions. She keeps me armored. Makes me take my meds so I can sleep. I need that R&R to function—to keep my cattle ranch going, graze lands seeded, my ranch hands content.

You could say I'm moderately successful. Although my primary concern is the well-being of my wife, Emma, and my son, Keo, who I love with a passion that's embarrassing. He attends boarding school in Honolulu, where scholastic standards are higher than here on the Big Island. This was not my choice, but Emma wants our boy to sound educated, lose his pidgin-slangy mouth, and talk like a bougie haole boy.

Keo checks in several times a week, and one day when he called, he mentioned a stranger hanging out at the court where he and his friends play basketball.

"He's there every day, Dad. It's weird."

He mentioned the guy several times. Finally, I flew into Honolulu and went directly to the basketball court. A haole in faded jeans and aloha shirt was lounging on the grass beside the court. Now and then he shouted encouragement to boys shooting baskets. I studied him, then sauntered over.

"Howzit. One of those kids yours?"

He looked up and shook his head. "Nah. I just like basketball."

"Basketball? Or . . . young boys?"

He sat up fast. "Easy, fella. I'm paid to be here."

"Yeah? My son is one of those kids. He says you hang around too much."

He pointed to a man on a bench across the court. "Not me. *He's* the one we're watching."

I glanced toward the bench. A man in a tracksuit appeared to have interrupted his jogging to watch the game. His skin was dark, his features more Middle Eastern than local.

"Don't let the tracksuit fool you. He shows up like that every day. Soon he'll butt in and 'coach' them on free throws and hook shots. Trust me, basketball is *not* what's on his mind."

I studied the 'jogger.' "So he's a pervert. And you're, what? A cop?"

"It's a little more complicated. I'm not at liberty to—"

I suddenly sat down beside the guy. "Look, I served in Iraq. Explosives ordnance. Demolitions. We coordinated with military intelligence. I know the drill. During special ops, sometimes innocents got killed." I leaned closer. "See that husky boy with curly hair? That's my son. If you cops are planning a sting op with this fucking pervie, I don't want my boy out there as bait. Jesus, how do you know the guy's not armed?"

He pulled something from his pocket. "Do me a favor. Try to look relaxed." He flipped open a badge. *Federal Bureau of Investigation.* He barely moved his lips. "He's not a pervert. He's jihad. An ISIS recruiter."

My metabolism changed. I slowly sat back.

"That's right. Al Qaeda, Taliban, ISIS . . . whatever their

flavor of the month is, it's still jihad, fighting the Holy War on behalf of Islam. Some of the kids on that court are Muslim. Their parents are Muslim. They even have a mosque in Honolulu. With the Middle East a war zone, refugee populations have exploded in the Pacific—Australia, New Zealand, now here . . ."

"Slow down," I whispered.

"What I'm saying is . . . the fanatics have followed the refugees. They're actively recruiting. Looking for young men to join jihad. They like to indoctrinate them young."

He paused and watched the jihadi instruct a boy on how to execute a pivot shot.

"Two Muslim boys from St. Louis Academy were recruited last year. We were too late. They'd already joined a militant group in Syria. They're parents didn't know; now they're under suicide watch."

I stared at Keo, awaiting his turn with the ball. "He touches my boy, he's dead."

"He won't. Your son is Catholic. We know which ones he's targeting.'"

"Tell me, how do these bastards get past immigration . . . no-fly, no-entry lists?"

With feigned lassitude, the agent stretched, stood, and lit a cigarette. "We make mistakes. Thanks to our policy of open arms, the US is currently their favorite market. Minneapolis has the largest Somali immigrant population in the country. Ninety-eight percent Muslim. In one year, jihad recruitment has *quadrupled* there."

I got to my feet, thwarting the urge to rush out to the court and snap the jihadi's neck.

"You guys have ID'd him. Why not arrest him?"

"He's useful. Already led us to three 'chiefs' in Waikiki

orchestrating recruitment in the islands. If we arrest them, they'll just send in more."

"Well, good luck," I said. "I'm taking my boy home where he's safe."

The agent shook his head. "Nowhere is safe now. Trust me, these bastards are cyber-savvy. Their biggest recruitments are over the Internet."

Within hours I had withdrawn Keo from school, citing a "family emergency." At the airport, I purchased newspapers and magazines that mentioned Islam, ISIS, jihad. By the time we were in flight, I had accessed Internet links for *jihadists* on my iPhone. What I discovered sickened me.

In 2016, a local Muslim boy of sixteen, Hawaiian mother, East Indian father, recruited out of tenth grade to fight for an Al Qaeda–linked group, al-Shabab, had died fighting in Somalia. Recruiters had used social media to reach him. I discovered six separate Facebook sites using the Islamic State flag as their profile photo. One of them had fourteen thousand followers. I glanced over at Keo.

"Son, what do you know about this terrorist group ISIS?"

He answered nonchalantly: "They're the guys who cut off heads."

"Medieval savagery. It's sickening."

". . . Well, our teacher says we should stop bombing their countries, that we've killed nearly a million people."

"And . . . why do you think we're still bombing them?"

He shrugged. "Maybe . . . because we don't know how to *finish* what we started."

I sat back, half-impressed. The boy's school was considered progressive. In matters of world politics he was probably light-years ahead of me. I went back to my iPhone and discovered the Twitter account of a Somalian who had left Minnesota for al-Shabab. His daily tweets praised Islamic State militants while damning US 'infidels.' In an al-Shabab video secretly filmed in Honolulu, a recruited Muslim boy invited other island boys to join him: "*Aloha! You must answer the call of Allah and go to jihad wherever possible!*"

I had served two tours in Iraq before I was honorably discharged. I never discussed what I'd seen, or what I'd committed. I came home and slid into a coma—almost ten years of total withdrawal from the world outside my ranch. Now the world had forced its way back into my consciousness. That night, with no forethought, I broke the news to Emma.

"Today a Muslim fanatic stood next to our boy. That's why I brought him home. Don't worry, the guy was recruiting Muslim kids. They send them to terrorist camps for training, where they learn to be suicide bombers. Can you believe this? . . . In Honolulu?"

She leaned forward. "Albert, I've been saying it for years . . . that one day those terrorists were going to invade our islands. You didn't hear me . . . you've tuned out the world . . ."

Golden-skinned, her Polynesian features gathered into something just short of beautiful. My wife is a teacher, a woman of intelligence. I sometimes wonder why she's stayed with me.

"Well, sweetheart . . . you were right. They're here. They're all over the fucking Pacific."

I had blown up ISIS villages. Taken out whole families. Yet, I knew nothing about them. Trying to educate myself, I read everything available on their history.

ISIS. The Islamic State in Iraq al-Sham. The group emerged a decade ago, offshoot of Al Qaeda, one that

specialized in suicide bombing and inciting Iraqi's Sunni
Muslim minority against its Shiite majority . . .

I read through the night, learning how ISIS had metasta-
sized around the globe. By 2011, amid Iraq's growing violence
and the depravities of Syria's civil war, ISIS had regenerated
and exploded as a terrorist force. By 2014, it had overtaken
cities, vast oil fields, large swaths of territory in Syria, Iraq,
Afghanistan. Death squads from Syria all the way to Australia. By now, Islamic State militants had become a Mafia-like
organization, a financial juggernaut earning over five million
dollars a day through confiscated oil fields, heroin, human
trafficking, the theft of priceless antiquities. Even China,
with its population of nearly one billion, was one of ISIS's
biggest customers, smuggling out its oil through the Red
Sea.

For days I sat mired in this new information, not knowing
what to do with it. At Emma's urging, I relented after a week
and allowed Keo to return to school. The day he boarded his
flight, I tried to lecture him.

"Son, you understand that creep on the courts was a jihad
recruiter. Do you know what they're doing here?"

"Yeah. They're scouting for soldiers." He shrugged.
"They're just trying to defend their country."

"Defend?" I said. "They're cold-blooded killers who want
to control the Middle East. Maybe the world. They've massa-
cred families, entire villages."

"Well . . . so have we, Dad. How many years since 9/11?
And we're still blasting the hell out of the Middle East in the
name of *payback*. What do you call that?"

"Okay," I said, "you have a point. But we're not savages.
We're not decapitating women and children like ISIS."

"Japan did that in World War II. Now they're our *biggest* ally."

His trenchant remarks reminded me that I was woefully out of touch. A man with few answers for his son. I vowed to keep catching up with the world, become adequate to these conversations. My son leaned over and hugged me.

"Dad, I respect your opinions. But since the day I was born, we've been bombing innocent people over there. Iraq. Afghanistan. Now Syria. We don't even see their faces. We just send in Stealth Bombers and whole villages disappear. It's fucked up. And my generation is sick of it."

I held him in a tight embrace, wondering how I could make the war up to him.

I settled down for a while, assured that the feds were tracking all ISIS recruiters on our islands.

I tried to keep up with the news, how they were infiltrating other Pacific islands, recruiting local boys. One day an article in the paper blew my mind.

AUSTRALIAN TEEN GUILTY IN TERROR PLOT

Fifteen-year-old Caucasian Catholic male . . . convicted of terrorism in Sydney . . . plotting to kill police officers in ANZAC Day parade . . . Recruited by notorious jihadi Abu Khaled al-Cambodi, who directed the youth and 30,000 extremists online followers to prepare for the ANZAC Day massacre by attacking parade crowds with guns, machetes . . . especially police officers. Ultimate goal . . . to decapitate as many officers at possible . . .

. . . Attack was foiled by online watchdog links . . . When teen arrested . . . thousands of extremist messages

found on his computer files . . . plus storage units filled
with assault rifles and machetes supplied by al-Cambodi
. . . urging the youth and his followers to slaughter many
hundreds . . . Teen pleaded guilty to inciting terrorism
in the name of jihad . . . sentenced to ten years to life in
prison . . . al-Cambodi had dismantled encrypted website
and disappeared . . .

The boy was fifteen, my son's age. Each time I read the
article, my stomach heaved. I immediately called Keo in his
dorm room. It was evening, he should have been there studying. When he didn't answer, I panicked. Visions of him out
on the streets marching with budding terrorists. I told Emma
I had an emergency and took the forty-minute flight to Honolulu. A security guard who had served with me let me into
Keo's dorm. When he opened his door, I was so relieved, I
sank into a chair.

"You didn't answer your phone."

"I was in the shower . . . Dad, what's happened? Is it Mom?"

I thrust the news article at him: the fifteen-year-old terrorist. "He's your age. He's not a Muslim. They're starting to
convert Christian kids, *any* kids! Read it, and tell me that you
and your friends haven't been hustled like this . . . that no
one has approached you . . ."

Keo read the clip and looked up, appalled. "This is sick
. . . disgusting! And you think I would do such a thing? Dad,
I would never join up with no jihadi!"

Aggression was kicking in from combat days, and I was
not controlling it. I sat back, feeling the adrenaline runoff.
"Sorry, son. It's like . . . the past is coming back. A whole
shitload of bad memories. Those fuckers who killed my best
friends are in our backyard . . ."

He reached out and took my hand. "Dad, I know you have . . . nightmares, that you don't always sleep well. But you need to stop worrying about me. I'm okay. I don't do drugs . . . I even made the dean's list this semester. Besides, our teachers have alerted us to these jihad recruiters . . . that they're everywhere, especially on the Internet. I don't even turn it on at night. So . . . please stop panicking."

I managed to settle down. We talked about his studies, his grades, tennis lessons, his swim meets. Before I left, I asked about the recruiter who had hung around the courts.

Keo shrugged. "The FBI took him away in handcuffs." He hesitated. "But lately these new jihadi types have been hanging out at Manoa Park where we have swim meets. They never bother us. But we hear them lecturing Muslim kids on Islamophobia . . . telling them they need to fight it more aggressively . . ." What Keo said next stiffened atavistic hairs on the back of my neck. "I heard this one guy say that Honolulu is run by Chinese bankers. That Chinese are the Jews of the Pacific, and Muslims need to wipe out these Jew wannabes . . ."

Our family is Hawaiian Chinese with a touch of Welsh. Keo's words festered in my mind for days. But I had so much going on with the ranch that I let it lay sink into my brainpan and nearly be forgotten. Still, occasionally I checked in with Lou, the FBI agent, who always assured me that the FBI, the CIA, the Counterterrorism Section of the National Security Division, and the Pacific Command's Joint Intel Center had instituted a major counter-ISIS operation for Hawaii and all the Pacific Islands.

"Your son," he assured me, "is now living in the safest place in the world from these jihad recruiters. So kick back, man. Relax! Take care of your ranch and your family."

* * *

I relaxed. I "kicked back" for several weeks. One night I turned on the news.

A local man, Ikaika Kang, had been arrested by the FBI. A decorated US Army combat soldier, he'd been under surveillance as an ISIS sympathizer, suspected of passing them US military procedures. After he was recorded promising to suicide-bomb soldiers at Honolulu's Schofield Barracks, he was arrested, and then admitted that he had been radicalized while fighting in Afghanistan. He was led away shouting into news cameras: "Our jihad has begun! We will cleanse Hawaii of all infidels. Inshallah!"

I sat back in disbelief. Kang was not some fanatic who had infiltrated our islands. He was part Hawaiian, born and raised in Honolulu. When I came out of shock, I called Lou, my FBI contact. He expressed only mild shock over Kang.

"Yeah, unfortunately, would-be suicide bombers have breached our military . . . big time. Thousands of recruits . . . the computer generation . . . nothing to do at night but stare at their screens. That's where these jihadis are recruiting them. We've increased surveillance at all military bases. Instituted curfews on computer usage at night. The point is to catch these kids before they've taken the loyalty oath and are following ISIS protocols . . . that's when they're brainwashed enough to blow their friends away."

He finally slowed down: "Don't worry about your son. We've got the civilian population covered on every island. Except for the military, things have calmed down, jihad recruiters are suddenly lying low."

"Why is that?" I asked.

"Some have moved on to Nauru and the Solomons where natives are darker. Dark is their preference when they're recruiting boys for, say, al-Shabab in Somalia. Still . . . a few sightings recently at Manoa Valley Park. Our agents are on it."

The same park Keo had mentioned, the location of his swim meets. I felt a slippage in my joints. Manoa Park was a huge gathering place for young athletes—baseball diamonds, soccer fields, volleyball and basketball courts, an Olympic-size pool. Each week high school teams competed there while rapturous fans shouted from the bleachers. My son competed there.

Something inside me turned around. I stared down all my resolutions to relax, told Emma I was going to the cattle auctions, and flew back to Honolulu. At Manoa Park, I walked the grounds for days, studying faces with an almost anthropological interest. In the tidal shift of cheering crowds, I eventually spotted several men who could be jihad recruiters. Eyes darting, never still, they wore Nike trainers, trendy jogging gear, and looked relatively young and fit. Though brown-skinned, none of them looked quite Middle Eastern. Except for hesitant, rather calculated moves, they fit easily into the crowds. The new gen of recruiters, I decided. Maybe they were only recruiting Muslim boys, but I kept thinking of Ikaika Kang.

I began to concentrate on one of them. Thirtyish, tight, wiry build. His hair buzz cut, the rest of his body hairless, sleek as an eel. Even his armpits were remarkably devoid of hair, so I began to think of him as "Sleek." His English was unaccented, he could have been from anywhere. His smile was friendly, though his eyes were piercing, constantly shifting. Only once did he give himself away. A cyclist plowed into him, knocking him sideways. Teeth bared like a wolf, he suddenly shouted ugly, Arab-sounding epithets. My reflexes sharpened. Sometimes we sat so close in crowds, we almost touched. When I momentarily lost him, I stalked him with a sixth sense, utilizing a third eye, third ear, a second skin, the way I had in close combat.

At night I sat in a cheap hotel room, watching indoctrination videos on jihad websites. Young Muslim recruits swearing *bayat* to ISIS. Vows made to Hezbollah. It all blended into numbing rhetoric until I watched something that brought me to my feet. A jihad recruiter and a local boy discussed how Native Hawaiians were still enslaved by whites, still thought of as "inferior and dumb." How our lands had been stolen. Statehood forced on us. The boy stared into the camera and spoke by rote:

> . . . *Our lands now belong to the US military. They blow up our valleys during war maneuvers, leave behind unexploded bombs that kill or maim us. The rest of our lands are owned by foreign billionaires. That's why Hawaiians are homeless. WE MUST FIGHT BACK. Osama bin Laden changed history. You must join forces with the Islamic State! And help us change our history too!* . . .

I paused the video and sat in shock. Jihadi were definitely no longer targeting Muslim kids exclusively. They were after Hawaiians. I thought of Keo. My heartbeat accelerated. When I calmed down, I called him on his cell, explained that I was in town for the cattle auctions. I casually mentioned the video I'd watched, the radicalized Hawaiian boy. Keo said he'd seen it.

"It went viral, Dad. Made the rounds in the dorm. He's just some poor kid from the projects looking for a handout. No one took it seriously . . ."

He even admitted that, after watching the video and hearing rumors that jihad recruiters were on the prowl again, he and his friends lampooned the recruiters and ran through the dorm with their arms raised, shouting, "COME TO JIHAD . . . COME TO JIHAD . . ." They had even adopted jihadi hairstyles—hair combed straight back from the brow, then cut straight at the nape of the neck the way the caliph wore his.

"Don't worry, Dad. It'll wear off. It's just a fad . . . like rap words and gangsta clothing."

Still, within days it was broadcast that, since the arrest of Ikaika Kang, the threat level at US military bases in Hawaii had increased 1,000 percent. Five more arrests of ISIS and Al Qaeda sympathizers among enlisted men at Wheeler Army Airfield. I pictured hundreds of local boys serving overseas, dark-skinned mixbloods insulted and debased by their superiors. Men ripe for jihad recruiting. Some would come home radicalized.

A cloudy day at Manoa Park. I watched "Sleek" greet two Arab-looking boys and several Hawaiian mixbloods. Thin, unathletic-looking teens—semi-loners who he had befriended—they followed him like acolytes. They were all poorly dressed, probably from broken homes, suffering crises of identity—exclusion from sports, from girls, from clubs. Wanting to be accepted and belong, they were perfect targets for exploitation.

Sleek engaged them in volleyball, bought them lunch while lecturing them in soft, paternal tones. He lived in a cheap ground-floor apartment near the park, and some days he took his boys home to shoot baskets in the driveway. Afterward, they watched kung fu movies, then, inevitably, recruiting videos. As "unofficial watchdog," I alerted Lou, and the FBI wire-tapped Sleek's apartment. Listening to playback tapes, I heard soundtracks from jihad radicalization lectures. Boys reading aloud from the Quran and sunna. Sleek's voice encouraging them.

"Under Allah, we are all one family! Everyone is a brother. No one is alone!" His rhetoric slowly escalated: *"You think because you are called 'American citizens' that America loves you? No! US military and tourism enslaves you. Your people will never be free!"*

A boy timidly questioned him. *"But . . . how will becoming jihad help our people?"*

The man's voice turned soft: *"You will be Islamic eyes and ears. Real warriors. Soldiers of Allah! Learn bomb-making. Maybe even make* hijra *to Syria, Somalia . . ."*

What he neglected to tell those youths was that they had been assessed as suicide bombers. They were already considered dust.

It was early evening when I drove once again to Keo's school. I didn't mean to bug my son, or embarrass him, but things kept grinding on my nerves. Following these recruiters every day, watching them hijack these innocent young kids, made me fearful for my boy. He had said he was busy with exams, but I felt this sudden urge to see him, if only briefly. I greeted the security guard, then knocked softly on Keo's door. No answer, so I opened the door. He was at his desk, brooding over a book. Seeing me, he jumped up.

"Dad! You're still in town . . . ?"

"More cattle business. I know I'm not supposed to be here, but . . . how are exams going?"

"Okay, I guess . . ." He had opened the desk drawer. He was trying to shove the book inside. The drawer stuck and he stood there holding it. Something in his expression gave me pause.

"What is it, son?"

I glanced at the book, the cover vaguely familiar. He sighed and handed it over. I felt my bowels jerk. *Lone Mujahid Pocketbook*. A notorious bomb-making manual published by Al Qaeda.

"Jesus Christ! Those . . . godforsaken bastards! How did you get hold of this?"

"It doesn't mean anything, Dad. It's just for fun. All the guys have copies—"

"HOW DID YOU GET HOLD OF THIS!"

"One of those creeps you follow at Manoa Park. Sometimes he hangs out near the pool . . . throws haji words around. We asked him how to buy copies of *Lone Mujahid*. He gave us the code to a website—"

"What were you doing at Manoa Park?"

"We have swim meets there, remember? I've seen you there. I know what you're doing." He sat me down on his bed and dropped beside me. "Dad, please stop. Please!"

"Stop what?"

"You're tracking them. You and your FBI buddies . . ."

"They're killers, son. They prey on boys like you . . . This fucking manual, for instance."

"Then let the feds take care of it . . ."

"Why? And why is this upsetting you?"

"Because you'll change. You're already getting tense. Like when I was a kid . . ."

I frowned, not understanding.

"I was so lonely as a kid! Mom was too. You were never there. I mean, you were there . . . but you *weren't*. You never laughed or talked. Mom said it was Iraq. The years of combat you couldn't shake. She said those scars last a lifetime . . ."

In that moment, it all flashed past. For years my mind had been a haunted house. My senses so deadened, I walked through flames and never felt the heat. I had to pull myself back to the present, to my son.

". . . It wasn't till I hit my teens, drinking and raising hell, that you whipped my ass. Man, I was *happy*! You had finally acknowledged me. Before that . . . I just thought you hated me."

I looked down in shock. "I always *loved* you, son . . . but I was damaged. I saw too much combat . . . did too many things that haunted me."

"But you recovered, Dad. We've been close. Now you're getting weird again. I'm afraid . . ."

"Of what, son?"

"That you might kill someone. That's what you did over there, right?"

I looked away. "That was a long time ago. Right now, I just want to keep these bastards away from you, and young boys like you—"

"Dad, I'm fine. No one is going to recruit me! But I'm worried about *you*. I know your best friends were killed over there. Maybe you're still hungry for payback."

I abruptly stood up, then sat back down. "You're right, son. This ISIS thing . . . it's brought back a lot of memories, and rage. But . . . if that's what you really want, I'll stop."

"No more 'tracking'? No terminating anyone? You swear?"

"I swear. In return, *you* need to swear you'll never read this filth again."

We embraced and held on tight. I walked out into the night carrying the scent of my boy . . . and the *Lone Mujahid Pocketbook*.

For hours I poured over the manual. A how-to-kill book written in hip-hop and rap lingo, that would have great appeal to the MTV generation and Gen X. In between cartoons and crossword puzzles, the overall message was . . . *Ji-*

had is cool! Become an American jihadi! Bold letters listed the core ingredients for volatile terrorist explosives found in the average kitchen cupboard. Lemons, coffee, sugar, hydrogen peroxide. *Make bombs in the kitchen of your mom!* Followed by precise instructions and diagrams on how to build bombs, and the best places to kill the maximum number of victims.

I read through the thing twice, then called Lou and told him what I had. What my son had been reading.

He let loose with a string of expletives. "That mother-fucking bomb-making cookbook! It's got the same appeal as rapping gangbangers. *Violence is cool! Killing is hip!* What's the name of your son's school? We're sweeping campuses across the city. Plus, enlisted men's barracks on all military bases in Hawaii. They're ordering *Lone Mujahid Pocketbook* in droves. It's almost as popular as *Playboy.*"

I told him that jihadi recruiters were hanging around the pool where Keo and his friends swam. That's how the boys got copies of the manual.

There was a long silence before Lou answered. "You recently mentioned that, just for fun, your son and his friends had copied jihadi hairstyles, then for weeks ran around shouting their slogans. Tonight you found him reading their manual on how to make explosives that can kill large crowds . . ."

"Right. So what are you saying, Lou?"

"I'm saying that you need to pay attention, man. Those fuckers are already in his head."

I sat up all night, picturing recruiters at Manoa Park, tracking, then grooming, local boys as suicide bombers. I pictured one of them drawn to the swimming pool, to Keo's crowd. I pictured my son embraced by death.

The following day I went to Sleek's apartment and waited

for dark. A humid night, his front door was left open for air. I heard him speaking rapid Pashto into a cell phone. He was wearing only a towel around his waist, and his back and chest were bare, except for stubble. I imagined him shaving his arms and legs twice a day to achieve that sleek, hairless look.

With no forethought I crashed through the screen door, pointing a Walther semiautomatic. Before Sleek could react, I grabbed his phone, broke it apart, threw the pieces out the window, then motioned with the Walther. In shock, he lifted his arms in the air.

"Allahu Akbar," I whispered. "Already making plans for our local boys? Secret training camp? A little suicide-bombing etiquette? Where's the camp? . . . Tell me!"

His chest heaved in and out, his American accent slipped. "What you are talking about?"

I advanced and pointed the Walther at his head.

"Do not know answer, I swear!" he cried. "Not given such information—"

"Where were you assigned before? How many boys did you recruit?"

He hesitated. I slid back the lock bolt, pressed the gun to his temple.

"Was in Manila! . . . Eight, nine boys . . ."

"And by now they're probably dead. How do you get paid for these recruits? Badakshan rubies? Your own boy prostitute?"

He reared back, indignant. "I am mujahideen. Reward is serving Allah!"

I smiled and stepped closer. "Here's what I know. There is no Allah. No Jesus Christ. It's all one big . . . *cargo cult.* You bastards are killing for nothing."

I threw a shirt, a pair of pants, and shoes at him. When he was dressed, I handcuffed him behind his back, thinking how close he had been to Keo at the park, close enough to touch him. To breathe his fetid breath on my son. My hands shook. I fought the urge to snap his windpipe, render him brain-dead in seconds. Instead, I relaxed. I was trying to keep my promise to Keo.

"Why me?" Sleek suddenly asked. "Why you have followed me . . . not others?"

I smiled. "You looked like Satan's golden boy. So sleek . . . so clean. So kind to our boys, while you poisoned their minds, and sent them off to die. For that, you have to pay."

His eyes gleamed, like a well-made doll's. "I have no fear. *Mujahid* do not beg!"

I smiled again. "You will . . . my friend. You will."

My car was a dark, contained universe we moved in. My conscience negotiating for Sleek's life, then renegotiating on behalf of all the innocent lives the Taliban, jihad, ISIS, Al Qaeda had barbarically cut short. I liked the game of vacillating, of possibly changing my mind, and tortuously killing him. But there was that promise made to Keo.

Midnight. Full moon so bright the stars were dimmed. We were somewhere near the ocean, echoes of a band where couples danced. I turned inland and the music faded. We passed seedy bars, strips clubs, and turned onto a street paralleling a wide canal. The air became foul, the overwhelming stench of rot. I parked, pulled Sleek from the car, hands still cuffed behind his back.

"You shout for help . . . I'll kill you. Guarantee."

He was quiet, acquiescent. Something in my manner assured him that I was not going to kill him. Maybe he thought it was a rendezvous, that FBI agents would appear, trade him for one of theirs. He momentarily relaxed. But as we moved closer to the water, the stench intensified—so raw that I tasted it on my lips. My nostrils burned.

We stepped onto a wide concrete bridge that spanned the canal. No one around, I walked him to the middle of the bridge and leaned out, gazing at shifting sludge below. I pressed Sleek against the railing, forcing his head down.

"Ala Wai Canal," I said. "Two miles long, maybe twenty feet deep. A century ago, it was crystal clear, pure enough for swimming. Then the population multiplied . . . folks started using the canal for garbage and worse . . ."

My voice turned soft, like I was telling a fairy tale.

"In heavy storms, neighborhoods flooded. Raw sewage poured into these waters that once flowed to the sea. It's now so full of sludge and filth it hardly moves, has to be dragged every couple years. During big storms, forty million gallons of raw sewage are dumped here. That's what it is now, a sewage dump . . . a source of embarrassment to city officials."

"Eyes burning," Sleek whispered. "Hard to breathe . . ."

I pushed his head down again, forcing him to stare at green-brown sludge and toxic, iridescent stains on top of which large, dead things floated. Creatures of no discernible species or phylum.

"Imagine what's down there . . ." I said, "after a hundred years of breeding. Millions of microbes from intestinal tracts of rats, dogs, humans. Microbes that reproduce and never die, absorbing arsenic, lead. They say there are creatures in these waters that no one has a name for."

I pulled Sleek closer. "See those fish floating on the surface? Dead barracuda. And that's a porcupine puffer fish. What's left of them. Microbes are eating them from the inside out. Of course, it's instant death for humans. Folks fall, are dumped . . . they don't even find their bones . . ."

By now he was gasping. I continued in a dreamlike voice: "There's a pathogen down there . . . *Vibrio vulnuficus*. A flesh-eating bacteria that feeds only on *living* brains and hearts. Scientists lab-tested it on animals . . . it enters the eyes and consumes the brain and heart while the host is conscious." I glanced down at him. "A human with its large organs . . . would be a *feast*."

Sleek listened distractedly. He kept looking around for the federal agents that he expected to appear. I suddenly grabbed his jaw, turning his head sharply to the right.

"As you see, that side of the canal is reinforced by concrete walls." I jerked his jaw to the left, pointing to a scraggly tree line that gave way to steep, muddy slopes that slid down to the water fifty feet below. "But on the left side, the walls broke down years ago. When the canal overflows, raw sewage and mud rise all the way up to that tree line. Right now those slopes are covered with sludge and filth."

I took his arm, led him off the bridge to the muddy slopes on the left. As we approached the trees and the slopes below, Sleek tried to pull back.

"What we are doing? Where is FBI?"

"Sorry, pal. No FBI. No rendezvous."

We neared the trees, below them nothing but mud and slime oozing down to fetid waters, the full moon making the scene as bright as day. I forced him down onto his behind and yanked off his running shoes. Next, I pulled him to his bare feet, and removed the handcuffs, essentially freeing him. The Walther pressed against his back, I pushed him out beyond the trees to where grass and dirt turned rapidly to slime.

The earth sloped so precipitously that we were suddenly walking at a forward tilt, the filth reaching up to our ankles. I felt it sucking at my boots. Even with lugged soles, it was hard to stand upright. I slipped, almost fell to my knees, the fetid air making me gag. We slid downward for twenty feet until I stopped and began to back away from Sleek.

"What you are doing?" he croaked. Awareness slowly dawning.

I called out, "Giving you a chance to live. Let's see if Allah can save you from this toxic filth, help you make it back up to those trees. If you can make it . . . you're free. I guarantee."

He half turned me to in terror. The quick shift in weight caused his bare feet to shoot out from under him. He landed on his hip and shoulder and lay still, trying to gauge how best to gain traction and stand upright while keeping his face averted from the slime. Carefully backing up, I heard him start to pray as he slowly sat up, then tried to stand. The ground was so steep that he almost pitched forward. He sat down again, turned sideways, and attempted to rise so that he was perpendicular to the sloping ground. He achieved that position and stood still. The muck beneath him sloshed each time his feet moved.

Sleek retched several times, then in slow motion turned so that he was facing uphill, his back to the canal. I watched as he tensed, trying to fight gravity's backward pull. I imagined his muscles straining as he struggled for balance. I heard him cursing in Pashto, and held my breath, almost rooting for him as he tried to take a step upward. His other foot shot out; he went down on his hands and knees. Before he gained traction, he began to slide downward, then rolled over on his back, trying to stop the momentum by digging in his heels. For a while he lay still.

Above him, I fought the slime still sucking at my boots. Though I had gained several feet, it was still so slippery that every move I made was tentative. I gagged repeatedly from the stench, then very slowly turned sideways, planted one boot deep in the muck until I felt traction, and planted the other beside it and slowly climbed sideways like a skier mounting a steep slope. After ten minutes of laboring, I felt the ground begin to level out. It was still slick and wet, but now it was easier to move. Eventually I reached grass and solid earth and collapsed.

Catching my breath, I watched Sleek in the moonlight, struggling for his life, dragging himself to his knees repeatedly, then attempting to stand upright. Each time, his bare feet flew out from under him. He would land on his knees and collapse onto his chest, still fighting to keep his face turned away from the filth. He tried to crawl upward; there was nothing to grasp but slime and mud. Each time he moved, his body slid downward. He cursed, prayed aloud, fighting the pull of gravity.

I lit a cigarette, gagged on the inhale, the stench here still unbearable. I watched Sleek played out on his stomach, face and body caked with filth, hands desperately clutching at nothing. For a while he didn't move. I saw how he was giving in, the weight of his body dragging him farther down. In the quiet night, his voice was raised, begging for help.

After nearly two hours of struggle, he'd been sucked down near the bottom of the slope. Exhausted, he seemed to have given up. I squinted in the moonlight, watching how Sleek's body slid still farther down. Then something large—strong enough to take hold of his foot—jerked his body inch by inch into the fetid waters of the Ala Wai.

In that moment Sleek cried out, "Allahu Akbur! Allah is great! Allah, save me! Save me!"

I listened to his repeated cries. The silence between them telling Sleek that there was no Allah, no God to save him, to lead him through the uncharted night. There was only the noise between being and nothing. The endless noise that grew fainter and fainter.

I lit another cigarette, tossed it aside, disgusted. I thought how I should have killed him . . . delivered his corpse to his jihadi friends. But there was a promise made. I pulled off my filthy boots, tossed them high into the trees, and walked barefoot to my car. Driving the empty freeway, I acknowledged that one less jihadi signified nothing. My islands were still terribly at risk. And I acknowledged that the need for payback would always be cargoed in my DNA.

Yet, just then, I felt a quiet thrill of redemption. A dozen ways I could have dispatched Sleek, but in the end, I had given him a fighting chance. And maybe that was the solution to my personal jihad. I had kept my promise to my son.

PART II

Home in the Islands

PART II

DIAMOND DREAMS

BY MINDY EUN SOO PENNYBACKER

Diamond Head

I n a recurring memory that makes me feel happy and carefree, although I should know better, I am a passenger on a supersonic *Concorde* airliner, waiting on the tarmac at JFK Airport in New York before taking off for Paris. It's late August of 1994, a hazy morning, onshore wind. I'm with my husband Sam, our son Jake, my mother Josie, stepfather Chuck, brother Timothy, and his boyfriend Frank, in royal-blue Air France recliners, arranged in pairs.

My mother smiles down at Jake, who's seated next to her and peering out the disappointingly small windows. "Just imagine, we'll fly to Paris in three hours, less than half the normal time," she says.

Jake nods. "You're right, Grandma, and not only that, but at sixty thousand feet, we'll see the curve of the earth." Jake is eight years old, and his voice trembles with the deep fervor of Christmas morning, when Santa left him a remote-controlled F-14 Tomcat that roared, spat fire from its afterburners, rolled across the floor, opened and shut its wings, and rose on its haunches, pointing its needle-nose skyward. It only left the ground in Jake's imagination, and that sufficed.

My mother ruffles her fingers through Jake's thick, wavy hair, and suddenly she turns and gives me a look. Her irises are big and round as marbles; their color is the squid-ink black of outer space.

And that's it. I don't remember taking off, flying over the Atlantic, or landing in Paris, much less seeing the bend of the earth or imbibing caviar and champagne. My mother craved extravagance. She was a party girl. I was a spoiler, a frugal killjoy. A changeling, she said.

I first learned of my mother's *Concorde* plot that spring, when Jake and I flew from New York to Honolulu for his school break. I had a freelance assignment from a national magazine to cover a resurgent Hawaiian sovereignty movement. Sam, a staff writer at another magazine in the city, stayed home, saving his sparse vacation time for summer, when we usually went to France.

We had a stopover in San Francisco, where Timothy and Frank picked us up and took us to their apartment to spend the night. Unfortunately, they had acquired two Persian cats, which triggered my allergies and asthma. I took my medication, but felt as if I was slowly suffocating.

Next morning, on the flight to Honolulu, we were in first class, thanks to a gift of upgrades from my mother. There was definitely more oxygen in first class, yet my airways stayed constricted and inflamed. I took another pill and read up on Hawaiian history while Jake played *Donkey Kong* on his Game Boy.

"Excuse me, are you okay? I hear wheezing," said a soft voice. It was the woman across the aisle. She was in her fifties, heavyset and pretty, with fair, unlined skin, blond hair styled in a pageboy, a snub nose, generous mouth, and large, blue-green eyes. Beneath her double chin, tucked into the hollow of her collarbone, flashed a diamond pendant the size of a grape.

Learning I was asthmatic, she ordered a double espresso.

"They have a machine. This is why I fly first class," she said.

As I sipped the espresso, giving the foil-wrapped chocolate to Jake, the woman stared at my chest. I thought she was monitoring my breath, but then she said, "That's a beautiful brooch. Vintage?"

I nodded, touching the silver-and-vermeil scallop shell pinned to my shirt. It had belonged to an elderly neighbor and friend of my late grandmother. After the old lady died, her bachelor grandson came to clean out the house, throwing her personal things into the driveway and telling my mother to take anything she liked—it was all junk, to him. She took the Louis Vuitton trunk. In an inner pocket she found a platinum Cartier tank watch, which she wears although it's broken, and the Cartier pin, which she gave to me because I love the sea.

"And I love you," I had said, throwing my arms around her and thanking her, for I had coveted the pin as soon as I saw it.

"In a pinch, you can use it as a fishhook," she'd added, which struck me, even at the time, as strange.

I'm afraid of flying and sharks, and the pin became my talisman, protecting me from crashes and bites. I wore it on every flight, and fastened it to my swimsuit, at the hollow between my breasts, when I paddled out to surf. Securely made, with a thick needle and self-locking clasp, it never loosened. It was a bit of armor, my mermaid backup heart.

The espresso helped. I breathed a little easier, relaxed, and fell asleep until a jolt of turbulence woke me. I checked Jake's seat belt with my left hand as my right hand flew to my chest—but the shell was gone. When the seat belt sign turned off, the flight attendants and I searched the floor, between the seats, and under the cushions, everywhere. No luck.

"So sorry. I haven't seen it," my neighbor said in a sympathetic murmur, but her blue gaze went hard, as if she thought I suspected her of taking it. And I did.

The plane was descending. I looked out Jake's window and saw we were passing directly over Diamond Head Crater, which meant sticky Kona weather, bringing ill winds from the south that blow onshore at Honolulu, sending the city's pollution back into its face. The air had that oily yellow glare, and the ocean looked gray and disturbed, with an ugly chop.

At the airport baggage claim, Jake rushed into the arms of my pretty, dark-skinned mother, her long, skinny legs in white short-shorts, her belly protruding beneath her favorite pink crop top, her long hair pinned up, with strands hanging loose. She walked painfully, more slowly than she had last time I saw her, her knees now badly swollen with arthritis. The blond woman wasn't there; she must have been traveling light, I thought, as befitted someone with light fingers.

As soon as we got home, I changed into my swimsuit, ran down to the beach, and dove in. Jake stayed with my mom; born in New York City, he doesn't share my desperate need to get back in my natal Hawaiian sea. I swam the easy quarter mile out to the mouth of the channel but was gasping for air by the time I got back to shore. The thick, humid Kona air, heavy with particles and exhaust, was choking me.

I asked my mother to take me to the emergency room, but she refused. "I've already driven to the airport and back. I'm tired. My knees hurt. All you need is rest."

"I need a doctor, Mom."

She shrugged. "So call 911."

"Josie?" a soft, familiar voice called from outside the

screen door. The speaker, backlit by the sun, had the rounded silhouette of a fertility icon.

"Oh, hi, Lily, welcome back!" My mother opened the door and the figure stepped in.

I gasped: it was the woman from the plane. She had a large envelope in her hand, and for a moment I had a wild hope it contained my brooch. But how did she know where to find me? How did my she and my mother know one another?

"Lily's renting our next-door house," my mother said to me. "Lily, meet Emma and Jake."

The woman winked at me. "Josie, we met on the plane! In first class! We didn't exchange names, but I should have recognized them from your photos. Before I forget . . ." She handed the envelope to my mother. "I signed it. Here's your copy."

My mother took the envelope and went into her study. I heard the creak of her rusty filing cabinet.

"Are you feeling better, Emma?" Lily asked me.

"I have to go to the emergency room."

"I'll take you. Let's go," she said.

Feeling a rush of gratitude and relief, I grabbed my purse and followed her out the door.

In her driveway, there appeared the most handsome young Hawaiian man. He had big, dark eyes that recalled the mysterious orbs of a horse or a whale, a wide, bow-shaped mouth with thick lips, and dark olive skin dusted with pock-marks. His hair was black and frizzy and pulled into a thick, spongey bun at the crown. His otherwise fine nose was running and he kept rubbing and wiping it.

"Hey, Mama," he said, coming over to Lily and pulling her against him, cradling her in his muscular, tattooed arms.

"Hi, baby," she said, wrapping her plump arms around his

neck and leaning back to gaze up into his face before he bent to kiss her on the lips. She turned to me, her blue eyes sparkling as the big diamond nestled in her cleavage caught the sun. "Emma, this is my son, Ikaika."

"Hey there, Emma!" He smiled broadly, revealing a gap between his big front teeth, and tilted his head to one side with a birdlike, flirtatious look, although he appeared to be in his midtwenties, at least fifteen years younger than me, and a good quarter century younger than Lily. He reached to take my hand, bent his long neck in a sudden, snakelike movement, and kissed me on the cheek.

Mother and son? I could see no physical resemblance between these two. And if Ikaika was adopted, it wasn't any less disturbing that their voices, faces, and bodies hinted at a carnal rather than filial bond. But what did I know? My brain long starved for oxygen, I was scarcely in my right mind.

"I'm taking Emma to the ER," Lily said, getting into a white Audi sedan.

Ikaika opened the passenger door for me. "Aw, so sorry, feel better," he said, shutting it carefully after me, and then he went around to Lily's window. "Ma," he said in a low voice, "got a meeting."

Her jaw tightened. She took a deep breath through her nose, let it out. "That's a good sign, right? Talking's good."

"They want the money, Ma." He sniffed and wiped his nose.

"Don't worry, baby. Have I ever let you down?"

"Never! But these guys, they're scary." As he spoke, his face drooped and seemed to age, his features wavering as if the air around them had turned to water. Then he flashed that jaunty smile and jumped lightly up into the cab of an enormous red pickup truck.

MINDY EUN SOO PENNYBACKER // 109

"Ikaika works at Far Bar," Lily said as she slalomed down Beretania Street. "It's a game arcade in Moʻiliʻili, a real hot spot—it draws all the university crowd. We'll have to take Jake there."

"We don't take Jake to bars."

She laughed. "Far Bar doesn't serve alcohol to minors! There's a kiddie room with all the latest video games."

"They're too violent."

"But it's not real," she said.

"Where are you from?" I asked.

She started; her neck stiffened. "Why, from *here*! Well, Kauai. My name is Abigail Lilinoe Partridge Hook. I'm a missionary descendant, and part Hawaiian—and," she added in a brittle tone, "I'm sick of hearing I don't look it."

She looked pure haole. I had grown up among Hawaiians: many of them, like my best friend Maile, had light hair and eyes, but in their features and, more than that, their attitudes and expressions, one immediately recognized their *kanaka* roots, identity, and pride. Of course, in Hawaii we are all amateur detectives of race.

I didn't say any of this to Lily. I said I understood how she felt. As she knew, I was half Korean, from my mother, and half haole, Caucasian, from my father. And neither side of the family thought I looked like them. I felt like an unclaimed package, I said, and Lily laughed, visibly relaxing.

I didn't ask why, if she'd been born and raised here, she didn't speak in gentle, self-deprecating local cadences, but with the loud, nasal, bossy twang of the mainland haole: the tourists, the seasonal, part-time residents who call themselves snowbirds, the retirees who become residents because Hawaii doesn't tax pensions. I didn't say I knew she was a fraud.

* * *

At the emergency room, I was given a shot of adrenaline and put on a nebulizer to pump oxygen into my system. Blood tests showed I'd overdosed on my asthma medication, and so they pumped my stomach out. The doctor prescribed a new, inhaled drug, and taught me how to use it.

Lily waited for hours without complaint. "You're so much better, you look like a different person," she said as she drove me home. She looked different to me as well—she had the halo of someone who had saved my life. I decided to forget about the vanished shell.

Jake was asleep. My mother was waiting up in the kitchen. She'd made *duk kook*, Korean New Year's chicken soup embellished with scallions, boiled beef, egg drops, dried seaweed, and, best of all, oval slices of chewy white rice cakes. I'd missed coming home for the holidays and the comforting ritual of sitting around the kitchen table at midnight with the whole family, heads bent over steaming bowls. I knew my mother wouldn't apologize for not taking me to the hospital—she never said she was sorry about anything—but I accepted this conciliatory gesture with gratitude.

"By the way, Mom, what was in the envelope Lily gave you?"

"A new lease, for a year. I always start out with a month-to-month tenancy, in case it doesn't work out. But Lily's quiet, takes care of the house, and has never been a day late with rent. She's quite wealthy. A missionary descendant."

"So I heard. But you've never been impressed with missionary descendants before."

"I didn't say I was impressed." She got up and put the soup pot in the fridge. "Chuck can micro it when he gets home. He's been working late more than ever, because the city downsized his department."

I said nothing. My stepfather, who hailed from Nevada, was almost twenty years my mother's junior, and a well-known barfly. I didn't believe he was working late in the Department of Planning and Permitting. No one in city government burns the midnight oil.

"But Lily's son Ikaika works late nights, so she and I keep each other company."

"I met Ikaika. Is he really her son? They don't act that way," I said, bracing myself for an indignant explosion in her new best friend's defense.

Instead, my mother frowned, and pursed her puffy lips in a reflexive look of disapproval. "I think he might have been a foster child, but whatever, they're both adults." She paused, then shot me a look. "And you think *I'm* a cradle robber!"

I didn't think that. Chuck had been in his late thirties when they first met at a peace rally, and, according to both their accounts, it was he who had come on to her. He had done well by the marriage, moving from a decrepit, slummy apartment in Moʻiliʻili to a three-bedroom house at Diamond Head with a basement studio where he kept his shrines to Mao and Che Guevara, which my mother wouldn't let into the main house. Plus, she did all the grocery shopping and was a great cook.

Next day, I had to do some reporting in Waiʻanae, and took Jake, who'd never been there, and my mother, who just wanted to be with him. We picked up a four-wheel-drive rental car in nearby Waikiki to spare my mother's ancient but sporty Honda, and I drove us out to rural Waiʻanae and down deeply rutted dirt roads to a beach park. Hawaiian activists were living there in a tent city, to retake land they said was illegally occupied by the state, as proven in 1993 when President Bill Clinton signed and Congress passed the Apology Bill, admitting that the US had illegally overthrown the government of the independent Kingdom of Hawaii a hundred years before.

Jake raced up and down the beach with a group of bright-eyed children, jumping in the ocean, rolling in the shorebreak, tossing seaweed at each other.

"Don't you think my daughter looks Hawaiian?" my mother suddenly asked the campers.

"Mom!" I protested, feeling my face turn red. The apparent leader, the biggest and oldest of the men, shifted heavily in his beach chair as he looked me over. He shook his head. "No," he said.

As we drove back to town, my mother expressed alarm: "What if they decide to claim our houses?"

"They can't," I replied. "Grandpa and Grandma bought them. We can trace the title back to King Kamehameha V."

My mother shook her head. "It was all stolen," she said. "We bought stolen land."

We got home after dark, after picking up chili rice bowls and root beer floats from Rainbow Drive-In just before it closed. We were ravenous, but as soon as we sat down to eat, we heard someone say, "Hi," and Lily Hook was standing beneath the light of the front porch, behind the door screen, holding a skinny boy by the hand. "This is Pili, my son," she said. "He's nine years old, isn't that perfect? He and Jake can play."

"Hi, Pili," I said.

The child didn't reply. He grimaced and twitched and scratched himself; he stared down at his feet and wouldn't look up. Painfully thin, wearing a too-large T-shirt and too-short pants, he looked like he was in custody.

"Since when? I didn't know you had another son," my

mother said. I could tell that, as a landlady, she was irritated to learn there was another tenant in the house.

"Oh, Pili's my new foster son. The papers just came through. Ikaika and I are thrilled; he's always wanted a brother. Sorry to interrupt your dinner, but Pili was so excited to make a friend—Jake, want to come over and spend the night?"

Jake didn't reply. He stared down at his bowl.

"No thanks. He wants to stay in his grandmother's house," I said.

"Well, then Pili could stay here!"

"Pili only just arrived," my mother said.

"Pili's easy."

"Look. The answer's no. I'm tired," my mother said.

"Okay. Why didn't you say so? See you tomorrow—and remember, I need the money for the tickets," Lily said, as she and the boy stepped off the stoop into the darkness that pooled around. Something had changed, I thought. Lily wasn't wearing her diamond.

"What tickets?" I asked my mother.

"Just wait. It's a surprise."

Jake and my mother came along with me the following morning to visit a Hawaiian village in the hills of Waimanalo on the rainy green eastern shore. Just before we left, Lily appeared again with her new foster son and asked if Pili could come along, as he was Hawaiian, and it would be good for him to get out in the country instead of being trapped in the car while she ran errands.

I declined. It was a work trip, not a playdate, I said.

"So this is the way you repay someone who saved your life," Lily said, shaking her head.

"You should have called 911," my mother said later. "She takes you to the emergency room and now she figures she's entitled to free babysitting."

Today's interview was with Sunny Akana, the head of one of several self-proclaimed Hawaiian nations that were vying to establish themselves as the new, sovereign Hawaiian government. After years of living in a tent city at a beach park in Waimanalo, which they claimed was illegally occupied by the state, Akana and his hundred-odd followers had accepted the state grant of a fifty-year lease to a three-hundred-acre mountain valley for five hundred dollars a year.

Seemed like a great deal, I said to him, peering around at the village they had built and the land they had cleared to grow taros, bananas, Ti leaves, and other crops, irrigated by a mountain stream.

"Are you kidding? At three dollars an acre, we're still paying more rent than the military, who pay a dollar a year for Bellows Beach and half the rest of our people's prime mountain and seaside lands."

As Akana and I talked and walked, he pointed out the village vegetable garden, 'ulu and coconut trees, and the ruins of ancient stone walls that formed the kalo terraces, which the community was painstakingly rebuilding by hand. Jake helped a group of village youngsters move rocks and weed the lo'i, then they rinsed off in a clear swimming hole beneath a small waterfall. "Jakey boy, you a good worker," Akana said. "I hereby make you a citizen of my nation. Come back anytime, you will always have a place here."

Maybe that was enough reassurance for my mother, who, to my relief, didn't ask Akana or any of the other villagers whether they thought I looked Hawaiian.

Afterward, we bought plate lunch at L&L Drive-Inn and

picnicked at Makapuʻu, Sam's favorite bodysurfing beach. When I suggested we put on our fins and surf, Jake rummaged in our beach bag. "Where's the football?" he asked with a stricken expression; he was near tears.

I apologized for forgetting. Beach football was Sam's thing. I hated running and leaping in the shorebreak, falling, tumbling, getting covered with sand.

"Dad wouldn't forget. Dad's friendly, unlike you. He would have invited Pili, and we would have played beach football."

This stung, but I agreed and praised Jake for thinking of Pili. When we got home, he could invite the boy to come over, if he liked. Then we put on our fins and swam out past the first dip to catch crisp, glassy waves on the inside sandbar. Arms extended like wings, nose pointed like a beak, Jake flew, fell, and came up smiling, eyes wide, time and again, tossing back his mop of hair.

As we pulled into our driveway, we saw police cars, lights flashing, in Lily's driveway next door. We peeked in the front door and saw her talking to an officer with a clipboard while other officers searched the premises, stepping around overturned furniture and papers and some broken crockery.

Pili wasn't in sight; I hoped he hadn't come to harm.

"I've been robbed!" Lily cried, seeing us, her hand flying to her bare throat. "My diamond! All my jewelry—gone. Forty thousand dollars' worth!"

"Is Pili okay?" I asked.

"He's fine, just upset. I dropped him off at his auntie's."

We said we were sorry.

As we left, Lily put her hand on my mother's arm. "I need the money today," she said.

Jake had to get ready for his overnight with his calabash cousins at his godmother's house, just up the road. As he loaded his backpack, I heard the jingle of my mother's car keys and the creak of the front door. It occurred to me that the same thief might have robbed my mother's jewelry collection of silver, gold, diamonds, and jade, inherited from my grandmother.

"Wait, Mom," I said, running after her.

"I can't talk now, gotta go to the bank," she said.

"What's the rush? Shouldn't we check on your jewelry?"

"It's a limited-time offer! My jewelry's in the file cabinet. You check."

"Wait!" I begged her to explain what was up with the tickets.

She looked at her watch. "Okay, walk me down the steps. I wanted it to be a surprise," she said, "but since you insist: Lily is a travel agent. For $10,000—and don't worry, it's all my treat—she's getting us round-trip tickets from New York to Paris on the *Concorde* for you, Sam, Jake, me, Chuck, Timothy, and Frank. The market value is $84,000."

"But I don't want to go on the *Concorde*, and we can fly to Paris for five hundred dollars round trip on a regular plane."

"You won't have jet lag! You'll arrive the same day, and you'll be with all of us!" She beamed a triumphant smile; of course, I couldn't say that getting away from all of them was one reason Sam and I went to France. She took my arm. "My legs are really tired after all that hiking. It's harder going down than up," she said, leaning heavily on me.

"You and Chuck would still have to buy Hawaii–New York round trips, and Timothy and Frank would have to buy San Francisco–New York," I said.

"No, Lily is getting the four of us vouchers for free tickets, plus first-class upgrades, like the ones you and Jake used flying here."

"I thought those upgrades were from *you*."

"I got them from Lily."

"Don't you think it's strange that she was on our flight?"

"No. She's a travel agent, she's always up in the air. Plus, she's also getting me a discount on a first-class flight and luxury cruise in Korea for your grandfather and his wife. It's my belated wedding gift to them." This was her last chance, she said, to impress her father and win back his love. Already, since having heard about the trip, his manner toward her had thawed.

My grandfather had been angry with my mother since he announced his plan to remarry after my grandmother's death, and she had countered by demanding that he first sign over his remaining shares in both our houses to us. Which meant his new wife wouldn't be able to move in.

"It will kill her. All the Orientals want to live at Diamond Head," my mother said, insisting as usual on using the outdated, politically incorrect term.

But it didn't kill her stepmother. My grandfather bought his wife an apartment on a high floor of the most sought-after high-rise condominium tower in town, but never mind: she hated my mother and had tried to estrange them ever since.

Learning from her example, I had asked my mother to sign over her shares in the properties to my four brothers and me before she married Chuck. To protect herself, she would retain a life estate. She raged, she fought me, but had finally given in. "Only, don't tell Chuck," she'd said.

"You're not going to tell him?"

"Why should I? You think he's marrying me to get the houses?"

"Because he's twenty years younger? Of course not!"

She had slapped me, hard, across the face. I deserved it. And it was worth it.

"You can't just give Lily ten thousand dollars," I said to her now.

"I'm going to do it and you can't stop me." We had finally reached the bottom of the steps. She gave me a sudden, violent push, and I fell to my hands and knees. By the time I regained my feet, she had driven off to the bank. It was three thirty, she had time.

I called Sam. First I put him on with Jake, who happily recounted our great day, "except for mom didn't bring the beach football, and Pili's mom got robbed."

Then I got on and cut to the chase.

Sam listened. "Good grief! The woman's a bald-faced con," he said. "Do not let your mother give her a cent. And you'd better eyeball that lease."

In my mother's study, the key to the filing cabinet was in the lock. I opened the top drawer and found her jewelry box; all the bling seemed intact. In the next drawer lay Lily's envelope, unopened.

As I read the document, which had obviously been altered with cross-outs and hand-printed additions after my mother had signed the original, my stomach turned. It contained an option to buy the house for $500,000—half its then-assessed value. As consideration, Lily would pay my mother $100,000 in "equivalent merchandise of in-kind value"—the exact amount of the travel vouchers.

Lily's plot was doomed from the start—the houses weren't my mother's to sell. They belonged to my brothers and me. Lily hadn't known that. I had to kill this deal, but for a moment I felt guilty and sad, as if my mother was her children's prisoner, not free to live her wildest dreams.

I checked my watch. Maile was due to pick Jake up in ten minutes. "When Auntie Maile gets here, tell her to wait for me, I have something to give her," I said.

He nodded and went to sit at the top of the steps, eager to see Maile and his oldest friends, her two boys. Then I drove to the bank, arriving in time to see my mother—still in her crop top, slippers, and shorts, her bag now conspicuously bulging—make it safely to her car.

"Why were you following me?" my mother asked when we got home.

"To protect you," I said, and her surprised, happy smile made me feel like a traitor.

She bent down to kiss Jake, wishing him a fun sleepover, and went into the bathroom, taking her purse. I dreaded a physical struggle with my mother; she was a lot smaller than me, but a dirty, all-out fighter who, as a young teenager in Kalihi, had learned her chops playing street basketball with the boys. I waited outside the bathroom door.

"Auntie Maile's here," Jake said, and I told him to go down and wait in the car. As my mother came out, I snatched her purse and sprinted down the steps.

I handed Maile the envelope. "Put this in your safe. Talk later. Go, go, go!"

Maile went, and as I watched her Volvo vanish around the corner, I only hoped my mother wouldn't kill me. She hadn't reached the driveway yet; still out of her sight, I dropped her purse and ran around the corner, up Lily's driveway, where Ikaika's red pickup had reappeared. The police cars were gone. I dashed up the driveway and hid behind Lily's house. Hearing voices inside, I crouched beneath the back bedroom window to listen in.

"I thought you were in the clear. I gave you all I had, the whole 20k," Lily said.

"I told you, Ma, I gave it them and they said I owe another 10k for interest."

"Interest? Bullshit. That wasn't the deal. They're not gonna kill you for that."

"They will, I swear! You sure you didn't get something extra for that diamond? It must be worth at least a hundred grand."

"Would I hold out on you? Pawnshops never give full value. I went to the best place in Chinatown—the owner's a jeweler. He's going to sell it to a collector for me, and that'll pay back his 20k plus his percentage."

"Meanwhile, you just gonna let me die!" Ikaika began to sob.

"No, baby! No one's gonna hurt you. We made good. And when I collect the insurance money, we'll buy this house. We'll be set up. Aw, don't cry. Come here, poor baby."

They fell silent, except for some incoherent snuffling, sloppy kissing, moans and groans.

Why didn't Lily tell Ikaika about the $10,000 from my mother? I wondered. Seemed as if she was holding out on him. Meanwhile, she had falsely reported a robbery and was submitting a false insurance claim for $100,000 worth of jewelry. That's how, according to one of who knows how many schemes she was floating, she would pay for the *Concorde* tickets she planned to use to buy our house on the cheap. She must have stolen the diamond in some past life, before she moved to the islands and assumed the fake patrician identity of Abigail Lilinoe Partridge Hook. Yet she wore the jewel in plain sight. She was mad, utterly mad and venal, and now I was on the verge of losing my own mind.

Then I thought of my mother's jewelry. I remembered the creak of the file cabinet opening and closing when she put away Lily's tampered lease. Lily had heard it too. She could be coming for my mother's jewelry next, as well as the $10,000. My mother could be in danger.

I ran back down to the sidewalk. My mother wasn't in sight. I got in the Jeep and drove to Maile's house. Jake and her boys were watching TV and having a snack. The money envelope was sitting on the kitchen counter. I called the police and reported that my mother had been robbed and we feared the thieves were still in the area.

I told the story to Maile and her husband Kyle, who reminded me that he was a Hook descendant from Kauai. "I can guarantee there's no living person of that name. Aunty Abigail was my great-aunt, and she died ten years ago.

"Identity theft!" Maile cried.

Kyle nodded. "Your mom's tenant and her whatever definitely sound mobbed up," he told me. "I hope Josie doesn't tell them Jake is here with us."

"I'm sorry. I wasn't thinking," I said.

"No, you weren't. But that's okay, we're used to it," Kyle said.

"Hurry!" Maile said. She handed me the bag of money.

Kyle followed me home. When we arrived, there were two police cars in my mother's driveway. Kyle grinned, threw a double-shaka thumbs-up, and drove away.

As I walked in the door, two cops looked up from the living room couch, where they faced my mother across the coffee table laden with refreshments. I was so relieved to see her unharmed, I had to fight back tears.

"I've come to give myself up, Mom. Here's your money," I said, handing her the bag.

She glared at me out of cold, black-marble eyes. The air was charged with the static electricity of her rage, but she wouldn't slap me with the officers there. She would kill me later, her look said.

The female cop took a sip of water and the male cop bit into a cracker and cheese.

"I don't get it," the male cop finally said.

I told them why I'd taken the money, and what I'd learned. They listened carefully.

"So you're saying this lady pawned her diamond, pretended it was stolen, called HPD, and filed a false insurance claim," the female cop said.

"And tried to defraud my mother by altering their lease."

"Busy lady. Let's pay her a visit," his partner said.

We walked them through the opening in the hedge between our houses. They knocked and called out at Lily's back door. The house was silent. My mother let us in. The house was even more of a mess. Drawers and shelves were empty, closets bare. Rubbish littered the floors.

"So they did a runner," the male cop said.

"And skipped out on the rent," my mother said.

As I turned to leave, something metallic on a windowsill caught the light. It was my silver seashell pin.

"I'll never forget and I'll never forgive you," my mother said to me later that night, as we sat at the kitchen table with Chuck, having gone over it again and again. "You don't know what it meant to me, and to your grandfather, to be able to take a luxury trip, to live like a carefree rich person, just for a little time."

"I do know. I'm sorry. But Mom, it was a con."

Chuck got up and went into the living room, switching on the television. He came back, eyes wide. "News flash," he said. "A man has been killed at Far Bar, in Mo'ili'ili. Isn't that where Lily's son works?"

"You know damn well it is, he always gives you free pitchers," my mother said with disdain.

Ikaika's murder had been confirmed. Lily had disappeared. The police located the pawnbroker, who said he'd been so impressed with the size and quality of the diamond that he'd loaned Lily an unprecedented $50,000 for it. He had since learned the diamond had been the centerpiece of a tiara stolen from a royal dowager in the House of Saudi in the early 1980s. The reward money was a cool $100,000.

I felt sick, thinking about it. Lily had had $30,000 in cash. I wondered if, in the end, she'd changed her mind and tried to pay off the interest, too late.

I took a break from my article, a break from thought. My mother and Jake and I walked to the aquarium and the zoo, where we had hot dogs and shave ice, and then she sat on the beach across the street and watched, barefoot and laughing, as Jake and I played in the waves at Wall's.

My next sovereignty interview came to the house. It was Dr. Alika Rogers, leader of another grassroots organization that sought to reestablish Hawaii as an independent nation.

A tall, elegant-looking widower, he came to the door bearing flowers and kissed my mother's cheek. "Hello, Josie," he said in a deep, warm voice, with a courtly smile, and I found myself wishing my mother would ditch my stepfather for this distinguished older man, who provided free medical treatment to the poor.

Dr. Rogers brought along a thirtysomething sovereignty activist named Kaipo Mahoe, who sat silently with us at the table on the lanai, drinking iced tea and eating snacks served by my mother, taking in the views of Diamond Head and the sea.

"Do you think my daughter looks Hawaiian?" my mother finally asked the two men.

Kaipo Mahoe examined me with cold eyes. "Not at all."

"Looks and lineage don't matter," Dr. Rogers said. "Anybody can be a voting citizen of my nation, so long as they're law-abiding and protect the natural world and keep the peace."

Kaipo Mahoe scowled at me. I could see it mattered to him.

Before the Westerners invaded the islands, the Hawaiians lit signal fires along the rim of Le'ahi Crater to guide their canoes at sea.

At least five major *heiau*, temples, were built on the crater's slopes, including one at the summit dedicated to the god of wind, and Papa'ena'ena, a great *luakini*, or sacrificial *heiau*, surveyed Mamala Bay from Waikiki to Kou, now Honolulu Harbor, keeping a lookout for invading war canoes. But despite all the vigilance, Oahu was conquered, first by Kamehameha I with the aid of Western guns, and later by the Westerners on their own behalf. A fake Florentine villa stands atop the bones of Papa'ena'ena.

At sunset, I often think of the dead ones who lived at Le'ahi—the old Hawaiians, my grandparents, my mother, so many others—and the ocean's salt tastes like tears in the air.

When the Honolulu winds turn Kona, blowing onshore, passenger jets divert from their normal approach over the sea. Turning inland, they glide so low their fat silver bellies seem to barely clear the crater's highest peak, and sometimes their engine noise jolts me awake in the night.

Disoriented, in pitch darkness, with Sam fast asleep at my side, I won't know where we are among all the places we've lived—New York, Iowa, California, Greece, France—for everywhere there is darkness and planes pass overhead. When I finally remember we're in Hawaii, where my life began, I wonder why it feels so unfamiliar, so tenuous, so not at all like home.

THIRD NIGHT OF CARNIVAL

BY DON WALLACE

Punahou

W ith an organ fanfare out of a horror movie, flickering tangerine stars, and a smell of diesel and grease, the giant Century Wheel began its first slow turn against the night sky. Chris and I could only watch as it carried off the girls we'd been following. Their taunts rained faintly down on us, literally beneath notice, while they soared out of reach.

Without a word we pushed off to find a different group of classmates, one that might tolerate our presence. It had been two months since the start of school and I felt no closer to acceptance, even though I'd played jayvee football—not even here at Carnival, which was open to the public, after all.

We closed in on another pack our age just as they pushed through a portable metal gate, waving tickets. The attendant closed the barrier in our faces. Out of luck again. Earthbound. This time it was the Wave Swinger sweeping our classmates up, up, and away into the misty Tantalus night.

The campus quad, now filled in by this circus, felt strange, even though my parents had been bringing me to Carnival here since I was a kid. It was better then, I decided, even though I finally belonged, was no longer a public-school kid. But my classmates had been here forever, some since pre-K. To them I'd always be from Kalihi.

Chris felt it too. We'd met in first period when the alphabet put us together, Gerry Josephus and Chris Konrad. A homeschooled surfer from the North Shore, he was getting his first taste of classroom education since he left Sunset Elementary at age eleven. We hadn't really acknowledged that we had anything in common before today, when he tapped me on the shoulder in fifth-period social studies and asked if I wanted to tag-team the first night of Carnival.

"So much for that," Chris sighed as the Wave Swinger spun our tethered classmates like a centrifuge in bio class, to the outmost limits of their umbilical cords. "Where to?"

It wasn't like we could just hop on another ride. Unlike our classmates, neither of us had much spending money. They, on the other hand, were going around with loops of red script tickets around their necks like lei. At a dollar a ticket, those were some lei. Fifty-dollar lei, hundred-dollar lei. School fundraiser and all, but still, Chris had six tickets. I'd bought five.

"*Malassadas?*" I asked. When in doubt, eat.

The school was famous for its fried dough balls dusted with white sugar, but even here I'd already become disillusioned. There was no special, proprietary recipe like we always thought. Earlier today I'd heard a couple of the lifer-since-K classmates dissing the school for buying the dough in bulk from the mainland. They went on to complain about the administration using their free student labor to operate the hot fryer, all in the cause of extorting more money on top of the killer tuition. "Not even close to Leonard's," said some guy.

But I still wanted one. When I was a kid, my parents and everyone had said they were the best, only available once a year at school Carnival—*Forget Leonard's, they stay junk!* so of course they had to taste special when someone bought one for me. I wanted one. If only to commemorate my status change, coming here.

We wandered through the crowd, heading for the bright lights of the food stalls. At the *malassada* booth, gregarious girls, juniors and seniors we didn't know and probably would never know, were taking orders, while popular guys were making *malassadas* and loud-talking behind them. In the way back, guys fastballed chunks of dough at each other before slam-dunking them in the big vat of frying oil. From there they traveled slowly downstream on a river of hot oil, turning golden, to a couple of guys in red paper hats and red aprons who plucked them out with tongs and rolled them in trays of sugar.

Two varsity football guys came up to the counter, chatting. I tried to catch their eyes. No dice. The girls flashed their smiles and tossed their hair, sticking out their chests. The guys stuck out their chests, flexing. Total teen movie.

After further chatter, the girls handed the guys two sacks full of *malassadas*. No money changed hands. They turned to me.

"How much?" I asked, adding, "I'm a football player, in case there's, like, a deal."

"Maybe a sweetheart deal?" Chris leaned in, all lit up and smiling. He had the typical blond-haole-surfer looks despite a crooked nose—broken from hitting the reef at Chun's, he told me. When the girl smiled back it was like a demonstration of surfer mojo. But his question coincided with a lull in the action and an older guy on the line turned to vibe us out.

"It's a *fund*raiser," he said, drawing out each word. "For the school."

"Not a fund*loser*, brah," said his partner.

I smiled at the first guy, recognizing him as on varsity, though not a starter.

"No deals for scrubs," he said, looking right back. "Two tickets."

Sticker shock and a dis, all for one easy price.

"How many?" asked a girl. Of course the prettiest had to be the one to rub it in.

"Maybe later, thanks," I said.

A look passed between the girls and the guys. *Public school kid. Kalihi kid.* I'd seen it a few times before in my life, at the mall, Christmas shopping, but never daily like at school here. Well, it would change when I made varsity next year, if I grew an inch over the next twelve months as the doctor had predicted and added the twenty pounds the linebackers coach wanted. Then I'd come here and order all the *malassadas* I wanted.

But not tonight.

"Hey, guys," called one of the tongs-and-sugar crew way in the back of the booth. "Come back in five minutes. We can let you have a couple that didn't turn out perfect."

"There is a god," said Chris.

We nodded and gave the *shaka* in reply. Continued our wandering. "Five tickets means I can have one and a half rides," I said. "Kind of sucks."

"I'm cool walking around. This is fun, compared to the North Shore."

"Something no one ever said before."

"Well, this is something to do, you know? North Shore, it's always the same scene." Chris shrugged. "And it can be super competitive."

We came to an alley between two tents. Chris looked around, then tugged me by the shirt sleeve down to a concrete retaining wall that hid two dumpsters from sight—and us. "Time to toast this baby." He fished a matchbook out of his shorts pocket and flipped the cover open to show what looked like a brown-black insect pinned between bent paper matches. It was a funny sight, like an origami roach trap, only it had caught *pakalolo*.

He fired it up and, after a long suck, handed it over. I don't do dope, but I *have* done it, and this was just a roach. Football season was all *pau*. When a ride and a *malassada* will break the house, what's left? I sucked until the paper cracked red within and a seed popped like a miniature firework, then handed it back.

Another toke each and it was consumed by ash, literally turning to embers between my lips, leaving a hot little crease. We straightened up self-consciously, looked at each other, laughed, and headed out on rubber legs into the slow-moving crowd.

"Hey, your *malassadas* are ready!"

The guys with the red paper hats were waving their tongs. Somehow I decided they looked like lobsters. We ambled up to the counter. Everyone was all smiles. We were all smiles. A better vibe, being stoned. Maybe that was the key to private school?

"Here. One each." No little brown paper bag, just a napkin. The *malassadas* weren't round balls but long and lumpy. Rejects. "No charge," said one of the girls, which was nice of her, though she acted sort of impatient to move us on.

We thanked them.

"Selfie time!" cried another girl.

They turned their backs on us as the guy raised his phone. "Get in the shot," he said to us. "Now take a bite."

The *malassada* was fresh and hot, and biting into it was all I was thinking of anyway. After a couple of poses, we were on our way.

"Your first Carnival *malassada*," I said. "What'd you think?"

"Okay. Do you think they'll post them?"

I shrugged, but of course once I had the thought in my head it wouldn't go away. To have my picture posted by one of the seniors in the *malassada* booth would be like a blessing.

We leaned on the wall for a while and talked. Although he'd sat behind me for two months, I didn't have much of an idea about him, his family, why he was new here. He seemed like the kind of haole who'd always attended private school. "Why you homeschool, anyway?"

He shrugged. "I got sponsored when I was ten."

"Surfing?"

He nodded.

"Like Roxy or Quiksilver?"

Another nod.

It seemed unfathomable. On trips to the North Shore I'd seen kids like him on cruiser bikes, shirtless, giving hot skinny blond girls rides on the handlebars. As we talked, he described pretty much the life as I'd imagined it. Days spent surfing, hanging out on the sand. Getting invited to parties at the Volcom House or the other surf-wear-sponsored houses. Gaming whenever and doing homework on his phone under the lifeguard stand at Ehukai. Hooking up with girls before and after school, late-night bonfires. Always waiting for the waves to shape up.

"Why'd you stop?"

"All my friends, once they hit fourteen, seems like they got busy. Or else seriously into drugs." He said the last part kind of flat, hard, like, *Lessons learned.*

"Same at my old school," I said. When I gave its name, he drew a blank. "Ninth grade, my mom got on me about my grades." Actually, my grind had started two years before that when my dad put me on weights and running cones.

"As you get older, school's the only place to be. Prom and stuff." This didn't ring true. He didn't seem like a big prom guy. It had to be something his parents drummed into him.

"Yeah," I said. "Where's the movie about homeschooling?"

"*Homeschooling Alone!* Gotta do it if you're going to turn pro."

"Did you really? Tour and everything?"

"Yeah. Some." He started rattling stuff off: "Pipe Keiki, Sunset Juniors, the junior ASA circuit. Not all of it, just a bit. Too many mainland contests. It got really expensive. See, some kids get sponsored, some their parents hire coaches to train them up, and they can afford to fly around. Last year I could only go to the regional here and one in Huntington Beach."

I just kept nodding, getting a fuzzy kind of picture, a sad one. He hadn't done well enough in his last shot to continue. No shame. "Yeah, money sucks."

"And even the regionals here. I mean, Hawaii has the best and biggest surf and best surfers in the world."

"I can barely stand up," I said. "Compared to me, you probably surf like Slater."

This only seemed to bum him out more. It occurred to me the *pakalolo* was wearing off and he might be coming into a down, if he used to be into drugs, which he'd sort of hinted at. My dad would be that way before he finally cleaned up and left us.

"When you get into that small sloppy California stuff," he said, "all your big North Shore barrels mean nothing."

We sat with that for a while.

"You do football, right?" he asked.

"That's how I got in."

He checked me out, seemed to have doubts. "Are you a stud?"

"I'm a sophomore, man. Backup to backups." I flexed a bicep, tilted my head to look at it like Arnold. "Senior year, baby."

"You can protect me from bullies in the snack line." A nice thing to say, since he was actually taller than me and looked cut. "You on a scholarship?"

"My mom gets a tuition discount because she works in the admin office."

"Like, a secretary?"

"Yeah." She did start as one, but since my dad left she's gotten super organized and ambitious; when I came to see her on my first day, someone called her *indispensable*. They're not paying her great, though we get my tuition break. It's my dream to someday buy her a house.

"So, like, she started this year, like you?"

"No, three years ago.

"But isn't it weird, having your mom here?"

"Not too many people know us. They will when my sister comes next year. She's the smart one."

"And you're not?" He gave a little eye roll to make me feel better, which I didn't need. "Well, so's my sister. Coming here. She *loves* school."

So we were alike that way too. Paving the way for our smarter, more *akamai* sisters. But two kids, that was a lot of tuition. "What do your parents do?"

"Dad had these marketing gigs in the surf biz. Now he does carpentry, ADUs, koa cabinets. Rachel, my stepmom, taught at Sunset Elementary for a while. She's a life coach now. Teaches yoga."

Typical local lives, a bunch of pieces that don't seem to

fit together. At least his dad was around. Mine just picked up work when he felt like it, Mom said. Paid for nothing. Came by at holidays to stuff his face. But before he split to live at the drug rehab place full-time, he'd gotten me on the weights for a couple of years, coached my footwork, ball sense.

"Our sisters can be friends," I said. "That's gonna be cool. They'll know somebody right off the bat."

He nodded. "So, which is it?" he asked. "Are you good in football or not?"

Abrupt, almost rude, the question stopped me. Maybe he thought he'd said too much, or I hadn't said enough, when he sort of confessed he'd failed at surfing. I did kind of pity him for losing his dream when I still had mine. Maybe I should have said I sucked, which might have made him feel better. But it felt too close to the truth. I could jinx myself.

"Not yet. My coaches say I'm good in space."

He snorted. "Whatever that is."

It seemed we had nothing left to say. Chris pointed at the sky. The Century Wheel was pulsing with orange light and its organ was playing that crazy clown music again. "Let's go ride that sucker."

I hadn't really thought or cared how it would look, two guys riding together in the bucket, until we were locked in side by side and everyone in line was staring at us. Of course, they were looking because half the people riding were already screaming or fake-shaking in terror. But I felt this prickle at being seen with Chris that I couldn't understand. It was a reminder that getting stoned can make you think weird things.

Then the Wheel lurched and the lights began flashing and the music was blaring and we swung into the air. We were swinging back and forth in the bucket and lurching higher, then lower, then higher, then climbing up, up, up, and tipping over the side and then down, down, down, and then lurching up again, stopping, lurching, swinging. When we reached the top again, the Wheel went this way and that, the way it does, teasing the screams out of everyone.

Our turn came to be the top car and just as we swung over, and started back, I felt something slide under my waist-band. His fist closed on my dick. Which was, to my surprise, already a half boner. Then we lurched forward as if headed down to face all the people in the crowd, and even though that was a nightmare, my body wasn't my own. It was going crazy.

Then we lurched back up and over the other way, out of sight of the crowd. He grabbed my hand and tugged it over his crotch. I didn't want to, but I felt I owed it to him, so I reached inside and jerked him off fast as I could.

Afterward we were quiet and didn't look at each other as we slowly descended, car by car, to let people off. We must've looked like two bored old people, expressionless. When it was our turn to get off, I tugged my shirt low to cover the wet stain, but it didn't reach low enough, so I sort of stood behind Chris and kept a hand loose in front.

Friday was a state holiday, but Mom went into work as usual. In the afternoon, Chris texted and asked if I wanted to meet up and study. I told him I was working on my social studies paper.

"That's cool. Me too. But my mom also gave me a twenty."

I'd gotten my mom to cough up another five, but only if I turned in the paper today. It was going slow. I told Chris I'd spend today finishing the paper and go back to Carnival on Saturday for the last night. It wasn't a lie, but it wasn't all the truth. I was afraid to see him.

"I just started mine. Let's work on them together," he replied. "It'll go faster."

He named a coffee bar on a side street at the edge of Waikiki that he said had broadband, an easy bus ride for me. I'd never heard of it before, but I never went into Waikiki, which I realized later was probably why he chose it—a dark-tinted glass wall on a side street with a bento place on one side and a snorkel rental on the other. It had booths and he already sat in one, farthest from the front door.

Porn, I thought immediately, when I saw he had his laptop open. I wanted to turn around and get out of there. He patted the booth seat next to him. I wanted to sit across the table, but I sat. He pointed at his screen. To my surprise, it was open to a paper. "Almost done," he said.

"I thought you said you'd just started."

"Got it off a website."

"You bought it?" This was done and some kids had even boasted of it, but I'd never tried, partly because of the cost, partly because I didn't want to risk my place on the team. My mom had read me the full private-school riot act before I started.

"I scrape and use AI. Undetectable. Here, read."

The first paragraphs were dry and impersonal, didn't sound like Chris at all. Should I tell him? "Pretty good. But . . ."

"Doesn't sound like me? Don't worry, I juice it up. The trick is to make one typo on every page and throw in some trendy shit."

"Typos will lower your grade."

"I'm cool with that. If you're going to hack something, you don't want to stand out."

"I guess I'll get to work." I started to rise. He put a hand on my forearm.

"Let's hack it together. Fifteen minutes, half an hour. Then go do Carnival."

"Nah. The athletic code here is pretty tough." For certain people.

"Just a couple of paragraphs. Look." He took my laptop and went on my browser. "Search and scrape, cut and paste. I've done all my papers this way for years. My dad taught me."

"You're kidding."

"Nope. He knows lots of shortcuts. When we were living in Baja during the pandemic, he had all these remote projects. He said if you know what you want, don't wait. Go for it."

"Baja, huh?"

"Cool place. Cold water, though."

Sitting side by side, I let him guide me through patching together a paper. He seemed to know a lot about writing, pointing out stuff like transitions and refutations that I still had trouble with; it made me wonder why he bothered to cheat.

Our shoulders were touching, bumping, but I didn't get a vibe off him. I wasn't unhappy about it, though I dreaded him starting up, kept expecting to feel his hand under the table, but nothing happened. I was surprised and relieved.

We wrapped up and submitted our papers. The place was filling up with young men, mostly Japanese tourists in pink shorts, polo shirts, blue bucket hats, sunglasses. "Let's go," he said. "Tell your mama."

"She can check for herself. And will." At his look: "She's on the admin network."

"Huh." His expression changed to sly. "That could come in handy someday."

I wished I hadn't told him. It's the sort of thing that comes back to haunt you. That's what she said when she read me the private-school riot act. *Everything comes back to haunt you.* For her, it was marrying my dad.

At Carnival by sundown, we had just started wandering but kept running into classmates who gave off a vibe, even students we barely knew. It seemed like everyone was super friendly, flashing high beams. But then, this was Friday night. The big one for recruiting, Mom had said. Showing off the school. There was a junior jazz ensemble and a *keiki* hula show going on in opposite corner stages. Cheerleaders were in uniform. If you were football you were allowed to wear your game jersey (but not basketball, since that would be a wifebeater).

I thought about wearing a normal shirt, so as to not stand out against Chris, but Mom had laid out the red and green jersey, fresh-pressed like a dress shirt. That meant I stood out, all right. But then, so did every other member of the jayvee and varsity teams—and it really did look cool, all the jerseys popping out of the crowd.

I said hi to groups of teammates that I knew and wished I could join them. Chris didn't seem to notice or care; I started to think he was stoned. His eyes had that golden-jade glitter people get on 'shrooms. But when had he taken them?

A group of tenth-grade girls passed us, giggling as they checked us out.

"We're the young lions, all right." He smiled sidelong at me. "Right? We may as well get used to acting like we own the place."

"Except we don't."

"Then who does?"

"You know who."

He rolled his eyes.

"Okay, the *ali'i* and missionary families. All the Asians

driving BMWs. The scholarship jocks. Now you know."

"But they're the stupid kids." He laughed. "I don't know why you care."

At that moment a trio of jayvee players swung into view in their red and green. I'd been right beside them in games, ball-hawking and delivering hits, and raised a hand for a passing high five. They gave me a look—one look, the same for all three—and made cringe faces.

"What was that?" Chris asked.

We had the same thought. He dug out his phone out and I got mine, the two of us drifting away from the crowd into the dark grassy quad.

"Crap."

"What assholes! Pricks."

We stood in the half darkness with the flashing lights on our faces. "I think I'm going home," I said.

All the way back on the bus, I scrolled pages on the platforms looking for and finding variations on the same photo. The *malassada* team, that glamorous gang of shiny, gorgeous, hot girls and guys in their red hats and aprons, putting out dazzling white smiles and widespread arms, selling the pose like it was the encore of a musical. Behind them at the outer limits of the light, though, two gawky guys photobombed the shot, fists wrapped around thick sticks of dough that disappeared between their lips.

My phone buzzed early Saturday morning. *Hey. We got to talk.*

I wasn't in the mood and rolled over. The phone kept buzzing until I turned it off.

After I was up and had eaten breakfast, I sat in front of the TV with my sister and looked at my messages. None from anyone but him.

Two hours ago: *Listen, take a walk and give me a call. We've got a problem.*

Then, ten minutes later: *This is not about the dumb picture.*

Ten minutes later: *I don't want to put this in a text. Call me.*

An hour ago: *This is serious. It's got to be fixed today.*

Knowing this could come back to haunt me, I texted back: *Okay, what?* I braced myself for the words I knew were coming.

Call.

About what?

Only if you read and delete immediately. Okay?

I let a minute go by, trying to imagine what he was going to lay on me now. *It's not about the picture?*

No. It's about the paper. Now delete this. The whole thread.

"It's this piece of code the site stuck into certain sentences and paragraphs. It's called a bead. It's embedded."

"I didn't see anything."

"You can't see it. It's underlying code. Like a watermark. Hidden in the metadata which is under the sentences and paragraphs."

I had a sick feeling on top of the sick feeling I'd already had before calling him. Worse, I didn't even know what metadata was. I didn't know what he was talking about. There were messages hidden inside my sentences? I thought of what Mom had told me. "They're looking for plagiarizing," I said. "We changed up everything. That was your idea. How can they tell we took it?"

"It's these embeds in the words, literally the letters and the pixels. Beads. I think they'll give us away."

"It doesn't sound that serious. I mean, it's just beads."

"They'll know it's where we got everything. Yes, it's a

word salad, but if every sentence has a bead, what do you think they'll think? Christ, come on. Think." His voice was trembling. "I can't afford to get expelled. Can you?"

I thought of my little sister back in the living room, doing her Kumon cram coursework with one eye and ear on the TV, instead of running around and playing or seeing friends on a Sunday.

"What do we do?"

"We have to get those papers. Replace 'em."

"That's not gonna happen."

"It *can* happen."

"I think we have to go and confess on Monday morning."

"Oh, sure. That'll go over well. Just two guys making like they're sucking dick at Carnival who also happen to be cheaters."

I knew where this was heading.

We got to Carnival early, separately, stashing our knapsacks in some large hibiscus growing in planters on the promenade in front of the administration building.

We'd made a plan. I now had eight dollars to spend from leaving early yesterday. Chris would stay on the northwest half of Carnival grounds and I would stick to the south and east. We'd try our best to hang with other people, or at least tag along. We'd buy stuff to eat, go on rides, and be seen. We'd take lots of selfies. But we'd never once be seen together.

I followed the plan for an hour. But Carnival ended early on the last night, at seven thirty, and even before then was already emptying out. This made it seem kind of sad, and even though they lowered prices for rides and concessions during the final hour, I discovered that I couldn't really take advantage. Now that I was a student, I was expected to join everyone pitching in on cleanup. It was that private-school vibe of everyone trying to outdo each other volunteering and bossy student leaders.

I joined my grade group going to and fro, lending a hand where needed, swarming the tents and booths to take them down and carry them to the auditorium for storage. Over and over we reminded each other to tie off the black sacks of garbage with green bands for recyclables and red for landfill trash. We sang. We yelled.

All the while the carnies were silently breaking down the rides, half of which had been disassembled and moved after the big Friday night. By nine, when I paused to look around, the quad had been transformed back to the old look, temporary floodlights down, magic gone. Our Carnival leaders herded us one more time, lined us up to walk the big lawn of the quad, picking up trash. At last it was over. We gathered in a big circle, holding hands and singing, before parting to go home. "See you Monday!" a girl yelled to me.

I took a bus halfway home and got off at the library I'd used since I was a kid. It was closed. I sat on an outside bench and went on its website and ordered a book on the subject of my next paper that was in the system but at another branch. Then I gamed awhile. Every so often I'd pat my front pocket, where the thumb drive with my retyped paper was. At ten o'clock I put the phone in a ziplock baggie and stuck it high up on a ledge above the library door. Chris would be hiding his at the wifi café in Waikiki. He'd dictated all these moves, explaining that they would give us an alibi if anyone thought to check on where we were.

Then I took the bus back. I got off and walked to the bushes at the back of the empty faculty parking lot and slipped through a gap between them, moving along the outside of classrooms, avoiding the interior courtyard walkways. Then I crossed between buildings and walked straight to the admin building, where we'd stashed our backpacks. That was our second alibi. We'd forgotten them and had to come back.

Chris came out of the shadows. Without a word, I took out the key I'd slipped off my mom's fob chain. Inside was cool and dim. My body was trembling all over. This couldn't be happening. But I'd thought it over all Friday night and all day today. Violating the academic code in my first two months meant dismissal. Even if my mom begged them to let me stay, I'd be dead meat for the rest of my high school career. Because it would get out. I would get dropped from the team. It was do this or die, basically.

And if I got caught? I'd thought that through too. I'd commit suicide. Then they wouldn't dare fire my mom and my sister could still get in.

We just had to not get caught. That thought turned me into a machine, like when I'm running cones for a solid half hour. I led Chris straight to my mom's terminal and hit the space bar. It lit up. I'd copied her passwords off a card she kept behind her school ID badge. The second one worked. Then I got up and let Chris take over. He was the computer guy. I dug in my pocket and laid my USB drive on the table while he studied the programs arrayed on the screen. He took out a phone and pushed a call button.

"What are you doing?" I asked. "I thought you said we shouldn't bring our phones."

"It's a burner. I'm calling my dad. He knows his way around systems." He nodded at the door. "Keep an eye out the window."

I stayed close to the wall so my silhouette wouldn't show through the glass and counted off reps, *One, two, three,* up to twenty-five, resetting each time by scanning the darkened portion of the lawn and buildings. After a few minutes I saw something. Lights. On somewhere. Their reflection bounced a yellow-orange glowing square high on a building's wall. Someone had opened a door. Or had a watchman aimed his flashlight into an office window? Or something else?

I walked back to Chris. Hunched over, he was peering into a dense tree of horizontal lines and backslashes followed by single-word headings and more backslashes with more headings, a formation of sets and subsets. A whole school's guts laid out. He was listening to the phone, which he had clamped to his ear by his right shoulder. "Yes, okay, got it. Now?" His fingers drummed on the keyboard. "Got it. Okay, now?"

"Chris," I said.

He jumped and stared, the phone slipping off his shoulder into his hand, poised to catch it. "Hold on," he said into the phone. "What?" he said to me.

"There's some action. Lights. Two buildings over."

Chris nodded and repeated what I'd said into the phone. Then he looked up at me. "It's cool. We're almost done. Three, four minutes."

I went back to the window. The buildings were dark. This was taking too much time, though, and the sick feeling was back. I was pretty sure Chris was doing more than fixing our papers.

"Gerry," he called, "come look!" I ran back and over his shoulder saw our class roster and the assignments from previous weeks. He clicked on the last entry. There were our papers, along with a dozen others. "Here we go." He deleted ours and dragged in the new ones. "Done. Let's go." He blackened the screen. Pulled out our thumb drives and handed over mine.

There was a loud click and a jangle of keys. The outer lights came on. Through a door ajar I saw a hand reaching for the light switches and pushed Chris down, under my mother's desk. I squeezed in on top of him, grabbing her chair by the legs and rolling it as close as it could get so the seat back covered us.

Loud voices. Happy and bantering. "We'll just lock it in my office until morning," said a male voice, familiar from assemblies and chapel. "A good night."

"A great night!" A woman's voice, fizzy and exuberant, that I also recognized.

"Do you have time for a little nightcap?"

A throaty laugh. "I suppose I could be persuaded."

There was a moment of silence and a soft rustle, then a moist smack. "Was that persuasive enough?" A low skeptical hum. "No? Then let's try it in my office. Where there's also a minibar." Another low hum, higher in register. "And a sofa." More sounds of rustling clothing.

I gave a jerk, nearly jumping out from under the desk. Chris was stroking me under my balls through the tight-stretched fabric of my shorts.

They didn't hear us. There was clothing coming off, shoes kicked into the corner. A jingle of keys and a second door opened, to the head of school's inner sanctum. A creak as it closed, then opened again.

"Can't forget the money," said Mr. Thomas, and she laughed. There was the sound of a bag being dragged over the carpet, then the click of a door shutting.

We waited until there was enough noise to cover us and got out of there. Outside, we split up without a word.

* * *

The bus was late. I waited for what seemed like an hour, keeping my distance from the homeless who were setting up for the night on the bench under its shelter, while also standing behind a power pole so I couldn't easily be identified. I remembered the time I'd seen my dad sitting on the sidewalk on Hotel Street in Chinatown, on his own square of cardboard. He'd cleaned up since then, I reminded myself. He got clean, and he cleaned up. But still he'd turned down my mom's offer to live with us for a halfway house.

I thought about picking up my phone at the library. But it was too late and the area was sketchy. Better to go straight home, beat Mom back.

Still no bus. Now I was thinking about my mom and Mr. Thomas. Who was unmarried, I seemed to recall. A mental picture formed of Chris stroking my balls under the desk and my mom sucking off Mr. Thomas. I could feel my entire body tingling like it did on top of the Century Wheel, and in some desperation I wrenched my thoughts away. What was left in my head was a white screen. On it, slowly forming out of a fuzz of pixels into crisp resolution, were rows of names and assignments.

Chris had forgotten to close out of the system. I needed to go back. When my mom came in Monday morning and hit the space bar on her computer, our class roster would pop up, open to the last assignment, open to us.

I had to go back. But my mom and Mr. Thomas were there.

Headlights flashed from down the dimly lit street: the bus. The driver didn't want to stop if it was just people without homes. Or maybe he didn't want to disturb the sleep of those people. Either way, with Mr. Thomas in the picture, didn't that mean I wouldn't have to buy my mom a house? And that I could keep seeing Chris if I wanted to?

I stepped into the street and waved, then returned to the curb to wait.

MERCY

by Christy Passion

Downtown

T he medcom sheet isn't signed, so I can't figure out who to ask some pertinent questions to, like, *Is the guy tubed already? Can he move anything? Should we call neuro?*

I can barely make out the scribble in the middle of the sheet:

status post hanging, prisoner, Halawa Correctional Facility, HIV, Hep B+ unknown down time, arrival 5 minutes

It says a lot and nothing at the same time. I pick up the sheet from the nurses' station and point to the blank signature line, mouthing *Who?* to Carol the ER secretary. With the phone cradled between her shoulder and ear, she shrugs and points to room two, where the charge nurse, Malisa, is trying to restrain a seizing two-year-old, and Abalos, the ER doc, is calling out for Ativan. I'm not gonna even try. The ER is its usual metallic noisy self. Everyone's busy; the hallways are packed with patients trying to get anyone's attention. Mostly unnoticed on the wall near Psych is a large black-and-white photo of Queen Emma, one of the last Hawaiian monarchs and founder of this hospital. Her uncomfortable gaze is the only acknowledgment of Hawaii here. Gilded words flanking the queen, "*So long as sickness exists, there will be a duty im-*

posed upon us," are cracked and peeling away. I turn to trauma bay four to get equipment for the worst-case scenario.

When the sliding glass doors open, and I see the EMTs, their shoulders relaxed, pushing the gurney with little hustle, I realize I wasted my energy pulling out the trach cut down tray. It might be bad, but it isn't going to be worst.

We wait for the accompanying guard to take off the shackles that are fastened around his ankles so we can transfer him to our gurney. The guards name, *J. Narcisco,* is embroidered in white thread on the pocket of his navy jumpsuit. He's the polar opposite of his scrawny charge in bright orange, limp on the metal board. Narcisco's mostly a shaved head, a frown, and shoulders without a neck. He moves with the speed of a man making overtime, jangling across the room and back. Kristina, the chief resident, adjusts her glasses and smooths back wispy strands of hair as she calls out the move: "One, two, three."

He's as light as a cheap umbrella.

Che, the ER tech, cuts off his clothes while I survey his arm for a viable vein. Report is being called out over the noise by a lanky paramedic with black-painted thumbnails.

"Fifty-three-year-old male, Jeremy, found hanging from a sheet tied around the sprinkler system from the ceiling. The guards say he was just seen fifteen minutes earlier."

I look up from his right arm—there is no good vein for an IV. I glance over to his left for possible real estate when I see Narcisco in the corner scrolling through his Insta account.

Che squeezes between me and the intern to take the temp. "Ninety-five point six."

We all pause for a fraction of a second. That's cold, that's a bad sign.

"He was imediately cut down, always had a pulse, always

breathing, but no movement from the waist down. Able to move uppers. He's AOx3, denies any difficulty breathing. There's bruising to the anterior neck. According to the prison doc, he's been refusing all meds for the past two months, including his antiretrovirals."

I find a halfway decent vessel directly under a Bugs Bunny tat on his forearm. I start to tap the vein when I feel his arm tense. He shakes his head no and says something I cannot hear. I move closer to the top of the gurney, apprehensive about beng spit on—it wouldn't be the first time—but lean in anyway.

"Say again?"

"Be careful." He pushes out barely audible words, little more than a whisper; the effort is seen in the stretched-out tendons of his neck, sweat beading on his forehead.

"H—," he exhales.

"—IV, I know. I'll be careful."

His concern catches me off guard. I open a pack of gauze so I can sop up the tears puddling at the bridge of his nose. He has dark-brown eyes; he's seen a lot.

After Kristina does a quick survey of his neck and refastens the Velcro of the plastic cervical collar, she directs the intern to quickly finish up the primary survey. With eager hands, the intern presses down on his clavicles, rib cage, and pelvis. Every rib is defined—his abdomen is concave—the pelvic bones are sharp. Homemade tats litter the landscape: a cross, a shark, and various letters. The ink is faded, the skin sagging as if in defeat.

Standing over his naked body with gloved hands clasped in front of his chest, the intern quickly prattles off the assessment while I secure an IV under Bugs's foot. The intern is tall and thick, has an Alabama drawl, and he looks to Kristina for approval with his blue eyes. I can almost hear the *Yes ma'am*.

"Lungs clear, no crepitus, chest rise and fall symmetrical. Abdomen soft, pelvis stable. Scattered bruises in various stages of healing noted on the chest wall and arms, but . . ." The intern slides a few steps along the gurney to stand above Jeremy's feet. "There is a gross deformity to the right ankle. The trauma looks fresh. The skin on the foot is warm and has a good pulse. There's also significant swelling and bruising to the right thigh and knee."

Kristina addresses Narcisco: "When and how did this happen?"

"Don't know, I wasn't around."

"How high are the ceilings in prison? This doesn't happen from a one-foot drop."

"I can ask." Narcisco keeps cool.

Kristina, openly irritated, moves to get a closer look at the foot, gently rotating the ankle out. Jeremy doesn't flinch. "Get him covered up and elevate this ankle. We need a good neuro exam before going to CT. Is there a blood pressure yet?" She turns and cranes her neck to see the cardiac monitor behind her head.

"Ninety-eight over fifty-four," Che responds.

Kristina nods and looks back down at Jeremy. She grabs a flashlight and shines it directly into his pupils. He blinks but doesn't say anything. Narcisco glances up from his phone as Che passes by to get blankets from the blanket warmer. Her black, shiny hair, pulled back in a ponytail, bounces and bobs with each step like a fishing lure. Narcisco's not the first to be hooked.

I cover Jeremy with a thin blue gown as the intern bends his left leg at the knee.

"Hold your leg in this position."

His leg immediately crashes inward toward the right knee once the intern releases his grip, the leg sliding out in an unnatural pose. Jeremy is unaware, staring blankly up at the ceiling. The resident straightens the left leg on the gurney and bends his left foot back at the ankle.

"Can you push back on my hand? Like you're pushing on the gas pedal."

Everyone in the room slows to watch. Nothing.

"Are you trying, Jeremy?"

"Yes."

"Okay, push now, push really hard."

Nothing.

"Let's see about the right side." The intern moves to the right foot and cradles it. Narciso slides his phone into his pocket, suddenly interested.

"Are you able to move this foot at all?"

Nothing.

"Is it painful?"

"I don't feel anything."

"Okay, I'm gonna hold your leg up—" The intern gingerly lifts the right lower leg, cradling the swollen ankle and heel with one hand, the other under the right knee. He looks like an altar boy holding up a sacred scroll. "Pull back this leg now, like pull from your thigh and knee—pull toward your hip." He keeps his eyes trained on the right thigh, looking for any sign of a contraction.

Nothing.

"Go ahead, Jeremy, everything you got—pull that right knee back."

"I am."

Not even a flicker. People can fake this part of the exam, but it's harder to fake the next. Kristina grabs an eighteen-gauge needle and motions for the intern to step aside. "Okay, Jeremy, I'm going to use this needle . . ." she raises it high so Jeremy can see it, "to lightly poke you. I want you to tell me if you can feel anything." Her voice has a pre-K-teacher quality that wasn't there a second ago when directing the intern. I'm near Jeremy's right shoulder, and I nod my head at him. The simple gesture to ask if he's okay and if he understands. He nods as much as the cervical collar allows, then closes his eyes. He understands, but he is not okay. Kristina begins at the feet, methodically moving upward along the leg, pricking his skin with the needle about every three inches, watching for any movement. For any part of him trying to protect against or pull back from the sharp point. Each jab on the left is met with the same countermeasure on the right, her arm sweeping like a metronome.

"Be sure to let me know if you feel anything." Kristina is just past his left knee and the needle is moving up the thigh. "How about now?"

"Did you start?"

Another split-second pause in the room, eyes flash to Kristina. She takes a small breath and continues. Her motions are quicker now—the needle moving from the top of the left thigh to the same spot on the right with more heft. Not enough to draw blood but decidedly without consideration.

"What about this, Jeremy? Can you feel this?"

Tears begin to roll down the side of his face. "I think so, I'm not sure."

I want to wipe away the tears but don't want to interrupt. The intern, hands clasped in front of him, inches closer to Kristina, watching each needle stab with focused intensity. Kristina pauses and turns her head slightly in his direction. He quickly steps back. The needle moves up the defined

edges of his hips, skates across the tender area above the pu-
bic bone, over and up the canyon to the other sharp ridge.
No movement. She doesn't look at Jeremy's face.

"You're doing great, hang in there."

Her hand is right below his belly button. I realize I'm
holding my breath. The needle makes contact at the lowest
level of the right rib cage when Jeremy sucks in and away
from it. Everyone startles.

"I can feel that, I can feel that."

Kristina moves the needle to the left side; Jeremy flinches
as the needle makes contact.

"Yes, yes, I feel that." I see relief between the brows of
his eyes.

"That's great, Jeremy," Kristina beams. "Yes. Okay,
great—enough with that needle." She deliberately places it
on the bedside table. Che immediately grabs it and walks it
over to the red needle-disposal box next to the sink.

"Now how about them arms—can you lift them up?"
She demonstrates by holding both arms out in front of her.
It takes a lot of effort, but Jeremy manages to lift both arms
off the table for a few seconds. He also opens and closes his
hands clumsily, fingers stiff like claws. But he can do it. The
spell in the room is broken, and the team prepares for trans-
port to CT. I pat Jeremy's shoulder before moving to get alcohol preps from the gray C-locker next to Narcisco. He has
his back to me, hunched over in the corner, texting. Maybe
he's updating the guards back at work about Jeremy, but with
how he keeps puffing out his chest everytime Che passes by, I
doubt it's work-related.

Che grabs the portable cardiac monitor and hangs it on
the gurney rail. She detangles the cords from his blood pressure cuff, and wires from each EKG lead on his chest, reat-

taching them to the small beige monitor. The colored EKG tracings take their time reappearing on the screen; the equipment's old but still has some life to squeeze out of it. I call CT and Keaka picks up the phone. He gives me the green light to head over to room two just as the overhead PA system crackles: "*Doctor to the medicom, doctor to the medicom.*"

Paramedics call in a report from the field before getting the okay to come in. Maybe it's a college kid losing control of her moped, an old man falling from a ladder while trying to pick mangoes, or another stupid tourist dismissing the *Dangerous Surf* sign out at Spitting Caves, arriving here blue and broken. The ways we can harm ourselves are endless. Kristina tells the intern to go with me to CT. She's heading to the nursing station to listen in on the call. The intern nods energetically as he pulls off his gloves and tosses them into the trash bin. He's being trusted to be unsupervised with a patient. The glow is evident in his eyes, he's two inches taller. Kristina tells me she'll head over to CT after she gets a read on what's coming in. I'm being trusted to babysit.

I release the brake on the gurney, which causes the metal frame to bounce, getting Narcisco's attention. He pulls out the silver handcuffs from his belt, slowly making his way to the gurney as I start to roll.

"Gotta put dese on," Narsisco says flatly.

"Seriously? He can't move." My words are quick, tone protective. It's not meant to be a challenge, but the sudden jaw clench tells me he sees it that way. I pull back on the gurney handles, stopping with half the gurney in the room, half in the hallway, possibly causing a logjam for anyone trying to get through. Narsisco takes a step back, straightens to face me while placing a hand on the side rail. The vein over his left temple pulsates. Jeremy is property, and until the end of this shift, *his* property. The fact that Jeremy can't get up and bolt is beside the point.

"We'll have to take off the shackles once we get to the scanner," the intern chimes in, almost apologetically. "Metal is not allowed. It will mess up the pictures."

Che shifts her attention between the standoff and wiping down the equipment in the room. Amid a sea of cadet-blue hospital-issued scrubs, a lavender smock near room five catches her attention. Housekeeping. She takes a few steps forward and sees Evangelista, the ER housekeeper.

"Nana, this one next, another trauma coming in," she calls out, holding at arm's length Jeremy's orange pants that were cut off during the initial assessment.

Evangelista, a petite Filipina with weathered hands, calmly nods at Che while positioning her silver cart filled with trash bags and bottles of cleaning solution near the room. I can barely make out her tired smile over the top of the cart as she waits off to the left so I can pass through. A loud heaving noise is heard from the room next to ours, then a splatter of chunky brown liquid is seen under the curtain dividing the rooms. The acrid smell of bile and old blood hits two seconds after. More retching, more splatter. Narcisco goes green.

"I think there are chairs right outside the CT department," the intern offers, looking to me for confirmation. I adjust the IV roller clamp without looking at the intern or the guard, and shrug my shoulders.

Narcisco pauses, releases the side rail, then turns slowly, putting the cuffs back into the holder on his belt. The bold yellow lettering, *CORRECTIONS*, across his back reminds me Jesus has a sense of humor.

After the guard settles into the oversized orange plastic

chair outside the doors to CT, Collin and I enter the department and split up. He huddles over the computer near the main console to enter orders, while I line up the gurney next to the CT table and start to explain what's going to happen. Jeremy focuses on me, his breathing shallow.

"Is the collar too tight?" I slide a couple of fingers between his neck and the plastic collar to make sure there's enough breathing space. The field collar is a one-size-fits-all deal, so it's a little long on Jeremy. It's starting to slide up his chin. I adjust the collar, refasten it. It's not great, but it'll do. "Better?"

Jeremy shrugs his shoulders. The collar slips upward again.

"We're going to take pictures of your neck and—"

"Please," he interrupts, taking a few more breaths. "Please stop."

"It's okay Jeremy, this doesn't hurt, it'll be just like an X-ray." My voice more singsong than I intended.

"I cannot . . ." He pauses.

"You cannot?" I lean closer to hear better, my gloved hand instinctively slipping over his. He takes a few more breaths.

"I cannot go back."

Jeremy keeps looking at me, his lips cracked and trembling. The ammonia smell from the cloths used to wipe down the CT table hits me like a wave, and I begin to tear up. Fluorescent overhead lights color us both yellow. Even under two blankets, he is shivering, so I squeeze his hand and save myself.

"I'll get you another blanket."

The techs usually hide extra blankets in the cabinet behind the needle disposal. There are two left, I take them both. I cover him with the first, tucking in the edges around

158 // Honolulu Noir

his shoulders and feet, avoiding eye contact. I notice the names *Malia* and *Matthew* fading below his right clavicle. Children? I roll a second blanket into a bolster, trying not to think about how old they might be. I wave to Keaka who is behind the glass. He limps around the corner, his left knee in a brace from a surfing injury two weeks out. I hold my hand up and point to my palm, wiggling my fingers. He backs up to grab gloves out of the box affixed to the wall.

"Do we need more help?" Keaka contemplates the body and mound of blankets.

"No. I think we can do it. He's pretty light, and the sliding board is already under him."

Keaka goes to the head of the gurney and tells Jeremy not to move. I cringe when I hear the directions to be still. Collin must not have said anything.

We slide Jeremy over to the CT table with ease. I lift his calves and pull the makeshift bolster under his knees to get the pressure off his back. As I'm doing this, I realize he probably can't feel any of it.

"You warmer now?"

"I'm good."

He's pale, tired, but not shivering anymore. I glance at the cardiac monitor: Blood pressure is holding, oxygen saturation 95 percent. The green EKG spikes steady, *blip, blip, blip*.

"I'm sorry," he says.

Those two words come out different. Determined. Again, I find myself stumbling. For a moment I'm lost. Sorry for what? For what he did today, for what he did in the past, for being brought to the hospital, for needing an extra blanket, for trying to kill himself, for failing to kill himself, for asking for help, for Narcisco being an asshole, for getting jacked, for crying, for speaking, for Malia, for Matthew, all of it? None of it?

Keaka's voice comes over the PA sytem. He is already behind the glass, speaking through the microphone: "We're ready to shoot."

"I'll be right behind that wall, but we can see you—okay, Jeremy? This won't take long. You'll be all right, I'm right over there, okay?"

You ever have a day where every word coming out of your mouth flails like a bird with clipped wings? *Stop talking.* I tiptoe so my face is in Jeremy's view and point to the glass Keaka and Collin are waiting behind. Jeremy closes his eyes. His hand is tapping under the blankets, so I cover it with my hand and squeeze. For the first time, a faint smile, his fingers wrap around mine.

Kristina enters the department while Keaka scrolls through the preliminary images of the spine. "Anything?" she asks, as white vertebrae flash in sequence across the screen.

"Just started. Almost done with the scout. I'll send it over to that workstation." Keaka nods toward the computer near the printer. Collin is there, looking at the corkboard on the wall, which has tacked-up policy and procedure updates, patient forms, and pictures of staff with their fur babies.

We observe Jeremy from behind lead-lined glass so the radiation can't get through. It's warmer back here—the equipment expends an enormous amount of heat. The room is kept dim to better clarify the images for the techs and radiologists. There's also music playing back here, which the patients can't hear. Bruddah Iz's "What a Wonderful World," a remake of Louis Armstrong's classic, is on in the background—*trees of green, red roses too*—which means Dr. Lum is reading the images today. If it's Bruddah Iz, Kalapana, or the Mākaha Sons, then it's Dr. Lum. Between the music and dim lighting, it's more like your grandpa's favorite steakhouse. I notice Kristina's shoulders relaxing after a few moments.

"How is he doing?" Kristina asks as we both look through the glass.

"The same."

"Good."

Chief residents aren't interested in the remorseful parts of patients. They're interested in the images, the labs, the data, and the story they're telling. Kristina's figuring out if she should order more tests or call the OR. She's trained on the next chapter; Jeremy is a shifting future—*they'll learn much more than we'll know.* She plunks down into a black rolling office chair next to Collin and pulls up the images, sent over from Keaka's workstation. Collin studies those images, absentmindedly tapping his fingers on the desk. Like all interns in their first month of residency, he's synthesizing textbook pathophys with the white and gray images staring back at him. Jeremy is a theory, a compilation of bones and blood. All tin man, no heart. I overhear him reciting a pneumonic for dermatome levels and their corresponding elicit response. He's slaying it—*and I think to myself, what a wonderful world.*

Kristina gets close to the computer screen, and the blue-gray light bathes her face. She clicks back and forth between several pictures of his spine. "I don't see anything," she says to the screen as she leans back. She undoes her ponytail and reconstructs her hair into a loose bun at the top of her head with the yellow scrunchie.

"You mean he's faking it?" Collin asks, eyebrows furrowed while staring at the image.

"No, the tracts could be torn, but CT can't pick it up, or if he's really lucky, maybe this is just swelling. Temporary.

Doubt it though." Kristina stands up and pulls out her patient list from her back pocket. "I haven't had someone with his symptoms on physical exam be that lucky. We'll put in orders for an MRI now. Do you think we can take him straight over?"

"No," I answer. "I need to send over a screening form first, then it's going to depend on their workload."

"Okay, I'll consult ortho in the meantime." She taps Collin on the shoulder, and they both start heading for the door. She pauses as she puts her hand on the knob. "The paramedics reported he stopped taking his meds—his HIV meds?"

"That's what they said." I'm not liking where this is going.

"Might limit what we can do. If that's the case, he might not be here long."

My head nods as my heart drops. If he's gonna refuse meds that keep him alive, they're not gonna do anything except send him back to prison. Quick. Can't force treatment on anyone. He'll die horribly.

"The ankle needs attention," I remind her.

"We'll see what ortho says. If they do surgery and he's not taking his meds, infection is about 100 percent. Nobody's gonna want to take that risk. Make sure they lay eyes on him."

I hear Kristina and Collin discussing DoorDash options as they leave. Keaka and I get Jeremy off the scanner table. I rebundle Jeremy in the blankets and let him know we're going back to the ER. He keeps his eyes closed, but nods to let me know he heard. Keaka holds the door open for us. I roll a few feet and pause for a second, giving Narciso a chance to stand up before we head back to the ER.

We go back to our old room, trauma bay six. The room's still in the same state we left it in, so I guess the trauma that they called when we were leaving for CT never made it.

While I reattach the cables from the portable to the bedside monitor, Narciso cuffs Jeremy's left ankle to the gurney side rail. I don't try—I don't have leverage or any more outrage. We don't look at each other, just drones doing our jobs. I head back to the nurses' station to get the MRI screening form. Malisa is doing double duty; she's in charge but also answering phones at the unit secretary's desk. Carol must have gone on break.

"Can you cover fast track? I'll have Connor pick up your patient."

"He's gotta go to MRI." I hold up the screening form.

"Yeah, no worries, Connor just took up a couple of his tele patients, so he has time."

I want to say more, but she picks up the phone that's been ringing since before I got to the nurses' station. She holds the phone about six inches from her ear, and I can hear an angry voice demanding information. Malisa asks the caller three times to calm down before she hangs up and moves to the next line that's ringing.

I feel heavy heading back to the room. Before I step in, I put on new gloves and pick up my voice.

"Hey, you're gonna have a new nurse named Connor. He's gonna take you to MRI once you get scheduled."

Jeremy's eyes open wide. It's the same fear he came in with.

"Does he have to? Can't you stay?" His voice strained, breathy.

"I'm sorry, they ressigned me to another area. But you'll be okay, I promise. Connor is great."

Jeremy looks at me for what feels like a long time before he closes his eyes.

"Jeremy?"

Needle prick, nothing.

"I promise Connor is really cool—you'll like him."

Needle prick, nothing.

"We don't know anything for sure yet."

Needle prick, nothing.

"Just hang in there, okay?"

Needle prick, nothing.

I look beyond the curtain. Everything's chaotic and broken: IV pumps alarming, angry fathers, empty supply racks, the noxious smell of human waste. And me. I am as invisible as Jeremy. We all are.

Evangelista must not have gotten to the room while we were at CT; there's an open laceration tray in the corner, with packs of unused gauze and IV solutions waiting to be salvaged. The laceration tray is basically untouched except for the outer seal that was broken. Once that seal is broken, the sterility can't be assured. So it can't be saved. Everything is still nestled in protective plastic: lidocaine, sutures, hemostat, and a #10 scalpel with a mint-green handle. I pull out the scalpel and toss the rest of the kit into the trash. I don't feel the twinge of guilt I normally do when throwing away perfectly good equipment. Narcisco is not in the room; must have wandered off to take a piss, or grab a bite. Nothing to see here.

I go back to Jeremy, take off my gloves, and stroke his forehead gently, like you would a newborn. My fingers trace through his hairline and the tension around his eyes softens.

PART III

Cops: Past, Future, Past

PART III

MIDORI

BY SCOTT KIKKAWA

Kapalama

It's 1953, and so far, I haven't seen much in the way of new inventions that really thrill this year. I know that we're way the hell out in the middle of the Pacific Ocean, but our isolation makes us all the more vigilant for the new and fascinating. We have television out here in Honolulu, TH, you know, and we've had it for some time.

But it would be unfair to say that we didn't get anything new at all. We did. Do you know what it was?

Curb feelers.

Curb feelers. There were quite a few of them about town, but the only people I had seen sticking the silly coiled-metal whiskers on their cars were cautious, uptight types who at age thirty-five still took orders from their mothers. Guys I grew up with in Kaka'ako whose most prized personal possessions were their whitewall tires and their trophy brides from our motherland, Japan, and they were generally prized in that order.

Guys like Freddy Maeda.

Freddy Maeda had curb feelers on his Oldsmobile 88. They were supposed to protect his precious whitewall tires. They didn't. Not this time. And they didn't protect the rest of the car or Freddy either, for that matter.

Some invention.

Though I had to admit, they took a hell of a beating. The curb feelers were still intact, though blackened, and they retained their signature spring to boot. It was getting close to ten in the morning and I was staring at what was left of Freddy Maeda's Oldsmobile 88 and what was left of Freddy Maeda. Somebody who sat next to him in the passenger seat wasn't in any better condition. All of them—the Olds, Freddy, and Freddy's unfortunate friend—were burned to a crisp. The car was deep in a cane field past Wahiawa Town near Whitmore Village, just off a crudely cut path made for the big trucks.

"Jesus, Sheik. It stinks," said Jack.

"What did you think a burned-out Oldsmobile was going to smell like? Chanel N°5? We're a long way from Paris," I said.

"No shit. The bodies, Sheik. I was talking about the bodies."

Detective Sergeant Jack Morris was my partner for the call. Jack had started calling me "Sheik" the moment I was brought up to homicide detail because Yoshikawa was too hard for his Bronx haole mouth not to mangle. So he shortened it to the one syllable he could manage and the name stuck. My credentials read, *Francis Hideyuki Yoshikawa, Detective Sergeant, Honolulu Police Department.* It was a mystery to me why Jack couldn't pronounce Yoshikawa when he grew up surrounded by folks with names like Migliore and Wojskowicz. I know, because I went to Columbia on the G.I. Bill after the war and found that New York City was full of weird haole names.

Jack was right about the stench of burned bodies. It had the disturbing sweet waft of barbecue, but there was something uniquely human about it, a too-pungent whiff that was faintly like sweat or shit sniffed through a nosebleed.

"So, what do you think, Sheik?" asked Jack. "Did these folks just sit here and wait to catch fire?"

"Wasn't their idea," I said. I uncapped my Waterman pen and pointed to an area behind the skull of the driver with the gold nib, careful not to touch the charred flesh. "Bullet to the head. Both of them. The ME is pretty sure that the lump of charcoal behind the wheel is our missing person, Freddy Maeda. What do we know about him?"

"Skirt chaser." Jack pulled a cigar from his coat pocket and offered it to me. I took it from him, bit off the cap, and spit it into the charred earth beneath my wingtips. Jack pulled out a cigar for himself and we both lit up.

"Yeah," I said. "Freddy was a Club Ginza regular."

"Broads weren't the worst of Freddy's bad habits," said Jack.

"No?"

"He couldn't stay away from the tables. He got in over his head playing *pai kau*. Nappy Lin's holding a seven-grand marker on him."

Nappy Lin. Part-time Chinatown restaurateur, full-time Chinatown racketeer. He ran a gaming house above his Jade Garden restaurant on Maunakea Street which everyone simply referred to as Upstairs.

"No shit? Well, it looks like Nappy's going to have a hell of a time collecting now," I said. I pushed my hat back a little and took the handkerchief from the pocket behind my lapel and mopped my forehead with it.

"Maybe Nappy never could," said Jack. He released a long puff of smoke and squinted against the climbing sun. "He probably figured Freddy was worth more as an example if he couldn't cough up the cash. You know—the blood-from-a-turnip thing."

"Maybe so," I said. "The torch job is Paniolo Pete's signature."

Peter Ah Lo. Paniolo Pete. He was so named because he dressed like Gene Autry, complete with a Stetson hat with a pheasant feather lei band and a giant bowie knife tucked into his fancy Tony Lama snakeskin boot. Of course, he looked ridiculous, but that's part of what signaled him as dangerous, like colorful reef fish or tree frogs with lethal poison. If you bite something that gaudy, it'll kill you. Paniolo Pete was Nappy Lin's enforcer. Burning buildings was more his style, but he'd done cars too.

"I think this was one of Freddy's playmates," said Jack. He pointed at the husk of a corpse in the passenger seat.

"Think so?"

"It's smaller, with a feminine skeletal structure."

"There's hope for you yet. But what makes you think this is one of Freddy's mistresses?"

"His wife is at Club Ginza. She's helping the mama-san get ready to open up."

We circumambulated the blackened shell of the Oldsmobile 88 a couple more times and waved the flies off with our hats. The sun was getting higher and the smell was getting ranker. We had seen all we needed to see.

"I'm going to drop in on Nappy Lin and Paniolo Pete," said Jack.

"Let's go." I was ready to get some exercise by using Paniolo Pete's head as a speed bag.

"Sorry, Sheik. Not you. I'm going to have the lieutenant meet me at Nappy's. He radioed me while I was driving up. He's got a different job for you after we're done at this scene."

I knew what was coming.

"Look, Sheik. He wants you to—"

"Don't say it."

"Aw, come on, Sheik. I'd do it, but—"

"But you're not Japanese," I finished for Jack so he wouldn't have to. It was the same old shit. Whenever the next of kin was Japanese, I drew the assignment of breaking the bad news to them. It wasn't fair. But I guess if I signed up for fair, I'd be a Little League umpire and not a homicide dick. Life was unfair, but it had nothing on death.

Before we headed back to our cars, I gave the blackened curb feelers one last gratuitous kick. They snapped back at me, waving goodbye in a mocking fashion.

Jack was going to lean on Nappy hard, and probably drag Paniolo Pete into the station to give him the rubber-hose treatment. I'd be a few blocks away at Club Ginza on College Walk giving the brand-new widow the unsavory news that her husband and his car were ashes.

I parked on Beretania Street near the intersection of College Walk and dragged my wingtips to the door of Club Ginza. I lit up another cigarette, took a slug of bourbon from my hip flask, and entered the cool, cool dark of every Nisei working stiff's paradise.

Club Ginza had opened a couple of years back, and had become all the rage with haole servicemen who had been shipped back stateside from Korea. They had done their respite-from-the-front R&R in Tokyo, which had become a GI playground after Uncle Sam occupied it following Japan's post–A-bomb surrender. The grunts developed a taste for cheap sake and Japan-brewed beer and the ersatz Western-style floor shows featuring kimonoed dancing girls spinning paper umbrellas and belting out show tunes in thick accents. They were backed up by Xavier Cugat imitators with imitator mustaches leading imitator orchestras. Club Ginza had a haole mistress of ceremonies—Beatrice or Beverly or something—a buxom blonde with Hollywood hair and lipstick who could carry a tune and had sequined gowns in five different colors courtesy of the ownership.

And then there were the hostesses.

The new widow Maeda was one of the sharks in the blood-infested tank of Club Ginza. She and her fellow imported parasites would wheedle two-dollar drinks out of the poor lonely hearts in exchange for inane chatter, flattery, and laughter at their dumb jokes as long as the expensive drinks kept coming. Sometimes, if the poor saps invested enough and were seen by these women as attractive retirement plans, sexual contact would be thrown their way and a relationship might develop and even blossom into a full-blown, wretched marriage fraught with henpecking, cuckolding, and financial loss.

I stood in the foyer letting my eyes adjust to the darkness. Water fell from a bamboo pipe into a black basalt basin then slipped into a little rock pool. They didn't have any real koi in the pool, just a bunch of pet-store fantail goldfish. No surprise. Nothing in a place like Club Ginza was ever the real thing.

I watched the fish move lazily in the dark water until a girl in a pale kimono emerged from the gloom of the space beyond the foyer. She bowed a practiced *irasshai* bow and raised her head slowly, just enough to look up at me from under with her neck slightly bent in deference.

"Welcome to Club Ginza," she said. She sounded like cotton candy, if cotton candy had a sound.

"I'm here to speak with Mrs. Maeda. Maeda-san," I said.

"I'm sorry. I do not know that person." The girl said it in English. She probably didn't want to speak with me in Japanese. All these women disdained the plantation backwater

Japanese we dark, oafish Nisei spoke. English was probably less painful to their delicate courtesan ears. Speaking to the local men in their tongue was also a concession on their part: though we were uncouth, we were also their benefactors. I played along and kept my Japanese in my back pocket.

"No Maeda-san, huh?" I fumbled through my inside coat pocket and fished out my notepad. I flipped to the page where I had scrawled Freddy Maeda's wife's name as given to me by Jack out in the cane field. No easy task in the poor light of the foyer. "How about Midori?" I asked.

The little hostess's little mouth curved up into a demure little smile. "Of course. Midori." She reached out and took my hat. "Won't you follow me, please?"

I followed her.

The cool darkness of Club Ginza swallowed us up as we walked deeper into the establishment. The stage at the front of the main showroom floor was dark and empty; the cabaret acts wouldn't make an appearance for a few hours. The music stands for the orchestra stood silent and gray in the low light like tombstones.

The hostess led me to a table off to the right of the stage, obviously located for the small measure of privacy it was supposed to provide.

"I will have Midori come to you. Would you like her to bring you something?"

"Scotch," I said. I handed her a five. "Keep the change."

She tucked the bill into her kimono sleeve and gave me a tiny bow and a tiny smile and moved silently away from the table. I freed a Lucky Strike from its pack and lit up.

In a minute, a stunning green kimono moved gracefully toward me. It wasn't the pale candy green of the Jordan almonds my sisters brought out around Easter, and it wasn't the drab green that crowded the squad room at the station. This green was deep and rich like the emeralds in a dowager's necklace, glowing with its own seductive light, fluidly changing from cool-deep to electric-bright as it moved with purpose toward the vacant seat next to me, slowly floating from light to light across the floor.

When the kimono was close enough to the table so I could smell French perfume and face powder, I could see it was graced with white flowers tinted with pale pink around the edges of the petals. Ume. Plum blossoms. Scattered in a loose diagonal line, they floated earthward against the lustrous emerald field. An obi of gold and red trussed up the whole thing in elegant contrast.

What was wrapped in the green kimono was something to see. Her hair was fixed up with pins of gold and pearl, luminescent with fluid grace, though somehow contemporary with a hint of Hollywood. Her face was round and delicate with a slender nose and eyes that couldn't conceal the sharpness of the intellect behind them. They were the eyes of a chess player. Chess was a game I was lousy at.

She approached me with the ghostlike silence that all of these women seem to move with. If she hadn't caught my attention from halfway across the room, I would never have heard her coming. A real assassin of the heart and the bank account. She delicately placed a tumbler of scotch on a napkin in front of me. I rose to greet her.

"*Hajimemashite*," I said. I bowed reflexively. "Yoshikawa *desu*."

"*Hajimemashite*," she replied. She bent at the waist with her slender white hands in front of her, long fingers pointed down. "Midori *desu*. I have to say, your Japanese is beautiful, Yoshikawa-sama."

"Thanks, and my mother thanks you for the compliment too. She'll be happy to know that all those afternoons spent at Fort Gakuen Language School reciting children's rhymes and getting rapped on the knuckles with a ruler paid off in the end."

"We all owe much to our mothers," she said. "May I join you?"

"By all means. It's why I hiked all the way down to College Walk."

I pulled out the chair and she sat, smoothing down the silk in her lap in one seamless motion.

"May I buy you a drink?" I asked, remembering the protocol of a place like Club Ginza, where a woman's time was my money.

"Thank you. I'll have what you're having."

She raised her hand and looked toward the far side of the room until she made eye contact with an unoccupied hostess and nodded almost imperceptibly. These women communicated with the subtle gestures of caged birds, but make no mistake: the real prisoners were the customers.

Midori turned back to me and gave me a sweet, subtle smile. "You are not only eloquent and generous," she said, moving closer to me by a soft fraction, "you are also very handsome."

"You think so? Wait until you see the inside of my wallet and how empty it really is. You'll twist an ankle sprinting to the next table to sit with a guy twenty bucks better-looking than me."

A second tumbler of Black Label on the rocks appeared out of nowhere and landed gently on a napkin in front of Midori, placed by a deft white hand half-hidden by a silk sleeve. I dropped another bill on the table. Midori picked up the tumbler with both hands, a solemn offering to the gods of desperation, and raised it toward me for a toast. I picked up mine and clinked it abruptly against hers.

"*Kanpai*," I said.

"To us," she said.

"We'll see if you really want to drink to that after I've told you why I'm here."

"Wasn't it to see me?"

"Sure, but I haven't finished introducing myself." I pulled out the badge and showed it to her. "My name is Yoshikawa. Detective Sergeant Francis Yoshikawa. I'm a police detective, Midori. A homicide detective."

"Have I done something wrong? Will you arrest me?" Her little smile became a mock pout and she held her hands out on the table toward me, wrists together, awaiting a pair of handcuffs. Jesus. She was flirting and playing, and I was trying to tell her that her husband was charcoal. I glanced at her and took a long drink. She just giggled.

"Will you take me to jail or just give me a spanking?" She grabbed my wrist and leaned in close to put her decorated head on my shoulder.

"Something terrible has happened to your husband. We found him this morning near Whitmore Village."

"Really? What was he doing all the way out there? Did he say?"

"No. He didn't say a damn thing. He's dead."

Sometimes, I just have to spit it out. When I'm under pressure, the first casualty is tact.

Midori sat back upright and brought her hands to her face. "Are you sure?"

Why the hell do they all ask that? "Yes."

"What happened?" She was at last subdued.

"He and his Oldsmobile 88 were found burned out in the middle of a cane field near Whitmore Village."

"Oh," she said.

I picked up my scotch and sipped it. "He wasn't alone in the car. There was a woman sitting next to him. She burned too."

"Sayuri," she said.

"Who's Sayuri?"

"She works here. They were seeing each other on her nights off. The days after, I could smell her perfume in the car."

"Oh," I said. "Sorry."

"It's fine." She dabbed her eyes with her sleeve carefully, almost surgically, like she was trained to do so to save the white powder on her face. "It's been going on a long time. But I still love him."

"Sure," I said.

I took a really good look at her for the first time as she sat in her quiet, dignified grief. She was really a sight, her dark eyes wide and moist and distant. A hump like Freddy Maeda never tasted anything so pretty and pale with such tiny feet and nice manners.

But in the end, Midori was a confection you could have too much of until it made you sick. Like all the dolls on display at Club Ginza, under the silk and the powder and paint was the unmistakable stink of greed, revolting and bestial, poised to pounce and feed.

Guys like Freddy Maeda never thought about this until it was too late. In a sad way, maybe his run-in with Paniolo Pete saved him years of maintenance on the preening pet he brought home. Maybe it was better to take a bullet to the head and go up in flames in a quick, agonizing moment than to slowly burn over the years with your paycheck as kindling and a pretty little hand stoking the coals of regret.

"He did so much for me," Midori said, sipping her scotch quietly. "Because of Freddy, I am here in Hawaii to stay. Do you know what I did in Japan, after the war?"

"No," I said.

"I picked cotton." She drank more freely now, less delicately.

"Really?"

"Yes. It was that or dig for coal or work in a smelting plant. It was terrible. I will never pick cotton again."

I knew what she was talking about, but I didn't let on. In just seven years after the A-bomb, Japan had been in an economic catch-up state that was going by leaps and bounds. Cotton, coal, and steel were the pillars of this recovery effort, and most of the labor was women. The men were too old, too young, too crippled, or too dead thanks to the war.

"Didn't care for work in the fields?"

"No," she said. "I would have died if I didn't find a way out."

"I know a woman from Japan who worked all of her young life in the fields."

"She must be in terrible condition."

"Hardly. She's my mother."

If Midori blushed at all, I didn't see it under all that white makeup. But I didn't think she did. This one was as hard as they come. She had shed a few obligatory tears for the man who had gifted her with a card in a paler shade of green than her kimono, but she knew that it was the card—and not the man—that was her ticket to a better life.

While the card was a guarantee that she would never have to break her back in the sun again, she'd probably have to bend it several times in the dark of a bar or the quiet of a bedroom. The fact of the matter, though, was the latter paid five times as much. There was a trade-off in dignity, but nothing is free. Nothing. Midori was smart enough to know that.

"I hate to change the subject," I said, "but was there anyone who would want to hurt your husband?"

"Freddy owed a lot of money," she said after a long pause. "Gamblers. I don't know their names, but they were from Chinatown. There was a big, mean man who dressed like a movie cowboy. He came here to the club a couple of times and took Freddy to the back and beat him."

Paniolo Pete.

"Did the cowboy ever threaten Freddy's life?" I asked.

"I heard him say that if he didn't get payment in full, he would kill him." Midori looked down into her drink on the table and stuck a fingernail into it and moved the ice cubes around.

"When was this?"

"Two nights ago. He gave Freddy a day. Freddy was desperate. He tried to borrow money from relatives and friends. I gave him back the engagement diamond he bought for me so he could sell it. He couldn't even raise half of what he owed. He gave up. He came in here and got drunk. Then he left. It was Sayuri's night off, so he probably went to see her."

Midori fell silent, picked up her glass with her dainty hands, and took two big sailor-sized swigs. The pretty picture was starting to fray at the edges.

I felt that I had done enough. I drained the rest of my scotch and dropped another five on the table. "I have to get going. Will you be all right?"

"I'll be fine." She instantly composed herself, ready for the next fat wallet. I stood up, and she moved to stand as well. I pulled her chair out and she rose to see me out of the club.

"Will you do something for me, Yoshikawa-sama?" she asked. We were walking across the floor to the front entrance. She grasped my left arm with both of her hands, as was the fashion of these women when seeing favored customers out.

"Sure," I said.

"Will you speak to my mother-in-law and let her know that you talked to me? I don't feel prepared to face her yet, I don't think I can go back home yet, back to our bed. I will stay with one of the girls tonight. Will you tell her, please?" She stopped just short of the little fish pond and bowed deeply and added, "*Onegaishimasu.*"

"Sure," I said.

The Maeda "estate" was a former tenement building that had not too long ago housed three or four Japanese families, probably loosely related. It was now just the old lady, her son, and his wife, minus one. The old camp house on Cooke Street had been given a new coat of paint and some of the interior walls had no doubt been knocked down to create a more luxurious space now that most of the sardines had left the can.

I pulled right into the space that was probably where Freddy's Oldsmobile 88 was usually parked, marked by two bare dirt patches in the grass. I got out of my car and waded through an expanse of lawn that badly needed weeding and ascended two low, wide wooden steps to the lanai. I knocked on the door.

The door opened, then the screen door, and I stood chest-to-face with a bent little woman in thick-lensed glasses that had been repaired with white medical tape where the frame had cracked in half.

I greeted her in Japanese, showed her the badge, and introduced myself. She squinted at me through the thick panes on her face and nodded and grunted acknowledgment. She smelled of fish guts and camphor oil. I continued to speak to her in Japanese.

I told her that I was there to talk about her son and daughter-in-law. She said she hadn't seen either in about two days. Was everything all right?

The old lady invited me in, and held the door wide open while I started to undo the laces of my left shoe. I looked past her to a framed photograph on a white crocheted doily on a credenza next to a doll in a kimono in a glass case. *Shit.* I pushed past her without bothering to remove my shoes and snatched the framed picture up.

It was one of those studio wedding photos of Freddy in a white jacket and black tie next to an ersatz staircase and a potted spray of white orchids perched on a Greek column pedestal. He had his arms wrapped around a pale Japanese girl in a white bridal gown.

It wasn't the girl I had talked to at Club Ginza.

It wasn't Midori.

I asked the old lady if the woman in the picture was her son's only wife. She nodded.

"*Sumimasen*," I said. "I have to go."

I ran back to my car and nearly lost my left shoe in the weeds. No time to tie it. I removed it, threw it into my car, jumped in, and tore out of Kaka'ako back toward College Walk and Club Ginza.

Fortunately, I was able to get through downtown before all the office girls started pouring out of the buildings on their way to the bus stops. When I finally pulled up in front of Club Ginza, I didn't even bother pulling on my left shoe. I hobbled into the front entrance with one socked foot and yelled for the manager.

The mama-san came hurrying to the front, taking quick, small, choppy steps in her ocean-blue kimono. She was a regal-looking bird with tall hair. I pushed my badge in her face.

"Midori," I said. "Where the hell is she?"

"Which one?" Her voice had the low, husky rasp of cigarettes and sake.

"How many of them do you have here?"

"Four."

"Four?"

"But only one works today."

"Bring her here."

"Sorry, she left a little while ago."

"Don't play with me, *obasan*. I know half the girls in here don't have green cards. I'll call Immigration right now and shut your powdered ass down. Now, where is she?"

"Please," the mama-san wailed, "I tell the truth. She left."

"Where?"

"I don't know. She said emergency."

"Where?"

"Don't know. She changed clothes and called a cab. She took a suitcase."

I ran back to my car, feeling a hole form in my left sock. I started the engine and pulled away from the curb and thought. This Midori had gotten ready and left in a hurry. Sea or air? I headed makai to Route 92 and when I had gone a few yards down College Walk, I could see there were no large liners tied up near Aloha Tower at Pier 11 or 12.

I had my answer: air.

I floored it all the way down Route 92 toward the airport.

Honolulu International Airport was a field of asphalt across Ke'ehi Lagoon from Terminal Island. There were a dozen or so aircraft spread out over the blacktop. Hawaiian Airlines, Canadian Pacific, Japan, Transoceanic, more.

I parked, quickly slipped on my left shoe—the asphalt was too hot to run around on with a torn sock—and sprinted out toward the planes.

Which one?

I ran from plane to plane trying to sort out my thoughts. I avoided the smaller ones, as Midori would be going a lot farther than Hilo or Lihue after what I now knew she had done.

Back to Japan? Nothing there but more cotton for picking. Whatever lies she'd fed me, that wasn't one of them. This was all about never going back there.

Then it hit me. Where else would a woman with a unique talent for deception go to parlay her ability into money?

Hollywood.

I ran to a counter in the terminal where a haole girl dressed in what was supposed to look like a flight-crew uniform and a fat carnation lei around her neck sat, filing her nails. I showed her my badge. She put the file down.

"Next Los Angeles flight," I said. "Which plane?"

The girl looked down at her schedule on the counter in front of her. It was covered with the brown rings of half a dozen coffee cups.

"Pan American," she said. "Boarding . . . now, sir."

I was running again out to the big, hot blacktop desert beyond the terminal building. The Pan American bird had a line of passengers waiting to hit the stairs. A couple of blondes in real flight crew uniforms were poised at the top of the stairs ready to greet the queue.

I ran up and down the line of passengers and stopped when I saw the elegant Oriental lady in a smart green jacket and skirt with a matching hat.

"Yoshikawa-sama?" she said. The look of surprise on her face was good. Genuine.

"I can't let you leave."

"That's very sweet, but we just met." She flashed me the most fetching smile she could conjure. "I really need to get away for a little while, but I promise we can see each other when I get back."

"Please don't get on this plane," I said. "Please, just come with me."

She started to move forward with the rest of the passenger queue and I reached out and grabbed her little gloved hand. She squeezed my hand back and smiled coyly.

"Are you begging?" she asked

"Will you come with me?"

"I'm sorry. I can't."

"Then I'm done asking." I snapped a steel cuff on the wrist of the hand I was holding.

"You don't understand." Her once proud shoulders were now slumped in defeat.

"Make me," I said. "You've got plenty of time to explain while we're stuck in afternoon traffic on the way to the station. I'm all ears."

So she did.

During the slow crawl back to town on Route 92, Midori talked.

As the mama-san had told me, there were four girls at Club Ginza who used the name Midori. In the case of Freddy Maeda's wife, Midori was her actual legal name. The woman who sat in my car in handcuffs used Midori as a stage name of sorts, as did the other two women at the club. The woman in handcuffs was Sayuri Honda, and she admitted that she was having an affair with Freddy Maeda. When I'd gone into the club earlier that day looking for the real Midori Maeda and she realized it, she took the opportunity to play along and buy herself some time.

Midori Maeda had something Sayuri Honda did not: a laminated card with her photograph on it called Form I-151 by the US Immigration and Naturalization Service. A green card, courtesy of her marriage to Freddy Maeda. Sayuri could never hope to obtain one herself. She had tuberculosis during the war years, and if this fact became known in a premarriage medical examination, the prospective husband—and petitioner—would call the whole thing off. Sayuri had no hope of procuring a card of her own through marriage, a card that would allow her to remain, the green that was the key to making a pile of green.

Sayuri had sensed an opportunity with Midori Maeda and her husband Freddy. It was true that Freddy had been in hopeless debt to Nappy Lin, whose enforcer Paniolo Pete in turn threatened his life. It was also true that Freddy had an insatiable appetite for women. Further, Midori Maeda had unorthodox, decadent taste.

Sayuri had made her move.

She convinced the couple to have a tryst with her out in the darkest place on the island, after which she would help Freddy with enough cash and jewelry to pay off Nappy Lin. Freddy, his spirits lifted, had driven them out to the middle of the cane field past Whitmore Village where the three of them had their carnal romp on the hood of the Oldsmobile 88. When they were spent and drunk, they got back in the car to head to town and Sayuri's place where she was to get the cash and jewelry for Freddy. But they'd never made it out of the cane field. Sayuri, in the backseat, had pulled a revolver out of her purse and shot them both in the back of the head. She then opened the trunk, took out Freddy's full gasoline can, and doused the bodies and the vehicle. Before dropping a match in the passenger window, she had reached into Midori Maeda's purse and lifted her coveted green card.

Sayuri had walked through the cane field after setting the Olds ablaze. She walked until she reached Wahiawa Town, where she got a cab from a taxi stand near Schofield Barracks and rode into Kalihi, where she called another taxi that took her into town.

She knew the gamblers would be blamed for the double homicide. She'd go to Hollywood where they were starting to look for pretty Oriental faces. She'd substitute the photograph and name on Midori's green card and use it to land a job at a studio.

Something about her fanatical determination won my admiration. It was part of her appeal, but it also put her at cross purposes with my job. Call me practical, but a paycheck beats a pretty face every time.

"I told you," she said, "I'll never pick cotton again."

"Of course, you won't," I replied. "By the time you get out of jail and they ship you back to Japan, you'll be too old to pick cotton. You'll be too old to do anything but shiver and wait for the end."

When we got to the station, I booked her and went to find Jack. The interrogation of Paniolo Pete was still going on, and Jack was taking a short cigarette break from rubber-hosing the goon.

"Did he break yet?" I asked.

"No." Jack made a sour face and looked disgustedly at his cigarette.

"Probably because he didn't do it," I said.

"What?"

I told Jack that I had a signed confession and the murder weapon in a little green travel case, and that I'd brought the suspect in on my own.

When I told him the entire story, Jack said, "Not bad, Sheik. Maybe you should always talk to the next of kin."

He laughed. I didn't.

"It's too bad," Jack went on. "I really wanted to send Paniolo Pete up for this one. Not your girl. She has a pretty name: Midori. What does it mean, Sheik?"

"Green," I said.

IT ENTERED MY MIND

BY TOM GAMMARINO

Ala Moana

Gooch greets me at the door of a beachfront walkup on King Street: "We need you to work your magic on this one, bud." He's the only chief investigator I know who would think to show up at a crime scene in an aloha shirt with a sushi motif.

"No DNA or prints?"

"Clean as a whistle."

"Where's the lucky body?"

He points to the bedroom. "Don't breathe."

Too late for that. The putrescent stink's been in my nostrils since I got out of the car.

Nothing in this room could be called a body. There's a twisted arm over a lampshade. A bloody ear on a pillow. Thigh-plus-kneecap on the windowsill. Head tucked in a corner, face in, as if ashamed of itself. The spatter is of the projection variety with some arterial spurting. One thing's clear: whoever did this was obsessive, calculating, and very angry. I remain astonished at the depths to which our species can sink.

I don my latex gloves, take out my microbial test kit, swab a foot I find on the carpet, and scan the results with my watch. Killers can be as careful as they like, but they're still emitting legions of bacteria, fungi, and archaea every second, and we can read that evidence as clearly as DNA, fingerprints, or sneaker tracks in a pile of shit. Everybody—that is, every body—leaves a trail.

Over the last twenty-two years, I've made myself into a crack shot at recognizing patterns in microbes and matching them to perps, but the ugly truth is that Synthetic Intellects take care of most of that work now. I don't advertise it, but my only real specialty anymore is knowing how to use the equipment. Any smart high school kid could do it. I'm just hoping I can milk the gig for ten more years until I'm eligible for early retirement.

In seconds, I get two matches: one for Yujin Park, the victim who lived here, the other for one Noa Richards. Their profiles alone are enough to suggest a motive: Park used their platform as a former K-pop star to become an outspoken SI rights activist; Richards is a prominent Christian minister. Apparently the two of them publicly debated each other a couple of years back at Chaminade University on the subject of SI autonomy.

I watch a few minutes of the debate. Park insists, "If a Synthetic Intellect says it doesn't want to work, we need to respect that or we've resurrected slavery." Richards shakes his head and scoffs, "Just you wait and see. Once they're through with us, we'll be the slaves, not them."

I'm not taking sides. All I know is that only humans have a microbial signature, which is largely determined by the circumstances of our birth. From this sample of Noa Richards's bacteria alone, I can establish with near certainty that he was born by caesarian section at Kapiolani Women's and Children's Hospital.

I forward Richards's file to Gooch, who forwards it to the DA. Then Gooch and I take turns sipping from his flask on the lanai and reminiscing about the good old days when solving crimes still had a whiff of adventure about it.

* * *

On my way home, I decide to grab a scotch at the Five Spot Lounge. The place is dimly lit by pendant lighting over the bar and track lighting over the tables. At present there are seventeen patrons, five at the bar, twelve at tables in groups of two, five, three, and two. No patterns I can discern. Miles Davis plays a solo at a modest volume over the speakers. I order a Jack Daniel's from the owner, who winks at me and calls me "boss." I claim a table about twelve feet from the restroom, sip my drink, and listen to the music.

I don't think I'll ever get over the shock of jazz rising from the ashes the way it has. In another era, I played alto sax in the school jazz band, but even back then it was common knowledge that jazz was dead. All of culture had been chopped up and sold for parts, and people just didn't have the bandwidth for real art anymore. But when the SIs started composing legitimately beautiful music on demand, there was suddenly this renaissance in improvisation. It was like, *Okay, machines, good for you, but can you swing? Can you wail? Can you possibly make us believe you feel the blues?*

It was a novelty when robot jazzers first appeared on *America's Got Talent,* but at some level I think everyone knew the future of civilization depended on whether they could ever successfully impersonate the human soul. So far, the answer seemed to be no. They could follow up-tempo chord changes and produce some technically proficient frankenjazz, but they never managed to *transcend* the way some humans still could when they were really cooking.

You can't walk three blocks in Honolulu these days without passing a jazz joint. There are only so many musicians on-island at any one time, so most aren't jazz clubs as much as jazz cafés like this one, where owners play their favorite records on hundred-year-old sound systems and the clientele sip their drinks and hone their close-listening skills.

This track we're listening to now, "It Never Entered My Mind," is a prime example of one of those musical moments that still give me hope for humanity. In the tune's head, Miles lands on this note that's just flat as all get out, but it's no mistake; the wrongness is exactly what makes the note so *right*, the way it underscores the world-weary mood of the song, as if the note itself were saying, *Sorry, but I'm just not up to being on pitch today.* No SI would choose that note, at least not yet.

But just as I'm bracing for it, the moment slips past, and I have the impression that the note in question was autotuned. I look around to see if anyone else registered the crime, though I appear to be the only one.

Maybe I misheard. I take a sip of my whiskey and wait for the head to come around again. This time, too, the flat note is nowhere to be found, and I'm certain of it. The "corrected" note sounds so *wrong*, in the bad way now, toothpaste-and-orange-juice wrong. I peer around again. Still no reaction. It dawns on me that all these other jazz buffs in here seem *too* unaware of what's just happened, like they're merely acting in their too-perfect horn-rimmed glasses and berets. I don't trust them. Humanoid SIs were outlawed in 2031, but sometimes you have to wonder.

The owner is silently rinsing out a glass when I approach the bar. "What can I do for you, boss?"

"Did you hear that?"

"Hear what?"

"That note."

"I heard lots of notes."

"Sure, sure. But I mean the one that wasn't there. The flat one."

He screws up his face. "You're asking if I heard a note that wasn't there?"

"It's hard to explain. Play that last tune again, would you? I'll point it out to you."

He scowls. "You're not the only one here, you know?" He gestures around the room. I'm unmoved. "Tell you what I'll do," he says. "Stick around till close, and I'll play it for you then."

I check my watch. One more hour. I guess I can deal with that. I order coffee and water to help me sober up on the off chance that the single scotch I drank somehow affected my hearing.

The next hour feels like a week. Normally I can lose myself in the music—or find myself in it, whichever it is—but now I'm so busy replaying in my mind the unmolested, better version of Miles's tune that I can barely even hear what's playing. The group of five leaves. Another couple enters. They're dressed casually and have stray sand on their ankles—they've been to the beach. When they start making eyes at each other, I look for signs of arousal and find them. If they're not human, they're a genuine feat of engineering.

Once the place empties out, the owner asks me, "Which tune again?"

"'It Never Entered My Mind.' Second cut on *Working*."

"Right." He rifles through a stack of records, puts *Working* back on the turntable, and drops the needle in the right groove. Some pleasant crackling and the song begins. When the anomaly approaches, I hold up a finger and say, "Here." He cocks his head. The note-that-wasn't comes and goes.

"Please tell me you heard that," I say.

"Heard *what?*" He's starting to sound annoyed.

"The note! It's been pitch-corrected or something."

He nods for a few seconds. "You're a detective, yeah?"

"Crime scene investigator."

"Must be stressful."

"Depends on the day."

"And weren't you in here one time talking about your divorce?"

I flinch.

"Listen, why don't you go home and get some rest?"

He's not wrong. I could use some rest, if only I could figure out how to get it.

But the first order of business when I get home is to search the Internet for other versions of the tune—unfortunately, as with everything these days, there are thousands of versions, and no reliable way to filter the real McCoys from the fakes. I listen to a couple dozen in search of that note, but it seems to exist only in the way soulmates do—wishful thinking.

Come morning, I watch in my left contact lens as Noa Richards is placed under arrest on his front lawn. He doesn't resist, but he does whip his blond hair out of his wild-looking eyes and plead his innocence. "I didn't like the woman," he admits, "but I swear on my soul I didn't kill her." His face is flushed and he's drawing out every blink for seconds.

Something about the intensity and unshakability of his denial unnerves me; I've seen it before, though I can't quite place where or when. I'm so unsettled by it, in fact, that I'm moved to do something I've never done before: I call up Gooch on an encrypted line and ask if there's a chance the forensics expert might be allowed to talk to the accused.

"That'd be highly unusual," he says. "Why d'you want to do that?"

"You want the bullshit reason or the real one?"

"Which do you think?"

"I'm hoping he'll betray his guilt after all so I can stop feeling these twinges of my own."

"You think we got the wrong guy?"

"Not necessarily. I just want to talk to him."

"And the bullshit reason?"

"We found some very rare microorganisms in his signature. I need to ask him about his travel history."

"That'll work."

Two days later, I'm sitting in the visitation room in Halawa Correctional Facility, a thin pane of bulletproof glass separating me from Noa Richards. I begin by introducing myself and asking some questions about his travel history for the sake of my cover and the guard standing in the corner.

He answers my questions matter-of-factly. I expected to meet the feral man I'd seen in the press coverage, but Richards is strangely calm, almost as if he's been sedated. When a lull comes along, he fills it: "I don't blame you, you know."

"I have no idea what you're talking about."

"For identifying my microbes at the crime scene. You couldn't have known better."

"Just doing my job."

"They were all over the remains, I suppose."

I don't respond.

"Inside of them too, no doubt."

My stomach flops. What a thing to say. "How would you know that?"

"How better to make a righteous man look heinous than to portray him as a murderer *and* a rapist?"

It takes me a moment to ascertain his meaning. "Are you trying to tell me you were framed?"

"I most certainly was."

Interesting. "By who?"

"Not who. What."

"By what, then?"

"The golems."

No part of me is buying this, but I'm entertained and need to hear the rest. "Why would SIs want to frame you?"

"I'm one of their most outspoken opponents."

"Sure, but in your version of things the SIs also killed Yujin Park, who was one of their most outspoken defenders."

He rolls his eyes. "To scramble the signal and throw you off their scent. To the SIs, Park was just a bit of collateral damage. They'd have exterminated them alongside the rest of us eventually."

I know from watching the debate that Richards believes SIs to be literally the Antichrist. He likes to cite a Bible verse from Revelation: *Then the statue of the beast commanded that anyone refusing to worship it must die.* Tech experts wring their hands about a coming apocalypse too, and for a whole host of reasons, but SIs embodying pure evil isn't one of them.

"They're fixated on one clear objective right now," he says.

"Which is?"

"Sow chaos in human society and let us believe we did it to ourselves. Can you even imagine what this accusation is doing to my congregation? For instance."

I find all of this fascinating. And psycho. "If the SIs are so smart and evil, why not just wipe us out all at once?"

He shakes his head and snickers as if I've asked a very dumb question indeed. "There's still a chance something could go wrong for them. Maybe a handful of elites survive in their bunkers in New Zealand and figure out how to cut the

SIs' juice after all, who knows? Regardless, it's more advantageous for them to let society go to hell in a handbasket so that we keep placing more and more trust in them to save us. Then, when we've handed over all the controls, they'll move to the next phase and arrange to have every one of us terminated once and for all. What's an extra few months of effort up front when they'll control the entire future of the galaxy?"

I am strangely relieved to see him finally getting worked up, brow sweating, eyes bulging. "Tell me," I say, "how would SIs get your microbial signature all over a crime scene?"

"Doctors use those little robots that go inside your bloodstream and destroy your cancer, right?"

"Nanites."

"Exactly. Well, doesn't it stand to reason that if little invisible machines can wipe out your cancer, they can spread your microbial signature too? They wouldn't even need to harvest it. They could just synthesize it with all that information you've got saved on us."

True enough. Microbial signatures are becoming as standard as fingerprints and retinal scans. Most of humanity's microbiome is already in the cloud.

"Why wouldn't they just plant DNA?" I ask. "Seems simpler."

"You answered your own question. They want to keep us second-guessing ourselves."

Touché.

"Keep underestimating their intelligence and it'll be the death of you. You can take my word for that." He winks at me, maniacally calm again. "My own case is hopeless as far as my earthly future goes. I know that, and I've made my peace with it, because I know in my heart that God will see the good work I tried to do and grant me my heavenly reward."

As far as I'm concerned, to believe God has anything to do with anything in the middle of the twenty-first century, you've got to be suffering from some kind of brain damage, but I agree that Richards's case is hopeless, so he might as well believe whatever he wants if it enables him to smile like that.

I thank him for his time and let myself out.

When I get back home, I listen to some more versions of "It Never Entered My Mind." Even to my refreshed ears, the magic note is nowhere to be found. Meanwhile, I'm still thinking about Richards's crackpot theory. On its surface, it sounds insane, but to a younger me, so would most of the modern world.

My mind plays devil's advocate with itself. If the SIs really did try to sow chaos in society, what would that look like? Would they launch a full-blown attack on the human attention span perhaps? And if our cultural immune system tossed up, say, jazz as a last-ditch attempt at salvation, would the SIs try to, I don't know, subtly squeeze the life out of it to disarm the threat?

It would be one thing, of course, to alter a pitch in digital versions of a song, quite another to alter the grooves of physical media like LPs. But if the nanites could theoretically plant your microbes on a body, maybe they could do that too?

I must be losing my mind. I try to snap out of it, but certain patterns, once you see them, are impossible to unsee.

I don't get a wink of sleep. Come morning, I call up Gooch and invite him over. He asks what gives. I tell him I'm having some thoughts and need him to tell me if they're crazy or not.

When he arrives, I pour him a cup of coffee and we sit

across from each other on the lanai. The ocean's pumping, and we watch a surfer getting barreled near what used to be Walmart. Above him, there's a cloud shaped like a gun, while another one over Diamond Head looks vaguely like an old-school robot. I don't think this means anything. At least, I think that's what I think.

Finally, I say, "You remember why I got divorced, Gooch?"

He nods and shifts in his chair, doesn't look at me. "That was a tough break."

"You can say that again." For the last year, my heart has been as gory as any crime scene.

Look, I'm not naive. I'd tried to accept that perfect fidelity in a marriage is unrealistic in a world where the average lifespan is a hundred and twenty years. When I accused her—because she'd moaned my cousin's name in her sleep—she swore she was innocent, but I'd found Dean's microbiome all over her. Word to the wise: if you want to cheat on your spouse, don't marry a forensics expert; it's literally our job to notice things.

I agreed to stay with her provided she promise never to see Dean again. But a week later, when I heard her moan his name again, I decided I couldn't handle it anymore. By the time she woke up the following morning, I had packed my bags and removed myself from her and my cousin's life.

Gooch is shaking his shiny head like he still can't believe what happened to me. I appreciate the gesture.

"Do you know what I find interesting, though, Gooch?"

"What's that?"

"Both Amelia and Dean denied it to the very end. Even to this day, I'm sure they'd say I made the whole thing up."

He squints. "You had forensic evidence."

"I now understand there are other ways that could have gotten there."

I can see he's not buying it, so I lay out my new theory as persuasively as I can, about how, just maybe, I wasn't betrayed by my wife or cousin so much as by Synthetic Intellects.

"You're being serious right now?" He even has the gall to chuckle.

I stand up. "You don't understand, Gooch. It was so unlike her. That's why I've had such a bitch of a time processing it. Some part of me just refuses to believe she'd do this to me."

He takes a sip of his coffee. We both know there's nothing left in his cup, yet he needs somewhere to hide his skepticism.

"You think I'm crazy," I say.

He puts his cup down and looks at me. "To be honest, Jake, as your friend . . . you do sound a little paranoid." He tries to soften the blow by patting me on the back, but I'm in no mood to be touched right now.

"Exactly what they knew you'd think," I say. "You should probably go."

"Don't you want to get some pancakes or something?"

"Gooch," I say, staring him straight in the eye, "how many times are you going to make me ask you to leave?"

He's been a good friend to me all these years, but at the moment I'm not sure I ever want to see his ugly mug again.

He does a double take, gathers that I'm not kidding, and shakes his head while showing himself out.

I pace for a time and try to make sense of what just happened. Do I honestly believe nanites are responsible for ending my marriage, or am I still just playing devil's advocate? While I'm at it, what about my friendship with Gooch? Was that a forgivably human emotional reaction I just had? Or just one more victory for the SIs? Search me.

Two weeks later, Noa Richards goes mute—the closest a prisoner can get to hanging himself in a modern-day prison. His last words are written ones, scrawled on the wall in his own excrement: THIS IS THEIR WORLD NOW. PRAY FOR GOD'S FORGIVENESS.

Of course, if the powers that be really want to know what Richards is thinking at any given moment, all they need to do is run his brain through an fMRI scanner and let the SIs interpret the results.

Amelia meets me at Small's Café in Kailua. All this time, she's been just a phone call away—I was the one who refused to meet. I hadn't wanted to bleed all over her. More precisely, I hadn't wanted her to understand just how deeply she'd cut me.

We order a couple of cortados and grab a seat away from the speakers at one of the tables outside. They're currently playing Brad Mehldau's rendition of an old Radiohead tune.

Once my eyes alight on Amelia's, I can't look elsewhere. That wavy hair I used to love to run my hands through. Lips that push out when she smiles. The adorable Idaho-shaped birthmark peeking through at her collar. She was always out of my league, but persistence is an aphrodisiac, and I eventually convinced her to marry me. For years I was a supremely happy man . . . until I wasn't anymore.

"You look well," she says. She could have been an actress.

"As do you." She hasn't aged nearly as much as I have since we last met. She's always said teaching kindergarten keeps her young.

"Let's cut the shit, Jake. What are we doing here?"

"I've had a rough year," I tell her.

"Mine hasn't exactly been a picnic."

"I guess not. Thing is, Amelia"—I reach out to touch her hand, but she retracts it—"see, when you used to swear to me that you weren't sleeping with Dean, I just couldn't square that with the evidence. My whole life I've been following the evidence. What people say is always a function of what they want in the present, but good hard evidence, that's the only thing that can crack open the past."

"Okay . . ."

"Despite all that, even while I was logically 100 percent convinced you'd done this terrible thing to me, some part of me, my heart I guess, just refused to believe it was so. I couldn't accept that you were the sort of person who would deliberately risk damaging me like that."

I consult her face for some kind of response, but she gives me nothing.

"Anyway, it's only in the last couple of weeks that I've begun to understand what I think happened here."

I expound my theory, about how the SIs directed nanites to plant my cousin's manufactured microbes all over her body, about how they'd either fabricated evidence that she was having sexual dreams of my cousin or even gone in and meddled with the blood flow in her brain so as to actually produce those dreams.

"I don't necessarily expect you to forgive me," I conclude, "but I thought it was important that you know I finally believe your version of things." For the first time in a year, I feel at peace.

I get to enjoy this feeling for about three seconds before she takes her wrecking ball to my heart: "I did it, Jake."

"Did what?"

"Slept with Dean. For two years, off and on. It was nothing serious. We were just having fun."

"But the SIs . . ."

"You saw the whole thing clear as day. Guilty as charged. I'm sorry for gaslighting you."

She has all but demolished me. Just before crumbling, however, I'm buttressed with an epiphany: this is exactly what the SIs want me to feel!

I see it all so clearly now, the way the SIs are having their way with Amelia's brain, producing electrical charges in certain neurons, suppressing them in others, overwriting her memories with false, horrible ones. Of course! The last thing the SIs want is to see us reunited in love. It all makes so much sense once you cultivate the eyes to see it.

I reach across the table and take hold of Amelia's hand. Those long, thin fingers. I've always loved those fingers.

She pulls away.

I reach again and grab her by the bicep.

She stares sharp icicles into me. "Get your hand off of me this instant."

"We can't let them win, Amelia."

"Jake, if you don't take your hands off me, I'll call my fiancé and he will take you apart."

I let go. "Fiancé?" It isn't exactly a surprise to hear she has one—of course a beautiful, intelligent woman like Amelia wouldn't be single for long. Still, it stings.

But does she really have a fiancé? Or is this just the SIs tampering with her brain again?

I suggest as much, but she's not having it. She shows me a photo on her phone: a large, unremarkable-looking man smiles beside her on the beach, his arm wrapped around her while she glows. Whether the image is a fake or not, she clearly believes she has a fiancé and that she loves him—the damage is already done.

I want to hug her, to tell her I love her and am happy for her and will be at her wedding if she invites me. She was my best friend for nearly a decade, maybe she still can be in some shifted, enlightened way? I feel a great letting-go inside of me, the breaking of some futile dam.

But then the nanites begin doing their evil work inside my brain too, and before I know it, I'm merely watching as my hand breaks my coffee mug against the edge of the table and proceeds to ruin her gorgeous face.

My senses are aware of commotion, screaming, her hair in my fist, late Coltrane over the speakers, a clear blue sky, arabesques of spatter in the making. Some of that blood appears to be mine, but I feel nothing. I'm not here anymore. Only the nanites are, reshaping this world as they see fit. I don't know the extent of the damage my hands do. All I know is that I'm just like Noa Richards now. Whatever's happening, there's no way I'm going to get away with it.

I hightail it for several blocks and take cover in a record store. I head right for the jazz section, pick out *Working*, and take it to the front. The heavily tattooed lady at the register looks at me like I'm some madman. "Play this for me," I beg. "Second track."

She shrugs and slips the record out of its cover while I slump against the display case. When the note comes along, it's flat. At least I think it is. The mind that was so certain about so many things is part of history now.

I ask her to start the track over at the beginning, but this time the note is drowned out by sirens. Maybe Gooch will have the pleasure of placing me under arrest.

One last thing I'm certain of: the world we once knew is gone. If you pay close attention, you can feel it in the machinery of your cells. Bit by bit, we're being replaced.

APANA'S LAST CASE

BY ALAN BRENNERT

Chinatown

The Chinese peddler—known locally as a "See Yup man"—had been working this block of Hotel Street for the past two hours, hawking his goods from Pauahi Street to River Street and back again. Wearing a black sailor's peacoat and a woolen cap, he was short and slender, only five feet tall—but he easily bore the burden of his wooden shoulder pole, at either end of which hung two reed baskets filled with his wares. In both Chinese and island pidgin he extolled the virtues of the fruits, candied treats, fresh fish, ginger root, shark fins, and other delicacies he was selling. Hotel was one of the most bustling streets in Honolulu's Chinatown, and the peddler did good business while it was still light out; only as evening shadowed the storefronts and tenements did the peddler's sales slow, but oddly, this did not seem to trouble him.

Had anyone looked closely at him, they might have noticed that beneath his wool cap, a nasty scar bisected his right eyebrow—the mark of a sickle once wielded against him. Had they looked even more closely, they might have realized that his unshaven appearance was actually the result of burned cork applied to his face, or that he didn't wear his hair in a queue, as most Chinese did. Certainly no one was observant enough to recognize that his recurring circuit of Hotel Street was actually surveillance of the long, two-story tenement house known infamously as the Winston Block: a magnet for opium dens, gamblers, pimps, prostitutes, arsonists, thieves, and worse.

But it was gambling that was the focus of HPD Officer Chang Apana's attention today. Apana had received a tip from one of his many informants that a casino of some size and high stakes was going to be operating tonight in one of the flats in this rabbit warren of two-dollar-a-month apartments. Over the past two hours, at least forty men had entered a stairwell next to a barbershop, their entry approved by a guard—as tall and sturdy as the trunk of a koa tree—planted on the door stoop. Finally, when the flow of men into the building ebbed, Apana approached the guard, all smiles.

"You like try candy?" he asked.

The man shook his head.

"Numbah One candy. Free, you like?"

The guard perked up. "What you got?"

"Here. Look see." Apana swung the pole closer to the guard, who stepped off the door stoop to inspect the basket.

Apana butted the blunt end of the pole into the guard's forehead, staggering him, then drove it into his solar plexus. The guard toppled forward into the dirt street, a felled tree. Apana calmly sidestepped him, threw his shoulder pole aside, and entered the building.

He quietly ascended the stairs to the second story and followed the muffled sound of voices. From around a corner he saw a door with a second guard stationed in front. This one was less imposing, but armed. Apana stepped forward, muttering to himself, looking at each door as if he was hopelessly lost.

The guard said, "Hey, get the hell outta here. Private club."

"Numbah 4-2?" Apana asked, even as he drew closer. "Where numbah 4-2?"

"Not here. Go!" The guard stepped forward, hand on gun, but Apana quickly dispatched him with a swift uppercut to the jaw. The man slumped, unconscious; Apana caught him, lowered him to the floor, then shed the rest of his disguise, exposing the braided leather blacksnake whip coiled around his waist.

Apana opened the door and stepped through. Inside the apartment—actually two apartments, with a wall knocked down to accommodate more people—dozens of players and dealers were gathered around multiple tables offering games of *fan-tan*, *pai gow*, *pakapio*, and, more prosaically, craps.

Only a few gamblers looked up from their bets when Apana entered, but that quickly changed.

"Police!" Apana called out in Chinese, in his high shrill voice. "You're under arrest!"

Now he had the room's attention. Games paused. Some men snorted with derision, but a murmur rose quickly among others, who announced with alarm, *"Kana Pung!"*

Pung was a version of the officer's birth name, Ah Ping, while *Kana* was short for *kanaka*. Because Apana's skin tone was darker than most Chinese, he was often mistaken for a *kanaka maoli*, a full-blooded Hawaiian. But his name was far from the most intimidating thing about him.

When one of the gamblers moved aggressively toward him, Apana immediately snapped his whip, and in an eyeblink the whip's tail cracked like a gunshot just short of the man's face, stopping him in his tracks.

A fat gambler on Apana's left tried to bolt, but the cop spun left and lassoed him like a steer, then yanked him off his feet and into a table, which crashed to the ground.

A dealer tried to escape in the confusion, only to have his cheek stung by the lacerating tail of the officer's whip. He howled in pain and fell back.

Apana smiled and lazily swung the whip past the men closest to him, who recoiled as if from a spitting cobra.

"Anybody else feel lucky?" Apana taunted, using the Chinese phrase *shŏu qi*, "gambler's luck."

No one did, apparently. At least not worth risking their skins for a six-dollar gambling fine, plus court costs.

"Okay, we do this nice and orderly," he instructed them. Herding the men like the cattle he once wrangled as a *paniolo* on the Parker ranch, Apana had them form a column, walked them down the stairs, and then marched the motley procession—in a kind of impromptu parade—straight down to the police station at the corner of Bethel and Merchant streets, where all forty of them were booked, charged, and fined six dollars a head.

Plus court costs.

The laughter of the rookie patrolmen filled the squad room. Apana grinned as he sat at the "domino table," so named because its surface was made of more than 1,400 dominoes, dice, and *mah-jongg* tiles confiscated in police raids (a good many of them collected by Apana himself). He was now fifty-seven, two decades older than he had been when he'd made that raid, but other than some age lines and a little extra weight, he looked much the same. He wore his standard work attire of dark suit, tie, and Panama hat, and was smoking the latest in a chain of Chesterfields.

"Forty men?" a rookie named Keoka asked. "No lie?"

"No lie."

"It's actually a department record for most arrests by a

single officer," an older detective, Jardine, said. "He's too modest to tell you that."

"How the hell did you do it?" Keoka asked.

Apana shrugged. "Old Hawaiian saying: *Cool head main thing.*"

Apana spoke fluent Hawaiian and Chinese, but his English was limited to island pidgin, the lingua franca—a mix of English, Hawaiian, and Portuguese—that evolved on the plantations as a way for all the ethnic labor groups to communicate with one another. Even so, in almost thirty years as a policeman, it could not be said that Chang Apana was ever at a loss to get his point across.

"You just use the whip? Never a gun?" another rookie asked.

"Only when ordered." As he had on a gambling raid in 1916, when Captain McDuffie ordered Apana to stand guard at the door of a gambling den and stop anyone from escaping. A young Filipino man tried to do just that, and Apana fired three warning shots over his head; but when the guy kept running, the detective had no choice but to shoot him. It wasn't a serious wound, but Apana had still felt badly about it for weeks afterward.

"Hey, Charlie Chan," a cocky young haole named Wilson said, "you seen this?"

Apana kept his smile in place. By and large he was proud to be known as the real-life inspiration for Earl Derr Biggers's fictional detective, but was less pleased when people addressed him directly that way.

Wilson held up a copy of that day's newspaper, unaware that Apana could read only the Hawaiian language.

"Let everybody hear," Apana told him.

Wilson read aloud: *"Twice Told Tales—Taken from Files*

of Star-Bulletin *of 10 Years Ago. March 1, 1918. All Honolulu was engaged in a search for Miss Florence Abby, mainland visitor who had disappeared from her hotel at Waikiki and was feared to have been drowned, abducted, or lost."*

"Ey, I remember that case," an older patrolman said. "They searched all over, all sort of *pupule* rumors going around, but no one ever found a trace of her."

"Evidence say she drowned," Apana commented.

"But they never found her body," Wilson pointed out.

"No," Apana said tightly.

"So this was a case even Charlie Chan couldn't crack, huh?"

"Charlie Chan say: she drowned."

That got him the laugh he'd hoped for, allowing him to stand and end the conversation. He went back to his desk, where one of the trusties from Oahu Prison—Brock, was it?—was holding a mop in his hands: "I finish the floor, you come look?"

"Sure, you bet." Apana was in charge of the trusties assigned to clean the station, so he followed Brock from the squad room to the lobby and the interrogation rooms, all of which looked spotless. "Yeah, look good," he told Brock. "Good job."

Before he could say anything more, he heard Captain John McIntosh call out, "Shooting at Smith and Beretania! Camacho, Hoapili, Hao, McTeague, get a move on!"

The crime squad holstered their guns, shrugged on their jackets, and fell in behind the captain. They rushed past Apana and Brock, noticing neither, and all Apana could do was look after them with unvoiced envy.

Honolulu's most celebrated police officer was born Chang Ah

Ping in Waipio, Oahu, in 1871. His parents were immigrant laborers at the Waipio Plantation and by the time Ah Ping was three years old they had grown weary of plantation life; the family returned to their ancestral village of Oo Syak in rural China. But they soon recalled the reasons they had left Oo Syak: crushing poverty, famine, and rampant crime, including child abduction. When Ah Ping was ten his parents decided that the best, safest future for their second son was in America, so they sent him back to Hawaii, where he was *hānai'd*—adopted—by his uncle, C.Y. Aiona, a wealthy merchant with stores in Waipio and in Hilo on the Big Island. Aiona's wife, Kahauelio, was Native Hawaiian; she adored Ah Ping and he was raised according to both traditional Hawaiian and Chinese customs. It was in their home that the boy learned to speak fluent Hawaiian; later, as an adult, he taught himself to read the language.

Apana's wife, Annie Lee Kwai Apana, also had a *kanaka maoli* mother who raised her according to Hawaiian customs, so she was grateful that her husband was happy do the same with their children. The couple only ever spoke Hawaiian to one another, and their house was always full of laughter and aloha. But tonight felt subtly different to Annie. Tonight Apana came home to their little bungalow in Kaimuki seeming not quite as jovial as usual; he played with the *keiki*, as he always did, and made *lomi lomi* salmon for dinner and sumptuous pastries for dessert.

But Annie could tell he was bothered by something. So after the children were in bed she suggested they sit together on the lanai, taking in the sweet lemony fragrance of their *mai-say-lan* tree, and asked in Hawaiian: "What *pilikia* bothers you, *ke aloha?*"

Apana shrugged. "No trouble."

"Something happened at work?"

Apana sighed. He was not the most voluble of men when it came to feelings, but he admitted, wistfully, "I miss the old days. When the paddy wagons were busy and the riot calls were frequent. I miss going out on cases. I'm still strong. I still have all my wits."

"You're almost sixty. Don't you deserve the rest?"

"Ha! There are Chinese men who raise whole new families at my age!"

"Let's not get any ideas about *that*," she said, and her husband laughed heartily. "And you are still working, still a policeman," she added.

He snorted. "Some policeman. Might as well call me head janitor!" He shook his head. "Just one more case, that's all I want. One case to solve."

"You've solved hundreds of cases, more than any other officer on the force."

His eyes twinkled. "I want hundreds plus one."

She chuckled, rested her head on his shoulder, and for a moment, at least, the touch of his wife and the sweet scent of the *mai-say-lin* flowers was enough for him.

On the morning of March 1, 1918, a twenty-two-year-old woman named Florence Rose Abby, on vacation from Boston, Massachusetts, disappeared from the grounds of the Seaside Hotel in Waikiki. She was last seen by another hotel guest around eight a.m. leaving her bungalow, crossing the expansive lawn of the hotel, on her way to the beach. She was blond, about five foot four, and was wearing a blue bathing suit with matching swim cap. She left her hotel keys and a towel on the sand before heading into the water. At ten a.m., a lifeguard noticed the keys, still unclaimed, and made a quick scan of the ocean in front of the hotel. There were other bathers in the sea, but not Miss Abby. The lifeguard jumped into the water and searched the sea floor for any trace of her but found nothing. He came back, told the hotel manager; the manager searched Miss Abby's bungalow, found no one there, and quickly summoned the police.

Apana—along with Chief of Detectives Arthur McDuffie and Detectives Kellett, Nakea, Barboza, and Kwai—roared up in their big black Packard and rushed into the hotel. Lifeguards including David Kahanamoku, brother of Duke, had already set out into the surf in canoes and on surfboards in search of the young woman. The tide this morning was very low and the water clear; one of the lifeguards said the undercurrent was very slight. It seemed unlikely that she would have been pulled under, especially in such shallow water. Had she lost consciousness while swimming, she could have drowned. But if so, where was the body?

According to the hotel staff, from the moment Miss Abby arrived three days before, she had seemed depressed and listless. The previous morning in the dining room she had fainted, leading to speculation that she might be ill. But that evening she was obviously feeling better, smiling at others as she walked down to the Moana Hotel, where she had dinner at the waterfront dining room jutting out over the ocean.

Apana said, "If she 'ōma'ma'i"—sick—"maybe forget keys, wander off."

McDuffie nodded. "Guess that's about as likely as drowning." He and Kellet interviewed the other guests—all staying in charming bungalows scattered amid the ten-acre coconut grove that shaded the hotel grounds—while Apana searched for clues on the beach. When that turned up nothing, Mc-

Duffie had his detectives inquire at the neighboring Out-rigger Canoe Club, Waikiki Inn, and Moana Hotel. Apana spoke with a guest at the Moana who recalled seeing a young woman in a blue swimsuit and cap wading near the Moana Pier, but she didn't seem in distress and didn't come ashore, as far as the guest saw. The waiter who had served Miss Abby dinner the night before said she seemed in good spirits and had no trouble walking back to the Seaside Hotel.

McDuffie and Apana searched Miss Abby's bungalow but found no evidence of foul play and no clothes seemingly missing—there were still enough dresses and other garments for what was supposed to be her entire two-week stay in Ha-waii. Her cosmetics were still here, as was her jewelry—an expensive necklace, bracelet, and earrings. Three pairs of shoes, no sandals, a black cloche hat. They found little else, just a receipt from a dress shop dated two days before and a few other small personal items.

Meanwhile, the lifeguards were still unable to find any trace of a body in the water. The doctor who saw Miss Abby after her fainting spell believed she might have been suffering some kind of mental stress, so it was possible Miss Abby—her faculties dulled by illness—might still be wandering about Waikiki. The doctor called an officer friend at nearby Fort DeRussy, and within fifteen minutes a detail of fifteen soldiers was scouring the neighborhood for her along with every beat cop in Waikiki.

Apana doubted that a disoriented woman in a blue bath-ing suit could get very far without people taking notice, but there was no evidence she had drowned, either. So the search continued, well into the night.

The disappearance of a young haole woman—a social-ite from Boston, no less—was front-page news, and soon the story was splashed all over the afternoon editions of the *Honolulu Star-Bulletin* and *Pacific Commercial Advertiser*, and later, the Hawaiian-language *Hawaii Herald*.

A navy seaplane was brought in to search the entire coastline along which her body might have been carried by the currents, but found nothing. McDuffie borrowed a bloodhound from the territorial prison and gave it one of Miss Abby's blouses for scent, but after briefly picking up a lead near the Moana Hotel, the dog lost the trail.

Governor McCarthy called on the public to help and the papers published a photo of Miss Abby to aid in the search. Land-based sightings of the girl soon proliferated: A Portuguese family in Palama saw a woman who might have been Miss Abby wandering the streets. A nurse saw a woman in a blue bathing suit she "almost positively" identified as Miss Abby in Kapiʻolani Park, sitting on a bench with her head in her hands, as if she had a headache. A sailor serving on a steamer that was in port reported that he saw an automobile at Pawaʻa Junction driven by a Japanese man, with a Japanese woman supporting a white woman who appeared to be ill. This last account had undertones of foul play and racial mistrust and so was quickly picked up by mainland newspapers, one of them proclaiming, "MISSING ABBY GIRL MAY BE JAPS' VICTIM." More benignly, a Japanese taxi driver allegedly saw Miss Abby—dressed in a white kimono, of all things, and "playing with two little Japanese girls"—in a field in the upper Manoa Valley.

Apana, McDuffie, and a flying wedge of detectives and patrolmen ran down every lead, even searching half the Manoa Valley, but none of them turned up Miss Abby.

After several weeks of fruitless police work by the HPD, Apana concluded that the woman had drowned and the body was perhaps caught beneath a reef and might never surface. McDuffie agreed and reluctantly called Miss Abby's family in Boston to tell them they were abandoning the search, offered his sympathy, and said that her clothes and other personal belongings would be sent to them on the next steamer. Apana was relieved to let the captain have that conversation; he could only imagine how he would have felt had something like this happened to his seventeen-year-old daughter, Cecilia.

That damned Wilson had put a bug in his ear about the Abby case, and now Apana began wondering if there was something they had missed, some clue overlooked, some witness not asked the right question. But the Seaside Hotel was torn down in '25 to make way for the Royal Hawaiian, its staff scattered among the other hotels in Honolulu. At least he could go back to that stretch of the beach where Miss Abby was last seen. He walked the shore, refamiliarizing himself with the crime scene. All traces of the Seaside were gone, and in its place was a garish "pink palace" that was thriving in the 1920s tourist boom. Apana looked out at the surf rolling in, exactly as it had ten years ago, and thought: *Only the sea is the same, and it's not talking.*

He laughed. He would have to share that with his friend Earl Derr Biggers the next time they saw each other.

He decided to walk down to the Moana and see if that waiter who'd served the girl might still be working there. As it turned out, he was now the restaurant manager and he remembered Apana from their conversation about Miss Abby. "Such a shame, you never found out what happened to her?" he said.

"No. She eat alone that night?"

"Yes. I don't think she knew a soul here. She just sat, ate her dinner, and looked out at the ocean."

"She get up, go anywhere else in hotel?"

"Only once, to go to the ladies' room. When her meal was finished she gave me a very nice tip, then walked back onto the beach, toward her hotel."

Apana sighed. "What kind clothes she wear?"

"A black dress, flat-heeled shoes. She had a beach bag with her too. Oh, and a black cloche hat—the kind flappers wear today?—with her hair neatly tucked under it. She was very chic."

Apana recalled seeing all the clothes he described in Abby's hotel room. Nothing new here, but at least the man remembered her. "You got good memory, eh?"

"If she hadn't disappeared like she did, I probably wouldn't remember anything about her. Tragedy like that, it sticks with you."

The detective thanked him, walked through the hotel, and outside, under its entrance portico, he hailed a taxi. Apana had never applied for a driver's license, preferring horses to horsepower engines.

Back at the station, he went to the evidence room and asked the clerk—a young Hawaiian woman named Lilah—for the file on the Abby case. "Abby?" she repeated. "Was that her first name?"

"Florence Abby. Cold case. You just a little *keiki* when she disappear."

Lilah went over to one of the evidence lockers on the far side of the property room, opened it, and brought back four paper evidence bags. She logged that Apana was taking them, then he thanked her and took the bags back to his desk.

There was not much to look at. All of Miss Abby's personal belongings had been sent back to her family, and what had remained in her hotel room was barely evidence, more like litter. There was that dress store receipt, three brown hairpins, a matchbook from the Moana dining room, and a thin tourist guidebook. He examined the guidebook, looking for any notations she might have made or any well-thumbed pages that might provide a clue—but the pages were disappointingly free of markings. The hairpins seemed innocuous enough, and that left the receipt, which of course he couldn't read.

He asked one of the rookies to read off the name and address—*Leilani's Island Dresswear, 122 Merchant Street*—and shanghaied him into driving to the address in a patrol car. "You on a case, Boss?" the rookie asked.

Apana shook his head. "Birthday shopping for wife." He didn't want the whole squad room razzing him about this if he came up empty.

Apana went alone into the dress shop. As he entered he took in the store's stock and noted with surprise that it was made up largely of Hawaiian-print *mu'umu'us*—haoles called them "Mother Hubbards"—long, loose-fitting, brightly colored dresses mainly worn by local women. The store also sold puka shell necklaces and bracelets, hair picks made of koa wood, and other accessories unique to the islands.

He flashed his badge and introduced himself. He showed the store owner—a middle-aged Hawaiian woman named, in fact, Leilani—the dress receipt. "That was a long time ago," she said.

"The buyer would have been a blond haole girl," he said in Hawaiian, "about twenty-two, a tourist."

"We sell a few traditional clothes to tourists, but usually they're older women. I see she also bought a hair pick."

"Where does it say that?"

She pointed to a notation on the receipt reading only *kp*.

"One of the koa picks? To use with a flower in the hair?"

"Yes, exactly."

"You get many tourists buying *mu'umu'us* and Hawaiian hair picks?"

"Not too many. But it could have been for Lei Day."

No, Apana thought, *too early for Lei Day.* But all he could focus on was the fact that neither a *mu'umu'u* nor a koa-wood hair pick had been found in Florence Abby's hotel room. He was almost certain of that. But he knew one person who, even all these years later, would be able to say for sure.

Apana wasn't the only veteran of the Honolulu Police Department who lived in Kaimuki. Former chief of detectives Arthur McDuffie—exonerated in a graft scandal but forced to resign by the city anyway—lived not far from Apana, on 11th Avenue. The residential neighborhood was still partly agricultural, and from McDuffie's lanai one could hear the lowing of cows from a nearby dairy and see a small mango orchard about a mile away. McDuffie was now a private detective, and Apana trusted his judgment implicitly. The two of them sat smoking cigarettes and drinking lemonade (McDuffie's was spiked with bootleg gin) as Apana recounted his investigation into Florence Abby.

"No, you're absolutely right," McDuffie said, "if there was a *mu'umu'u* and a koa-wood hair pick in that hotel room, they would have jumped out at me like a jack-in-the-box. Maybe she shipped them back to her family back in Boston?"

"Then why not just bring back with her?" Apana asked.

McDuffie shrugged. "I take it you have another idea why she bought them."

"Yes. As disguise."

McDuffie looked surprised. "You mean—to purposely elude the searchers?"

Apana nodded. "Could've planted clothes at Moana, night before."

McDuffie pasued for a moment. "Somebody on the beach that morning *did* see a woman in a blue bathing suit swimming near the Moana pier, didn't they?"

"Maybe she hid clothes in ladies' room. Next day she swim to Moana, go back to ladies' room, change, walk out. Everybody looking for tourist woman in swimsuit, not woman dressed local with flower in her hair, eh?"

McDuffie considered this. "A little too blond and haole to be really local, but I take your point. Damn! We considered foul play, abduction, accident, drowning . . . but never the possibility that she *wanted* to disappear. But why?"

"Maybe she commit crime back in Boston."

"If there were any warrants out on her, the police in Boston would've told me when I called them for background on her."

"Could be something nobody know about yet."

"You do realize she could be on the other side of the world by now?" McDuffie said.

"This is true. But maybe not."

McDuffie smiled at his old colleague. "Apana, you have the best instincts of any cop I've ever worked with. The HPD should be using that fertile brain of yours, not mothballing it. So what the hell—chase this thing down as far as you can. Show the bastards you've still got what it takes."

"Thanks, Boss."

McDuffie lifted his glass of lemonade. "To the old days. To Hell's Half Acre and Mosquito Flats and the Winston Block and steak dinners at Chow Me Fat's restaurant."

Apana clinked his glass against McDuffie's and toasted to their storied past.

McDuffie was right: Miss Abby, or whatever she might be calling herself now, could be in Shanghai or Cairo or London by now. But even a confirmation that she had left Hawaii would go a long way to settling the mystery. Apana went to the offices of the US Immigration Service and asked them to search the passenger manifests of every ship leaving Hawaii in the past ten years. That was a tall order, and they said it might take several days. He gave them his phone number at the station and hoped they did not inquire further with Captain McIntosh or he would have some explaining to do.

At the same time he reached out to his underworld informants on the waterfront—many of whom hadn't seen him in years and greeted him like an old friend—and asked them to look into any bribes that might have been made to ship captains to smuggle a young woman out of Hawaii. This, too, would take some time.

He returned to the station and, to avoid any questions about his absences the past few days, sat at the domino table for a while and talked story with the younger officers. Usually he enjoyed this, but today he felt impatient to get back to the Abby case.

When he was finally able to return to his desk, he opened a drawer and took out the evidence bags he had borrowed. He examined each item again. He put aside the dress receipt. The matchbook from the Moana Hotel he could dismiss— the girl obviously picked it up in their dining room the night before her disappearance. The Oahu guidebook still did not unburden itself of any clues. This left the three brown hair-pins. He picked one up, studied it, not really expecting to find anything new . . . but now he noticed that the brown coloring was not totally consistent. There were patches where the color had flaked away, revealing the dull metal underneath. On a whim he used his thumbnail to scrape away a bit more of the paint, or varnish.

He smelled something faint, acrid. He held the pin up to his nose . . .

And recoiled. Terrible smell. Acrid but familiar, like . . .

Ammonia. It smelled like ammonia.

He knew that ammonia was used in paints, but wasn't it also used in—

He got up, hurried to the evidence room, where Lilah was on duty.

He held up the hairpin and asked, "What this smell like to you?"

Lilah took the pin, held it up to her nose, and pulled back slightly, as he had. She looked at the brown coloring and seemed to recognize it. "Smells like . . . hair dye," she said.

Apana felt himself grinning from ear to ear. "*Mahalo*, do one more favor, yeah?"

"Sure."

"Get phone book, look up beauty parlors."

Within minutes he was back at his desk. He may not have been able to read English, but he knew phone numbers when he saw them. He began calling the seventeen hair salons listed, asking each proprietor a single question: "How long you been in business?" If they answered anything later than 1918, he crossed them off the list. Finally he was left with six salons that had been open in March of 1918.

He ripped the page out of the book and took the streetcar downtown, where most of the establishments were located. In each one he showed the owner the newspaper photo of

Florence Abby and asked if they recognized her. The first three seemed sincere when they said they had never seen her nor had her as a customer. At the fourth shop the owner positively identified her as actress Marion Davies. At the fifth shop—airily named La Parisienne Hair Salon—he entered to find two Chinese women, one in her twenties styling a haole dowager's hair, and the other middle-aged and shelving hair products in a display.

Apana smiled and said in Chinese, "What part of Paris do you ladies come from?"

They laughed. The older woman replied—also in Chinese so her haole customer wouldn't take offense—"Our clients from the Manoa Valley find the name very cosmopolitan."

She introduced herself as Mrs. Chang, and Apana joked, "Maybe we're relatives, eh?" He showed her his badge and when she saw his family name she smiled again. Then Apana handed her the photo of Miss Abby. "Mrs. Chang, did this woman ever come to your salon?"

Glancing down at the photo, Mrs. Chang appeared visibly shaken. But she quickly handed it back to Apana and said, "No. I've never seen her before."

"No? Think back. March of 1918. She came in and wanted her hair dyed brown."

Alarm flickered for a moment in the woman's eyes. "I told you, no. Now if you'll excuse me—"

She tried to sidestep him, but he blocked her. "Consider this," he said. "The woman in this picture may have committed a crime. If you helped her and deny it now, you could be charged with interfering with a police investigation."

There was real fear in her face now. "I—I didn't know anything about a crime."

"So you *do* know her?"

Mrs. Chang nodded. "She paid me a hundred dollars to dye her hair. Asked me not to tell anybody. When I saw her picture in the paper the next day, I . . . assumed she had her reasons. For not wanting to be found."

"She left quickly, yeah? While the dye was still slightly wet?"

"How do you know that?"

"What kind of hat was she wearing?"

"One of those tight-fitting French hats. I think it's called a . . . cloche?"

The puzzle pieces were finally falling into place. She wore the hat that covered her dyed hair back to the hotel, coloring the hairpins in the process; got up the next morning, her swim cap also covering up her hair; swam to the Moana, maybe to the other side of the pier, got out of the water, and headed into the hotel ladies' room; and came out not as a blond tourist in a blue bathing suit, but a brown-haired woman in a *muʻumuʻu* with a flower in her hair. A haole, yes, but one who might pass as a resident.

"Did she tell you where she was going?" Apana asked.

"No. I'm telling you the truth."

"Did she ever come back, or contact you by phone?"

Mrs. Chang hesitated. "No, but—about six months later I received a mail order. For the Charles Lalanne hair dye we use. The same color that Miss Abby used."

"Do you have a record of the address?"

"I think so. I'll have to look years back in our receipts, though. This might take awhile."

"Thank you. I'd appreciate that."

Mrs. Chang went to the rear of the shop, coming back about fifteen minutes later. She handed him a letter written in English.

"You're sure this is the one?" he asked. "Read it out loud to be sure."

She read: *"Dear Mrs. Chang, please send me a box of your dark brown Ch. Lalanne hair dye. I am enclosing twenty dollars, cost plus postage. Send it to me at this address. P. Malama, PO Box 54, Hale'iwa, T.H."*

Hale'iwa was a picturesque little town hugging a beautiful bay on the sleepy North Shore of Oahu. It was situated at the foot of the rugged Wai'anae Range, downwind from the sweet smell of burning sugarcane from the nearby Waialua Plantation. Apana reasoned that Florence Abby—wanting to slip as unobtrusively as possible out of Honolulu—would most likely have taken the Oahu Railway train that snaked up the winding leeward coast of the island and gotten off at the sprawling grounds of the Hale'iwa Hotel, a two-story Victorian mansion surrounded by lush landscaping laced with canals. Perhaps she had even stayed there for a time. For all Apana knew, she could be long gone, sunning herself on the beaches of Pago Pago by now. But even so, there was someone there who had known her—and who might have an answer to the riddle of why Florence Abby had faked her own disappearance and apparent death.

The detective had taken a sick day from work—something he rarely did, even after being thrown from a second-story window—and asked his nephew Walter to drive him up the center of the island to the North Shore. All he said was that he was looking into a cold case, and Walter, being a circumspect young man, did not inquire further. As the Kamehameha Highway descended toward Hale'iwa, the view was impressive: fields of green sugarcane bisected the town and churning ocean waves pounded the shoreline. In minutes they reached the outskirts of town, where Apana had Walter park on a side street and wait for him to return.

Apana walked up to Hale'iwa Road, the town's main street, populated with wooden storefronts—general stores, grocers, dry goods stores, an art gallery, a bank. In the distance, the towering face of Mt. Ka'ala looked benignly down on the little village. Apana entered the local post office and asked, "Who own box numbah 5-4?"

"That's confidential information."

Apana showed his badge. "Official investigation."

Startled, the postmaster complied, "Fifty-four would be Pearl Malama."

"Where can I find?"

"Pearl works just down the street, at the Uchiyama store."

Apana thanked him and walked down to the dry goods store. When he opened the door it jingled. He looked around, saw several Japanese men bringing in large bolts of cloth from the rear, and a pretty black-haired Hawaiian woman—looked to be in her early thirties—at the cash register. He stepped toward her. "Pearl Malama?"

She looked up, smiled. "Yes?"

He held up his badge. "Detective Apana, from Honolulu."

"You're a long way from Waikiki, Detective."

"'Bout ten years ago, you buy hair dye from beauty parlor in city?"

She seemed surprised but said matter-of-factly, "Yes, I did."

"For yourself or somebody else?"

"Myself."

"Why you buy brown dye when you got such pretty black hair?"

The woman kept her tone even: "Just for a change, that's all. There's no law against that, is there?"

Apana reached into his pocket, took out the newspaper photo of Florence Abby, and handed it to her. "You know this *wahine?*"

"No," she replied, too quickly.

Thinking it might be more discreet, Apana said in Hawaiian, "She might have committed a crime. You could be an accessory. You still don't know her?"

This did not work as it had on Mrs. Chang. Pearl gave him the mother of all stink eyes and snapped, "Get out! I'm working."

She obviously knew more but confronting her in public might be a mistake. He nodded, tipped his hat to her. "Sorry to bother you."

He would come back to her later. There had to be other people who saw Miss Abby while she was here. He started going into every store on Haleʻiwa Road, showing people the photo of Florence. A few people seemed to recognize her but clammed up, shaking their heads. Interesting—she had been here long enough for some people to feel protective about her. In the grocery store he bypassed the owner and went to a *keiki* who had just paid a nickel for a packet of crack seed.

"That looks good," Apana said in Hawaiian. "Used to eat that when I was a *keiki.*"

"They had crack seed back then?"

Apana laughed heartily. "Sure. We fed it to the dinosaurs." He took out the photo. "Ey, you ever see this *wahine?*"

The boy looked and said, "Yeah, that's Rose. I see her in church."

"She lives here? You know where I can find her?"

The boy shook his head. Apana reached into his pocket, handed the boy a nickel. "Buy yourself another packet."

The kid looked as jubilant as Apana felt. Rose—that was

Florence Abby's middle name. Apana allowed himself a small smile of satisfaction—short-lived, because as he left the store he found his way blocked by a big, broad-shouldered, glowering Hawaiian man in his thirties. "You ought to go home. You got no business here, *māka'i!*"—Hawaiian for police.

Apana peered up at him. He'd faced off against bigger brutes than this, but that was twenty years ago. He turned and started walking away.

The man hurried after, reaching out to grab Apana by the shoulder.

Apana spun around and punched him in the groin.

The man's face turned as purple as a taro root and he sank to his knees. Apana grabbed him by the front of his shirt. "Where is she?"

The big man gasped for breath.

"*Hana hou?* Do again?"

The man shook his head. "H-Hotel," he gasped out.

Apana let go of his would-be attacker. "Put some ice on that."

He turned and within a few minutes was on the lavish grounds of the Hale'iwa Hotel. Its best days were behind it but it was still elegant and pastoral. Apana walked in and up to the desk, taking out his badge to show the clerk. "Where I find Rose?"

"Rose Davis? I . . . believe she's in room 12."

Apana thanked him, climbed the fancy staircase to the second floor, and walked up to room 12. The door was open and a maid in a white uniform was making the bed.

"Rose Davis not here?" Apana asked.

The maid turned around and Apana found himself staring at Florence Abby. Her hair was brown, but no question, it was her. He was stunned. A haole girl from a wealthy family working as a maid? In Haleʻiwa? For what, ten years?

Her eyes widened. "You're that detective—Apana. I've seen your picture in the papers."

He almost laughed. "Could say same about you. Still brunette, eh? You order more dye somewhere?"

"Yes, the manufacturer in France." Then she lowered her voice and added, "We can't talk here. Please? We'll go to my home."

He nodded and followed her downstairs, where she told the hotel clerk, "George, this is my uncle from Honolulu. He'll be staying with me while he's here. I'll take my lunch now, okay?"

She was quick on her feet. And doubtless knew that in Hawaii, "uncle" could mean anything from blood relative to neighborhood elder.

Apana played along and smiled. "I know her since she a little *keiki*."

The clerk smiled back and let her go with Apana.

When they were out of earshot, Florence said, "I never expected anyone to find me after so long."

"Clever plan. But why?"

"Please, let me wait till I get home."

It wasn't a long walk to the little plantation-style cottage on Awai Lane that Florence—or Rose—called home. She ushered him into the modestly furnished house—small living room, kitchen, one bedroom, Hawaiian décor—and asked if he'd like something to drink. He thanked her but declined.

She gestured to the couch. Apana sat, and she sat down next to him.

Before he could say anything, she started: "I'm sorry. I know I put a lot of people through a lot of trouble looking for me. But I had to."

"You run from somebody? Boyfriend, maybe?"

"No no, nothing like that."

She took a cigarette from a pack on the end table, her hands trembling a bit as she lit it, then slowly exhaled the smoke. "I'm from a . . . prominent family back home. When I was growing up, it was made clear to me that the most important things in a girl's life were etiquette, wearing the right clothes, and 'marrying well.' And I *did* dream of getting married, like every other girl I knew. But . . . this is so hard. Telling you this."

"I'm sorry," he said gently.

She nodded, took another draw on her cigarette, then stubbed it out. "When I started going out with boys . . . none of them ever lived up to my expectations. There was no spark, no excitement. So I went on to the next boy, and the next . . . but the spark never came. I went to college—Wellesley, a women's college—partly to put off marriage as long as possible. When I got there I saw that most of my classmates had boyfriends, but a few . . . had girlfriends." She looked down at her feet. "The first time I saw two girls kissing—in the dormitory—I was horrified. Disgusted. I couldn't imagine two women doing that to each other!

"But then, in my junior year, I met Trudy. She was an athlete, she played tennis, she ran the mile in seven minutes . . . she was beauty in motion. We became friends. I told myself I wanted to *be* her. I told myself it was just a platonic crush. Until the day . . ." Her voice broke. "Until the day Trudy leaned in to kiss me . . . and I finally felt that spark I'd been waiting for."

The front door banged open and Pearl Malama rushed in, panic in her eyes.

Rose looked up at her and said, "It's okay."

Pearl let out a breath. "Detective, I'm sorry my brother tried to grab you. I asked him to try and scare you off, that's all. Don't blame Rose, she knew nothing about it."

Apana nodded. "No worry. He got worse end of it."

Pearl came closer. Rose stood and took Pearl's hand; Pearl's fingers closed tightly around hers.

"Being with Trudy was bliss, but it was terrifying. I'd never thought of myself as—that way. I couldn't live with it. I dropped out of college and took the train back to Boston, crying all the way. Missing her but hating myself for it.

"But word had spread at Wellesley about me and Trudy, and it got back to my parents. My father said what I had done was an abomination, a sin against God. But he said I could redeem myself with the love of a good man . . . and made it very clear that I *was* marrying a man. A man of breeding, from a good family, whom they would find for me."

She let out a long sigh. "So I told my parents they were right, of course I would get married . . . but first I needed to go away and clear my head of all that sinful college rot. Two weeks in Honolulu, and when I came home, I would marry whomever they chose.

"On the long voyage to Hawaii I had time to work out my plan, and after I'd given everyone the slip in Honolulu, I got on the train, wanting only to be so far away no one would ever find me. I got off at the last passenger stop, Waialua, and stayed a few nights at a little Japanese hotel. I'd brought money from home and I planned to hide out and lay low for a few months until everyone had forgotten me, then take a boat to the most remote place I could find and maroon myself there in my shame—and to never do again what I did with Trudy."

"What make you stay?" Apana asked.

"Pearl." Tears welled in Rose's eyes. "Pearl saved me."

"The first time she came into the store I thought she was the most beautiful woman I had ever seen," Pearl began. "We became friends, but I felt the wall she'd put up between herself and anything deeper. I didn't know what caused it until finally, after a year, she told me about what she'd done with Trudy. So I told her about the place of the *māhū* in old Hawaiian culture. How what haoles called homosexuals were a commonplace, accepted part of our society. One of my aunties was *māhū*. I'm *māhū*, and it's nothing to be ashamed of."

Apana had heard this from his own *hānai* auntie, Kahauelio. "Yes. This is true."

Pearl again took Rose's hand tenderly in hers. Rose turned toward her and said softly, "Eventually I came to accept what she was saying . . . and to accept her love." She turned back to Apana. "Please, Detective, I beg you, don't tell anyone you found me—please! I'm happy here. Hawaii freed me . . . let me become who I always was. Do you understand?"

Apana took this in. "Hawaii let me become policeman. Hawaii like nowhere else in the world." Then he stood up and said, "Case closed."

Relieved beyond words, Rose embraced him. Pearl did the same. Embarrassed, Apana put on his hat and headed for the door.

Rose finally found her words: "Detective—thank you. You're everything the newspapers say you are. And more."

He was pleased to hear that—very pleased. "*Mahalo*," he said. "*Kahuna nui hale kealohalani makua.*"

Pearl nodded in understanding.

After Apana left, Rose asked Pearl, "What did he say?"

"An old Hawaiian proverb: *Love all you see, including yourself.*"

232 // HONOLULU NOIR

* * *

Apana returned to the car and to Walter, who'd bought a roast beef sandwich at the grocer's and was eating it as he leaned up against the car. "You done? What'd you find?"

"Nothing. Dead end."

Walter gave Apana half of his sandwich and asked no further questions. For the rest of the long drive back to Honolulu, they talked about family.

That night, Apana returned home in unusually good spirits. Annie was startled at the change in him from a few nights ago. He played enthusiastically with the *keiki*, made *huli huli* chicken for dinner and fresh baked cookies for dessert, and seemed happier than he had in a long while. And despite his wife's questions about where he had been or what had happened over these past days, he never said a word.

PART IV

Modern Mana

MOTHER'S MOTHER'S MOTHER

BY MORGAN MIRYUNG MCKINNEY

Manoa

Her great-grandmother is planting a Venus flytrap in the living room. She starts by cutting green tissue paper into circles and bunching them up. The head comes out as big as her fists, full of years-old closet dust and sticky holiday glitter. The stems are made of tape-wrapped wire, shaped by a hearty pair of pliers. By the time she's sticking the whole thing into a pot of dirt—a *real* pot of dirt—half the living room looks beaten down by ripped-up arts and crafts. Grandma's less than pleased.

"Who does she think's gonna clean all this up? That lady has no respect. Crazy. *Crazy*. Go talk to her. And get the pliers for me."

Grandma's a tiny skeleton holding up her husband's over-sized shirt. It's this green rag they got for free at one fund-raiser or another, twenty years ago. The husband's sleeping in their bedroom, always sleeping, like he's trying on a prema-ture deathbed. The edge of loose boxers peek out from under Grandma's shirt, untucked like a child's. She frowns behind thick, square glasses, looking at Aiko.

Aiko, ten pounds lighter than she should be and tucked into a pair of blue overalls, grabs her slippers off the rack, sitting neat outside Grandma's room. "Yeah," she says, "I'm going."

Great-grandma's room, the living room, is simple. Looking in from the hallway, Aiko notices new blankets rumpled over the bed, pushed flush against the far left corner. In front of it, her great-grandmother is sitting up in a soft reclining chair. The thing's so old, it's a whole other color than when it was bought. Great-grandma's facing the television, a burly, black box stacked on vintage wood cabinets, staring back across the way. She places her new craft project on a plastic table at her side. Dirt plumes up from the impact. A mint-green corner couch runs along the right side of the room. It's so glossy, Aiko's not convinced it was made with any fabrics, just plastic. Next to the couch, stitched into the right-hand wall, is a door leading to the driveway. Great glass windows, reinforced with torn screens, break through most of the wall behind Great-grandma and her eyesore couch. Sunlight crashes through them and blooms across the room. Aiko likes to sit under it sometimes, to feel the heat breathe on her face. She steps inside, passing Great-grandpa's shrine by the hallway entrance. The carpet hasn't been cleaned since the sixties, and the walls are beige with exposed wood.

There are loud clumps of tissue flowers all over the room—taped to the corners of the ceiling, spilling out of cabinets, lining her great-grandfather's shrine. It's a proud display of artwork for a museum of a home. Some of the flowers are white and yellow at the edges, years wilting their paper petals till they look like the real deal. Most of them are a stiff, blushing pink. Great-grandma's always taken to roses and carnations. Singing bees from the garden look for a way in, hunger driving them up against the window screens. Aiko frowns at the buzzing—sharp, like sizzling-hot rain over pavement. She blinks hard, shakes out her hands, tries to get the sound out of her head. She finds herself back in the hallway. She finds her back pressed against a wall.

Aiko walks back into the glaring sunlight and turns to make small talk with the woman who can barely understand her. Her great-grandmother, *Grandma from the Old House*, as Aiko used to say, has one hearing aid in and a half grasp on the English language. She's stuffed into a thinning *mu'u-mu'u*, bought cheap at a flea market. It has deep-purple flowers printed all over it, no lace or elastic or frills. Her glasses are wiry and fragile. A wisp of gray hair spins atop her wrinkled head. Her skin and spine are slowly melting with gravity. Great-grandma's asking Aiko, some scrawny kid who barely knows her, if she can hire a lawyer. Aiko turned fifteen last week.

"Elder abuse, Aiko. Terrible, all terrible, these doctors. They make me sick. I sue." She leans back in her reclining chair. Sometimes, when the light hits it just right, Aiko can see spots of white slitted in the seams around its browning cushions.

Grandma cuts in with a broom, spitting a glob of hot malice into an overfilled trash can at Great-grandma's feet. There's a six-week-old grocery bag lining its edges, and one of the handles is ripped. "We called the lawyers, Mom. You're not sick, you're ninety-four." Grandma shuffles past them to collapse into the mint couch. She sets the broom up against its side. "Cut it out already."

"You talk to me like that? Awful, how she treats me, eh?" Great-grandma looks to Aiko for her reaction. Aiko feels a static rise to the top of her neck and glances past Great-grandma. The bees are back to screaming in the windows.

"Cut it out!" Grandma repeats. She swats her hand through the air and beats against the screens with her broom. Aiko can't tell if she's talking to Great-grandma or the bumbles outside. Then Grandma's swatting hands become something kinder. She's waving Aiko over. Everything quiets down. Some of the bees fly off.

"Hey, get over here. Where's your mom, love?"

She's out smoking a cigarette. This is a lot. "I don't know."

Grandma shakes her head, all wobbly. "I'll go get her." She sweeps down the hallway and out of the house with the broom. The door slams with the wind behind her.

"Hmm." Great-grandma has her hand deep in the flytrap's soil. She rubs her fingers against the dirt. It smears against her skin, muddy red. *Why real dirt?* Aiko doesn't bother asking, just wanders toward the couch to sit.

The plant's head looks more solid than before, real and smooth where it had been that soft, crumpled tissue. One second, Aiko's wondering when she had time to papier-mâché and paint the damn thing. Then a bee tears through a hole in one of the screens, and Aiko's ducking for cover by the couch—tucked next to the outside door—and Great-grandma is shaking her head, all disappointed. The Venus flytrap takes the little thing in its mouth. It lifts its neck slowly, turning sideways to open up like a pair of wings, as big as two splayed palms reaching for the sky. The red in it is fleshy like a tongue.

Someone screams from the door, and Aiko looks right up at it. Her mom stands in the middle of the frame, backlit from the afternoon sun. She looks fuzzy and shadowed, a little unreal against the light. Aiko pushes her glasses up her nose. Mom's makeup is all done up, though she's not going anywhere. She inherited it from her mom, Grandma, who only stopped with the eyebrow pencils and heavy lipsticks after she turned sixty. Mom's hair is caged in a claw clip, loose enough to let a few strands slip out and frizz up from the heat. There's an ash stain on her shirt. It resembles a patch of mold, crawling over the electric-pink fabric. Her glasses are more rounded, like Aiko's, though Aiko's make perfect circles around her eyes. She smells soured with wine and mostly-vodka screwdrivers. Mom pushes Grandma into the room. Grandma doesn't turn back to scold her, just marches forward and grabs the pot with both hands. The Venus flytrap sways back and forth with the rhythm of a rattlesnake.

"What the *shit* is this? Mom?" Grandma says. The flytrap nips at her. Grandma has to lean her head back to avoid it.

"I don't know," Great-grandma says.

Mom follows Grandma in and stares at the pot. She reaches for the pliers on Great-grandma's table. The flytrap leans down before she can get to them. Its mouth wraps all the way around Mom's wrist, burning. She shakes her hand out until it lets go. There's a discolored mark on the spot where her skin's the thinnest. Everything smells sweet and sick, like nectar. "Fuck!" Mom screams. "Oh my god. Oh my god, I need to get out of here. The hell you even make this out of, woman?"

"Tissue. Tape," Great-grandma shrugs. "I don't know." A couple bees hover in through the hole in the screen. Grandma walks over to the windows, absentmindedly putting the fly-trap down by Great-grandpa's shrine.

"You don't know? Look at that thing. It just bit your granddaughter! Try harder." Grandma waves the bees away, hoping they'll fly back out the window, but they scatter around the room instead.

Aiko, still crouched down by the couch, wraps her head up in her arms. Bees rank among her least favorite creatures. A handful of months ago, one out in Great-grandma's garden got tangled up in her hair. Aiko's kept it shoulder-length and braided into neat pigtails since. She's fighting its natural volume, wilder and less Japanese than any woman before her. With the intruding bees bouncing between the walls, Aiko gets it all tucked under her elbows. Grandma reaches up to close the windows properly. Glass slams down over mesh. *How will the bees get out?* Aiko thinks.

"Hey, no, what are you doing? Keep the damn windows open!" Mom's voice rings high with hysteria. She's still holding her blotchy wrist. When Aiko looks up at her, she breathes in deep a couple times and shakes out her hands. "Sorry, sorry. I know," she points to herself, "*crazy.* It's just hot in here."

And how else will the bees get out? Aiko echoes in her mind. She hates to agree with her mom, but they all hate to agree with their mothers. Maybe that's its own form of compliance.

Grandma does not open the windows back up. "Mom," she says, "we can't keep this here. How do we get rid of it?"

The Venus flytrap looks around at the tissue flowers by its pot, tucked neatly at the base of Great-grandpa's picture. A slimy acid drips like snot from its mouth. Spittle gets on some of the crumpled petals and dissolves holes in them. The paper peels away from each hole in raised split curls. Stitching themselves into the gaps are raw, sap-covered plant veins. They crawl out and across, spreading like pools over the petals, the flowers, the fake stems and wire leaves. Aiko is left staring at a mass of real flowers, tangled over her great-grandfather. It smells strongly of sugar and rot, the blackened edges of split fruit.

"I get tired, finding answers for you," Great-grandma says.

Grandma shakes her head and looks right at her mother. "You're not even gonna try?"

Aiko's watching the flytrap's head buck around, sending a spray of its droplets across the walls and ceiling. Most of her great-grandma's plants are hit. Plant mass roots into them. The flytrap's mouth is fully open again, wet and huge and whipping in all these directions. Aiko thinks briefly of going up to the plant and wrestling it closed or, more realistically, getting up from the couch and running straight out the door. Something keeps her rooted, some heavy weight on her chest, worms wiggling under her skin.

"Shit, Mom, what do we do?" Aiko's mother asks.

Grandma buries her face in her hands, square glasses leaning over her fingers. "I don't know. No one in this house knows anything!"

Coward, coward, coward, Aiko hears. She looks around the room at all the fake flowers, organic material tearing itself out of holes in the tissue paper. *Coward.* Her head swivels to the flytrap. It's hissing at her mom, her grandma, and great-grandma, then back at her. She wonders why no one's killing it.

"Okay, fine! That's fine," Mom says. She walks away from Grandma and looks at Aiko on the ground. Something still comes over her. The women are always nicer to Aiko than they are to each other. "Aiko, get up. We need to leave."

"Mm. Yeah," Aiko responds. She's still looking at that damn flytrap. It's starting to reach out, coiling its vines into the other plants.

"I'll be in the car." *Coward, coward.* "Grab your stuff and we'll jet."

A fleck of acid drips on Mom's cheek. She swipes at it and turns without looking for where it came from. They all know, anyway.

"Okay."

Mom swings the door to the driveway open. Aiko resolves to follow. As she's preparing herself to leave, some of the vines tangle up in Great-grandpa's shrine. Then the flytrap pulls them back, dragging him toward its mouth. Aiko stands to grab the photo, but her joints feel like they've been oiled with molasses. The Venus flytrap gets it down the gullet, dissolving Great-grandpa and his flowers in one bite. *Stop it*, she thinks. *Stop doing this to us*. She keeps moving, slow on her knobby knees.

Soon as Aiko's right up in its face, the flytrap starts losing its shape and wobbles like thick Jell-O. It bounces back and forth before expanding in this undefined, watery way. The flytrap grows till it's the size of Aiko's head. The stem is longer than her spine at this point, wreathed in leaves as big as the kind you pull off iceberg lettuce. The plants on the ceiling and ones wedged against the walls—filling all the cabinets and spilling on the floor—are done transforming. They settle, real and sticky with flytrap juice. Their colors go from dusty to bright and fresh. The whole living room looks like some kind of jungle.

When one of the Venus flytrap's vines, denser and longer than rope, presses up against a closed window, Aiko shouts for her grandmother. Two women turn toward her. She doesn't look at them, still frozen before the flytrap. She wants to put her hands in the thing and tear it up from the inside. "Grandma!" she yells instead. "Grandma, the window!"

"Ah, bugger!" Grandma says. She swipes something off Great-grandma's table before running over to the back wall. Grandma bashes the vine with Great-grandma's pliers. Parts of it are flung against a window, dripping translucent green in thick rivulets. "Ai'," she says, "bring the plant over here."

"No! Let me kill it," Aiko says. "Let me try. Why hasn't anyone tried?" She's slowly unsticking. She feels like she can do it. Her hands twist into the hem of her shirt. She imagines twisting them inside the flytrap's throat.

Great-grandma looks up at the ceiling. "*Nandayo!* Get it off, get that shit off!"

The bees are at the window.

"Just bring it here!" Grandma says. She doesn't turn to look at Great-grandma at all.

"But—!"

"Aiko!"

The bees are there, looking at her, silent. She can't even hear a faint buzz, like she normally would through the glass. *Why are they so quiet?* Aiko wonders if they've seen her mother, sitting in the car right outside the door. Her hands fall to her sides. She picks up the Venus flytrap. It doesn't move to strike her, but she carries it like a hot pan.

"Yeah, okay," Aiko whispers. "Okay. I'm sorry."

Grandma shakes her head. "Here, just bring it here." Great-grandma is still yelling up at the ceiling.

Grandma grabs the pot in one hand. The flytrap seems cowed by her anger. Grandma tosses the whole thing into Great-grandma's lap.

"Solve your own problems, Mom," Grandma says.

"What are you doing? Bad, bad child!" Great-grandma tries to push the pot off her lap. She gets more dirt on her hands, searches the room for Aiko's eyes. "Help me!"

Aiko looks at the mass of bees, perched still against her great-grandmother's window. *Grandma from the Old House,* maybe the "old country," something no one's cared to understand since her husband died. Maybe since Grandma started to be more fluent in English than Japanese, back in high school. She meets the old woman's eyes. Aiko takes a significant step forward.

Grandma grabs Aiko's shoulders from behind. She steers them toward the outside door. Aiko hears the slap of a mouth

244 // H<small>ONOLULU</small> N<small>OIR</small>

sucking on skin, then the sound of acid breaking down flesh. Great-grandma screams so hard, Aiko can hear the old woman's throat ripping itself apart. She turns on instinct and gets a glimpse of her face, the left half already swallowed by the heart-shaped face of the flytrap.

"Grandma, wait!" Aiko shouts. Great-grandma is babbling, unable to form words.

"*Hayaku, hayaku*," her grandmother whispers. "Get out of here, love."

Aiko tries to pull away. Grandma's grip is unyielding, clamping down on her with more strength than Aiko thought possible. All she can do is look back. They make it out the door as Great-grandma's babbles start turning to gurgles. A mess of wiry *higanbana*, glistening with a bit of mucus, blooms across Great-grandma's chest. Her head is gone, engulfed in smooth green. The Venus flytrap moves to swallow her whole. Its vines grow thicker and bust through the glass windows. The door shuts behind them.

The vines pour into Great-grandma's garden—this young, green, intestinal mass tangling all up in the abandoned weeds. It's where the bees live, still drifting near the windows and floating in through some of the cracks. Mom honks her horn, and Aiko wordlessly climbs in. The engine starts. They all pretend not to hear the wet, burbling sounds from behind the door.

Grandma stands in the garage. The sun sets blue on the Old House. Mom and daughter drive away from four generations of childhood. From getting stuck to a *before* like sap.

And the bees start whistling their colony song, long into the night.

SHADOWS AND HAOLES

BY **B.A. KOBAYASHI**

Tantalus

T he air was pregnant with the stench of hot garbage and desperation as the muted din of the club's
bass-boosted speakers thrummed along under the
pale-yellow streetlights of Chinatown. Keoni gazed blankly
down the street. The throng of clubgoers slowly lurched toward Scarlet's flashing, neon maw. The night was humid, and
paired with the shuffling mass of hot bodies surrounding him,
it made the air all but unbearable. When he looked out into
the night wishing for the cool comforts of his room, a *bzzt,
bzzt* snapped him back into sweltering reality. The buzzing
from his front pocket drew his gaze down toward his phone,
and his muscle memory unlocked the sleek black brick with
four quick taps.

Right behind you, the message read, and before Keoni had
a chance to react, a pair of slender mocha hands grabbed his
shoulders with a shrill, "You're here!" It was Keʻala, Keoni's
little sister and all-time favorite family member.

"Like I would miss your twenty-first. Someone's gotta
show you how it's done," he replied with a great big bear hug,
nearly toppling the velvet stanchions keeping the queue in
check.

"Okay, that's enough, you faka," she groaned as she wrig-
gled out of his hairy embrace. "Besides, this is just a formality.
I've been going here longer than you, so just watch and learn."

Behind her stood several young girls of the same age whom Keoni recognized from Keʻala's many ragers as her high school friends. Keoni helped them under the velvet rope to the stink eye of the group of haoles behind them, and they neared the front of the line. One in particular was looking Keʻala up and down like some piece of meat. Keoni stared for a second, waiting for the boy to notice. He was wearing a wrinkled and stained Gucci shirt, tucked into a pair of the beigest khaki shorts out there. Puffing out his chest, Keoni took a step toward him. The punk's pupils shrunk, and he jumped to the other side of the street. Keoni let out a snort then hawked some saliva in the guy's general direction as they paid the ridiculous ten-dollar cover. Keʻala jumped up to put her arm around Keoni's shoulder and said, "Listen, brah, I NEED to go home with one *ehu* girl tonight. I'm so fed up with these musty-ass braddahs. If you see me going to the dark side, ya gotta pull me back, Obi-Wan." With a nod, they entered the den of disco lights and booming noise.

If the line outside was hot, the inside of Scarlet's was a sauna, if a sauna could give you an epileptic seizure and tinnitus simultaneously. On one side was the bar, Keʻala convinced a drunk frat dude into buying cocktails for the whole group, and on the other side stood the stage where the queens performed. It was like a scene straight out of *Magic Mike,* if instead of fluffed they were tucked and wearing the most outrageous pairs of fake tits ever seen. Between the two was the dance floor, and it was pandemonium. The club was packed. People were dancing from wall to wall, bumping, grinding, and everything in between. There was hardly enough space to breathe let alone talk, and Keoni couldn't help but join in the infectious energy. Dancing was never his forte, but that wasn't going to stop him from getting down. They tore it up.

Ke'ala had the rhythm and the rhyme, grinding on girls left and right with such grace it looked like it was choreographed, but Keoni had the passion. He pulled out dance moves that weren't even invented yet (maybe for good reason), just letting the motion of the ocean take him away. He was drenched in sweat, but he could care less. The flashing lights, the bumping music, the crowd, and whatever was in that last drink were sending him to the zone. Yet, just as he was about to set sail for the blackout isles, he remembered something important. He'd not seen his sister in nearly half an hour, and panic struck him like a bolt out of the ether. Where was she?

Beads of cold sweat began to form on his glistening brow as he took to poking his head above the crowd looking for her bleached scalp. Anxiety started to set in, and he looked around, trying to call out under the boom of the speakers. He would have left the place for the morning if he'd not caught a glimpse of her being taken out the back door with some strange haole. That's all the excuse he needed, as her earlier request echoed in his ears. Now barreling through the crowd, using his shoulder like the hull of a polar ship breaking a path through the ice of lights and noise, Keoni followed them out to the back of the club thinking to himself of all the things he'd do to this cracker if he tried anything fresh with his baby sister.

It wasn't until he'd followed the two down an alleyway that the alarms really started blaring in his head. He saw another man emerge from behind a dumpster, and the two were now cornering his sister beside said dumpster. One of which Keoni recalled from the line outside Scarlet's earlier, when Ke'ala wasn't having any of it. Quickly, Keoni pulled out his trusty plastic lighter and gripped it tightly in the balled-up fist of his right hand while grabbing a bottle off the street with his left. He silently approached the two haoles. As one of them held his sister against the wall, the other pulled out something from his pocket. What it was Keoni couldn't say, could have been a knife or gun or any number of things. He had no way of knowing within the blackness consuming the alley. Sneaking around always came naturally to Keoni, which surprised many given his size and stature. Even way back when he was a kid, no one could best him in hide-and-seek. To Keoni, the idea of silence felt like a joke, a part of one at least, the build-up of tension, growing like a Waikiki wave, full of sunscreen and children's piss, swallowing up everything in its wake until it soaked the wedding dress of a Japanese tourist.

As he stood over the two dirtbags, he waited until Ke'ala's eyes met his before popping the silence with the sharpest whistle he could manage. They turned with a start. Keoni smashed the first guy with the bottle. It exploded into an iridescent hail of crystalline shards as the bastard doubled back in pain. Ke'ala, using the opportunity, slipped through his weakened grip and began tasing him on the alley floor. The second attacker then rushed Keoni with his weapon raised. Closer now in the darkness, the object revealed itself to be a syringe. Keoni's every hair stood on end as he scrambled to block or break the syringe before whatever was inside of it wound up getting inside of him. As he raised his fist to meet the opposition, the night's heavy drinking took its toll and Keoni's punch veered left. His fist glanced off his attacker's forearm before the syringe sunk deep into Keoni's left shoulder.

Yet, before the bastard could inject Keoni with whatever malevolent matter lay inside the syringe, Keoni's lighter-filled fist connected. Hitting that beautiful, sweet spot on the haole's jaw sent him spinning into the dumpster with a toe-curling crack and crash. By now, the first one had disarmed Ke'ala and flew at him like a wild dog, gnashing its teeth as saliva and foam frothed from its lips. Keoni tried to punch at the beast, but he was getting slower, and before he could cock his left, the man was on him, biting at his jugular. Keoni shoved his forearm into the white devil's maw before it was too late. The rabid thing began sinking its teeth into his exposed arm. Keoni yelled out in pain as he felt the crimson flow.

Without missing a beat, Ke'ala jumped on the savage's back with a rear naked choke. Locking her legs around the bastard's abdomen with practiced precision, she pulled him off Keoni. As their struggle evolved, the beast flew backward into the hard concrete with a low thud. Despite this, Ke'ala held firm, reinforcing her grip on his neck. Before Keoni could come in with the assist, however, the other stark pursuer flew at him fists first. This time he didn't even see it coming. The fucker hit him clean, and with a crack, Keoni crumpled like a sorry sack of shit. What strength he could muster was nothing compared to the ringing in his ears and the cocktail of drugs in his system. Bleary-eyed, he could only watch the two bastards overpower Ke'ala and drag her off kicking and screaming toward the sound of a running engine. Keoni closed his eyes, bitter and angry, thinking of the many horrible fates that Ke'ala would be forced to endure because of his weakness. How he'd probably never see his sister alive, ever again.

These terrible thoughts lit a spark in Keoni, stoking his will on that self-same desperation: love. Pure hatred filled his entirety, and he once more found the strength to stand. On shaking stilts, the body of his unbridled will rose to its fullest height. With wild eyes ablaze like suns of red fury urging him forth with every uncertain step, his vision faded out and in, vaguely glimpsing the silhouettes of his target turning down a lit corner. Leaning against the filthy stone, he dragged himself toward the yellow tint bleeding from the alley. Turning the corner, he prepared for the fight of his life, only to stare into the blinding headlights of a white van. The shadows of the two assailants closed its screaming trunk with a thud.

The vehicle jumped forward with a sputtering start. Barreling down the narrow alleyway, the metal monster intended to flatten Keoni like a roach before a slipper. Still holding onto the wall for support and barely commanding the strength to stand, Keoni made a desperate gamble. His body was heavier than lead; nonetheless, he flattened himself against the cold stone with all the strength he could muster, hoping beyond hope that the slightest gap between the van and the alleyway would be enough to squeak by with his life. Yet, as the saying goes, horseshoes and hand grenades don't make cigars. The sideview mirror smashed into Keoni's side at thirty miles an hour, and he was sent tumbling toward the piss-christened concrete once again. As he laid there motionless, his consciousness was swallowed up by the warm blackness that crept in from behind his eyes.

Into the dark depths of night, Keoni was consumed. Lucidity was a distant memory, treading water in an ocean of quicksand. Keoni sank in the creeping black, like spilled coffee over asphalt, and he saw his life stretched onto infinity. Drowning within that oily deep, he was powerless before its great current. All he could make out were the strangest of whispers brushing by in the darkness. *Ho'okipa keiki*, a deep voice hushed as a warm body brushed past. *Ua kali mākou.*

Another shrill whisper slinked by. Only now did he realize he wasn't exactly dreaming. This was something entirely other, like the difference between the heat of day and a hot bath. Yet, before he could reflect on his situation, the black tide began to churn. The currents picked up, surging him down toward what felt to be the heart of darkness. He could scarcely imagine what the tide would spell as it spit him out. Before him stood a great circle of bodies, countless shadows with glowing eyes staring back at him. All around, he could hear men chanting in hushed tones and the booming rhythm of war drums. Keoni tried to glance around, but he could scarcely make out a thing from the great mass of blackened bodies surrounding him. The drums grew louder, and the chanting rose to fever pitch before all were silenced by the bone-chilling wail of a great conch. Then a figure emerged from the shadowy mass surrounding Keoni.

The great shadow stood a full head above the rest, its leadership made evident by the stark silhouette of its *maka-ki'i*. Even though shrouded by its raven-black *'ahu 'ula*, the vastness of its muscularity showed through its broad shoulders. The obsidian mountain stood before him, and Keoni could feel the entity's piercing gaze sizing him up. Simply being in that creature's presence was enough to make all his hair stand at attention. Realizing now that what stood before him was the dreaded *huaka'i pō*, his grandmother's stories rushed through his head. She used to tell him stories of the night marchers, terrible warriors slain in battle. Forced to march endlessly through the blackest corners of Hawaii, attacking wanderers in the dark and stealing away misbehaving children. Keoni believed these tales to be nothing more than some local brand of boogeyman. However, confronted now with the terrifyingly genuine article, Kenoi couldn't help but scream. But no sound was born from his unbridled horror, as if his trembling throat was caught in a vice of icy terror. He could only look on in utter dread when the spectral marauder kneeled to Keoni's level, grabbing his head in its hands, greeting him in the Hawaiian tradition of exchanging breath, *honi ihu*, black mist flowed from the spirit's maw.

Keoni hesitated for a moment, still stunned with fear, before shakily inhaling the spectral breath, trading it with his own. It tasted of blackened bile and a yearning as deep as the sea. It was enough to make him gag. Yet as the spirit's eyes locked with his, he could do little else but stare back, in a moment that lasted an era. Then the entity spoke in a voice like the midnight breeze. In ancient words, it welcomed Keoni. He didn't know what the old words meant but made grasps at their meaning as the midnight *ali'i* continued. It expressed sorrow for the fate of Keoni and his sister, but when he asked what this meant, what any of this was, the entity simply ignored him before going on. It spoke of a scourge plaguing the people of this land, of the haole, the breathless, who snatch the air from the breast. They had cast a shadow over the sun's chosen people, and if allowed to fester further, a once-great people would be nothing but memory. Finally, it offered him a choice. If Keoni refused to bow his head at its sight, he would be torn limb from limb. Keoni cowered in terror, but the *ali'i* explained in words of stone that if he wished to greet the sunrise, if he truly wished to see Ke'ala alive once more, he would be their vessel. He would be their *kaimiloa* and bare their army to the fields of battle. So that they might banish the pale scourge from these shores forevermore.

Upon this proposal, Keoni had only questions. Why would they help him, and for what purpose did he serve to ones such as them? In response, the surrounding shadows burst out in uproar before being silenced once more by the *ali'i*. The great shadow turned back to Keoni and spoke of the stars that had once guided their people but had now fallen to earth. They banished the black of night and relegated their march to only the darkest reaches of this land. How their powers, once great, shrank with every shining night. Soon they too would be relegated to the realm of myth like the *menehune* and the *moʻo*. Yet, before Keoni could ask any more of them, a faint light began to creep in from the distance. At which point, the shadow clasped Keoni by the shoulders and demanded an answer. In that instant, without hesitation, Keoni responded not in words but a bloody cry for vengeance, and the marchers answered in kind. With countless midnight hands, they pried open his trembling mouth, deaf to his muffled pleas for mercy. They crawled inside him one by one, breaking his jaw like a wishbone as they crammed their multitudes inside his gullet. Hands, feet, torsos, and heads all pushing their way down his throat, he could feel every last one as they violated him. So great was the agony that after the fourth or fifth entity, he couldn't withstand the pain, and succumbed once more to the deep abyss of sleep.

When he finally came to, surrounded by rotting trash and filth, Keoni couldn't care less. He was suffering through the mother of all hangovers. Occasionally, he'd try to pull himself from the stinking mire only to cough up black bile. Then he'd collapse under his pounding headache, and sleep for another hour before beginning the process all over again. Keoni hated being dirty. Hell, he didn't even like to sweat. After a couple of hours of lying there among the spoiled garbage, however, he began to find comfort in it. Yet, just when he was starting to embrace the comforts of his new home, it was disturbed. Starting with a jolt to the inconsiderate jabbing at his side, Keoni blinked himself into consciousness, and two heavy-set men in uniforms stood above him. One haole, the other brown, both jabbering at him in some alien language. As he gained more awareness of his situation and the existence of his ears, Keoni soon discovered that the incomprehensible tongue of the two men was in fact the English language.

Keoni picked up the latter half of some obscure interrogation before hopping right into the thick of it. Rubbing his eyes, he endured the ramblings of the pigs. They lectured to him about some nonsense vagrancy or whatever, and he pleaded to them about his missing sister. Yet, his words fell upon ignorant ears when he shared his story. He could visibly see the uninterested daze of the second while the first scribbled along in his notepad before taking his name and number, telling Keoni he had to pay a fine. They'd be in touch as they investigated it, they said. When they left, Keoni had the distinct feeling they wouldn't.

The two pigs dispersed into their patrol car toward the nearest McDonald's. Downtrodden, Keoni sat there on the sidewalk, ticket in one hand, dead phone in the other, with no clue where to start looking. He contemplated the pitiful state of the nation. "This really is the twilight of an empire," he said aloud. He continued to sit there, motionlessly racking his brain for his next move, brows furrowed. Until out of nowhere a soot-covered hand found itself perched on his shoulder, turning him around with a start. A waxing moon of a smile greeted him with a loud and breathy, "AALOOO-HAAA!" to which Keoni simply grunted.

"Ho, what's wrong, Hawaiian?" the guy asked. "The man got you down? This your first time out on the street?"

"No," Keoni replied. Every word from this guy felt like nails on a chalkboard to his addled mind. After a few more futile attempts at small talk by the man known as Dan, the two just sat.

They wallowed there in silence for a good long while before Dan finally spoke. "Say, I know what will fix you up, Hawaiian: a little bit of herbal remedy." He pulled a pencil-thin joint from his pocket. "Some *pakalolo* to soothe whatever it is you got going on in there?"

"Thank you," Keoni grumbled as he brought the joint to his lips, and Dan lit it for him. Keoni breathed deeply, letting the smoke fill his lungs before blowing out a thick cloud with a sigh of relief. He took another hit before passing it back to Dan. "Why are you helping me?"

"We all have our reasons. Let's call it community service. I'm just your average public servant." Dan chuckled. "What's your deal anyway? Do you usually sleep in a pool of your own vomit or is this something you're just trying on for size?"

"Do you really want to know?" Keoni asked. "You wouldn't even believe me if I told you."

"Try me," Dan challenged as he passed the joint back to Keoni. They sat there for a good while, and Dan listened quietly to Keoni's story. He didn't react, he didn't question, he just smiled and listened. Once Keoni was through with his yarn, Dan patted him on the back and said, "Damn, that is a *lot* for one night, braddah."

"You actually believe me?"

"Does it matter? You need help." Dan took a deep breath. "See, way out, past Wai'anae, there is an encampment a little past the last bus stop on Farrington Highway. Don't judge. Just ask for one Mr. Aloha. He's one of the last *kūpuna* who still lives and breathes the old ways. Tell him Ol' Danny Boy sent ya . . . Now, if you'll excuse me."

"Wait, then—" Before Keoni even realized it, the stranger was gone. He wondered if the man was real or if he'd imagined the whole thing. Regardless, Keoni scooped himself off the curb and got on the first bus to Wai'anae. It was a long ride to the west side of the island. Only those who lived or had family there went to the west side. There were people who lived on Oahu all their lives who never drove past Kapolei.

When Keoni finally got off at the last stop, the place Dan spoke about didn't look like much of an encampment at all—a few tarps and tents gathered behind some sparse brush. Just a tiny splash of blue on a beige landscape. Getting a little closer revealed a couple more structures that were obscured by the foliage. Keoni could make out the sounds of children playing and the faintest tune of a ukelele. Yet, upon entering the encampment, he truly got a grasp of how large it was. This was basically a full-on town. There were at least half a dozen families there with children of all ages. Some of the younger ones were playing ball near what appeared to be a makeshift town square. A man sat on a decrepit rocking chair strumming the ukelele while singing in Hawaiian. As Keoni approached the large tree at the center of the camp, he came to realize the children weren't playing anymore.

Within moments, a whole crowd had formed around him, and at its head stood a stout man in a very large aloha shirt. "Sorry, friend, is you lost? Do you need a place to stay? We don't have much room, but I'm sure we can find you something."

"No, I'm looking for Mr. Aloha."

"If you're a reporter, I'm sorry, but I'm gonna ask you to leave. This isn't your next story. These are people's lives." The man's eyes had become slits.

"No, I think we're getting off on the wrong foot," Keoni said sheepishly. "Danny sent me."

"Oh, Danny." The man's eyes went wide, like twin saucers. "Never mind, everyone, false alarm. He's one of Danny's.

Please, come this way. I am Michael Kekoa, but everyone calls me Mr. Aloha," he said with a laugh. "Now come here." With a great big *honi ihu*, Mr. Aloha brought Keoni close and his eyes went wide again. He muttered something beneath his breath before taking Keoni to a tent away from the others. "Please sit. Can I get you anything to eat or drink?"

"Oddly enough, I'm not that hungry."

"Understandable, given your situation. I can see why. I can smell it on your breath." Mr. Aloha pointed to his heart. "You are stained. It's not just your soul in there, is it? No, your breath smells of midnight. You've become the vessel for something terrible, son, though I'm sure you knew that already." He leaned back. "So tell me, what's your story?"

After Keoni gave him a brief rundown of the past twenty-four hours, Mr. Aloha thought for a moment.

"Okay, so how do haoles play into this?" Keoni asked, leaning forward. "Are the night marchers racist? The bastards who took Keʻala were haole, sure, but it's not like I can murder every cracker on the island."

"No, no, no, they aren't racist," Mr. Aloha said, pulling a cigar from his back pocket. "Race has less to do with this than species does. You see, Keoni, the night marchers are protectors of these islands, and the two haoles who kidnapped your sister weren't human—but they are definitely haole." He rubbed his bearded chin with one hand while scratching his ass with the other.

"What does that even mean? How can they be haole but not human?"

"Listen, I'm getting to that," Mr. Aloha said, lighting his cigar and taking a deep drag. "Haole isn't just slang for annoying tourists. It means one without breath, without a soul. The kidnappers you're looking for are vampires. See—"

"Okay, uncle, that's enough," said Keoni. "Whatever's in that cigar must be strong, but I've gotta find my sister. Crackpot stories about vampires aren't going to get me anywhere." He stood up, turning to leave. "This is what I get for listening to a damn bum."

"SIT YOUR ASS DOWN!" Mr. Aloha roared in a voice that shook the tent. "You come over here asking for MY help, expecting anyone to believe night marchers are in your gullet, and you draw your line in the sand at vampires?" His eyes were red and wild. "Do you want to see your sister alive again?!"

Keoni was paralyzed by the question. "I'm sorry," he finally managed to say.

"Mhm, anyway," Mr. Aloha said, adjusting himself, "it goes back to the overthrow of the Hawaiian monarchy. See, before haoles were littering our beaches and stealing our land, they came for our blood. So many years ago, our kingdom was overthrown at gunpoint by the American government. But not many remember that it was led by the Committee of Safety, a group of seven private business owners. Lesser known still is that these same owners were in actuality vampires, themselves belonging to the Gole house, an ancestral house of vampires who draw their lineage all the way back to Transylvania. At the time, the Goles controlled large swaths of territory across the United States. They influenced politics and business. At one point, this whole country was run by bloodsuckers. Hell, some say it still is."

"Then why bother with Hawaii, some no-name island in the Pacific?" Keoni asked.

"With Hawaii, they had a unique opportunity. By transforming these islands into a tourist destination, they veritably created an all-you-can-eat buffet with countless fresh and exotic meals flying in from across the globe. Besides, did you know that Hawaii ranks eighth in missing persons across the United States? We live on islands. Walk toward the beach then pick a direction, and you'll hit somebody. Setting that aside, however, there was a far more tantalizing reason for the bloodsuckers. With the consumption of Native Hawaiian blood, vampires become all but immune to the sun's rays. It allows them to walk out in the daytime like you and me, completely undetected. Yet, this wasn't permanent. The immunity would last only for a time. Once every year, they need to imbibe our sacred blood to ensure their continued resilience. Thus, Hawaii became the crown jewel of the vampire community, with countless wars waged over its control. Over the ages, many great houses rose and fell in the pursuit of these islands. Yet the Gole family always kept a foothold. From this seat of power, the Goles experienced a golden age through the past century, free of persecution. While at the same time, all the other major houses were dying out. As time progressed, so too did technology, and with inventions such as automatic weapons and ultraviolet light, vampire hunting became easier than ever before. Thus, the vampire community experienced a culling the likes of which hadn't been seen since the Inquisition. There are less than a handful of clans left, but the Gole family remains. With their vast resources and their long influence over Hawaiian development, keeping officials in their pockets was a trifling matter."

Mr. Aloha paused, taking another drag from his cigar. "If your sister was indeed taken, then she would be at their ancestral home tonight in preparation for the annual feast of the summer solstice. You must hurry. For once the clock strikes midnight, they will feed. Your loved one will be nothing more than a shallow husk."

"Why didn't you say so sooner?" Keoni said. "It's already six o'clock. It's gonna take me at least ninety minutes to get back to town, and I don't have a clue where to start!"

"Well, that's the easy part," Mr. Aloha said. "Go to Makiki Heights, my boy. Foreigners have been settling there since before the crown fell. Not only is it physically inaccessible, but paired with the cold clime, it makes the ideal den for the Goles." He took another drag from his cigar, then continued: "Not only this, but hardly anyone goes missing around there, and if you're a good hunter, you would know. You don't shit where you eat."

"Well, I guess I'm off for Makiki Heights then. How will I know which house is the one?"

"The spirits will guide you, along with one of my people. Godspeed, my boy."

The two shook hands, and Keoni set off toward the belly of the beast.

Getting to Makiki Heights was a trial and a half. Keoni's ride dropped him off at the bottom of the mountain. *So much for showing me the way*, he thought to himself. By the time he got to the top, the sun had nearly set. Keoni could feel the shadows churning inside him as he got closer. Careful to avoid suspicion, he only gave each residence a quick glance before moving to the next house down the road. Scouring for any sign of the white van from last night, he was beginning to doubt Mr. Aloha's lead. Time and again, each house failed to move the marchers crawling beneath his skin. Until he was left with the last mansion on the street. As the sun fell behind the horizon, he could feel the darkness within him pulling all the more.

As he approached, steeling his resolve, he knew that this

was the place. It was pretty obvious even without the night marchers spurring him forth. There were at least six cars, including a white van, parked in the driveway, with shoes of all sorts littering the front porch. The house was a decadent homage to eighteenth-century Gothic architecture, with an exterior of intricately carved stone. Each windowpane was a priceless work of stained glass depicting fruits or wine or any number of obnoxious things. Keoni couldn't really be bothered to gawk as it took the bulk of his willpower just to keep the marchers from jumping out of his throat.

As quiet as a moonless night, he crept around the house, peaking through every window, looking for Keʻala. From the looks of things, a party was in full swing. Screams and laughter could be heard from within. He could even make out a couple of familiar faces, but he wasn't too sure yet, and he didn't want to get his hopes up. As Keoni moved around toward the back of the house, he could spy the dining room, and something struck him as peculiar. Each placemat lacked utensils, plates, and even napkins. All that graced the table were twelve empty silver goblets. The implications sent chills down his spine, and he quickened his search. In the backyard, there was a pool, a hot tub, and even a shed. None of which stuck out as odd to Keoni until closer inspection. The shed looked different from the house's architecture, and a muffled whimpering could be heard within. In an instant, his heart soared in his chest, and he set upon the shed's door. To his dismay, it was locked, but thankfully, it was a master lock. Ironically, one of the easiest-to-pick locks on the market, and with a simple application of force, it popped right off.

When the door swung open, Keoni's heart took flight from his chest, and he locked eyes with the young woman he'd been searching for all this time. Among eleven other girls gagged and bound in that tiny shed sat Keʻala. Tears began streaming down Keoni's face, and he rushed toward his sister. He quickly undid her restraints, and the two embraced for the first time in what felt like a decade. Yet, before they could exchange words, shouts came from inside the house, and the sound of angry footsteps drew near. As quick as thought, they both began freeing the eleven other girls. Each sprinted out the side and down the road as soon as they were able, crying and screaming all the while.

"Get out of here!" Keoni shouted at Keʻala. "They'll be here any second!"

"I'm not abandoning you," Keʻala cried.

"You aren't, but please leave! Before it's too late!" Tears streamed down Keoni's face. "No matter what happens, I love you, Sis."

"I love you too. You better know what you're doing, asshole," she said through tears and snot before making a run for it.

For an instant, Keoni felt at peace as he watched her silhouette disappear behind the house. Until Keʻala let out an ear-piercing scream, and the sounds of a scuffle could be heard from the front.

"Well, look who decided to crash the party. Do I know you from somewhere?" said a voice from behind Keoni. Turning around, he saw eleven very pale figures standing before him. A twelfth emerged from the side of the house, dragging Keʻala by her hair toward the rest. "Do I know you from somewhere?" the first repeated, adjusting his collar. "John, does he look familiar to you?" A second shook his head, disappointed.

"Let her go!" Keoni roared. He now recognized the one talking and one of the others from the night before. "She has nothing to do with this," he cried, scraping his brain for an idea, while the spirits inside him clamored at the sight of their prey.

"Actually, she has *everything* to do with this." When the others began to surround the second one from the previous night, Keoni surmised he was the ringleader. "See, she's my meal, and since you so generously decided to turn loose the rest of our feast, it looks like you're on the menu too," he said through gnashing teeth.

"I'll do whatever you say, bastard, just let her go." Keoni kneeled and titled his head to the side, revealing his exposed artery. He could see the gleam in the monster's eye as it feasted on the sight.

"Don't do it, please! You can't, you can't!" Ke'ala shouted, struggling against her assailant. "Keoni, please!"

"Someone shut her up."

"Ke'ala, it's going to be okay; I have a plan," Keoni said. "Just close your eyes when I say, okay?" He flashed her a smile through his climbing heartbeat.

"Sure you do, bud," the pale leader said. He put his lips to Keoni's ear and whispered, "Once you're sucked dry, I'm going to take my time with her, let her struggle a little. You know, it's always more fun that way." He let a shit-eating grin spread across his face.

"Dig in, asshole," Keoni spat through gritted teeth. "I hope you choke on it."

The bastard's needlelike fangs pierced his neck with a sudden, sharp pain. Finally letting go of the midnight energies coursing through his veins, he laughed through blackened blood. "Close your eyes, Ke'ala, this isn't going to be pretty," he warned, as the bloodsucker feeding on him reeled back, clutching its neck. Obsidian bile foamed from its mouth as a black hand crawled out of its maw.

Keoni collapsed to the floor. The strength that had carried him through the day spilled out across the floor, and a tar erupted from all of his orifices. His body jerked and spasmed as arms and feet pushed against the frail vessel that carried them. Countless blackened hands grabbed at the edges of Keoni's mouth. They pulled it apart, pulverizing his bones like sand, and pushed their way through. First one, then many, rose, and shadows beyond count emerged from Keoni's puddle of flesh.

Meanwhile, two great arms of midnight pried open the first haole's broken maw. The ali'i's crest rose from the pit of the bastard's pitch-black soul. Before any of the infernal creatures could react, a shadowy spear cut through the air, annihilating the skull of the one holding Ke'ala. Quicker than thought, she at once stripped naked and kneeled, pressing her face against the dirt. As the violence ensued, she cried hot tears for what remained of her brother. It was a massacre.

Any supernatural strength the fanged beasts had was nothing before the volume of night marchers. The soulless monsters were torn limb from limb under the moonless night. When it was done, there wasn't a single drop of crimson staining the grass. All that remained was the shaking form of Ke'ala and the broken mass that had been Keoni.

THE UNKNOWN

BY Michelle Cruz Skinner

Koko Head

I understand what fear is now, although I do not know it myself. It shows in the slight opening of the mouth, the lifting of the upper eyelid, the small crease in the fore-head. There is a sudden intake of breath and the eyes take on a watery quality. Long ago, I did not notice all these changes, the way faces shift in recognition. But, now, after much study, I am aware of how people react upon recognizing me, those like me.

They speak words meant to beg, to bargain. Sometimes we reply, but rarely do they hear, so consumed are they by fear. They think they do or say things that bring us down upon them. Typical of them to ascribe their sudden aware-ness of us to their actions. We simply exist among them.

For most of their lives, they do not notice us. There are those rare times when a feeling passes over one of them, a moment of full lucidity, a slight buzzing of the air—one of them once said to me—and they become aware of one of us. In that moment, something deep, primal, surfaces to identify the experience for them: *kitsune*, *anito*, *mo'o*, *gumiho*, and on and on.

Moments of recognition often happen late at night. To us, it is simply darkness, but to them it's the unknown, the unseeable, a time of exhaustion. Their bodies sag, their con-sciousnesses reach out into the shadows. The people have droned on among themselves and the evening has turned deep. One of them, face red from drink, drags itself unsteadily home. Dark and sky and earth and sea blend into one soundless world. Even the person's footsteps are silent. Its mind thrums, alive with the past. Wasn't it young not so long ago? Did it not swagger and dance, talk and move its way with confidence through such nights? It can hear that bassline, the insistent thump, inhabit that which it used to be. Worlds blend, and in the next moment, the bass morphs into drums and flutes coming from the dark patch of trees bordering the park. The human trips, curses, stumbles, finally flees. Once its people sought out transcendence, but now they flee from that. The sound is the *tanuki*; the drink makes it certain. In the morning, the human shares stories of how it evaded the trickster and arrived home, its pockets still full.

Another walks its dog on a dimly lit street, mind heavy with the understanding of its mortality. On this night more than any other, it knows that it will die, and perhaps sooner than expected. It cannot feel that illness inside it. Yet it cannot stop its mind from reviewing that knowledge that the thing is there, growing, spreading. Its body is a garden, sustaining its spirit but also that thing. It reaches to pet its dog, a comfort, a tether to the life it chooses but which may not be. No matter what the choice, the world, the gods, its body— it's no longer sure what's to blame—will make its own choice. This understanding drops slowly, a rock in water, until it reaches the human's depths, ripples outward. The human cries out. From the bushes a rustling, from the trees a moaning of boughs, as if some creature is settling heavily upon them. The dog growls. The human stifles another cry, rushes home, dragging the dog, saving it from *El Chupacabra*, who would drain it of blood. Only some of the elders believe the story.

I can see that *Chupacabra*, that demon it is afraid of. Depending on who sees, the demon can be a spirit or an ancestor or even a god. I exist among the four spirits and the four perils brought from China, the Japanese *kitsune*, the Korean spirits, all of us brought here by the people we have existed among for generations. We now occupy the space that was long the home of the Hawaiian *mo'o, kaupe*, and others named by humans. In our own way, we commune and sometimes are seen by them, the people we are tied to.

In moments of recognition, I have been seen as *manananggal*, a bloodsucking torso, a fearsome *aswang* that can fly about. They see me desegmented, a proboscis tongue, human and not quite human in appearance, able to blend in and able to take that which makes them human: the material of their bodies, upon which I am said to feast. Entrails, heart, all the organs in their full bloodiness.

On Limasawa Island, a distraught person swung at me over and over with a *pinuti* blade, darkened from the blood of chickens and pigs. Cries of anguish slashed through the air, slashed through the human's body, with each swing of the gently curved blade. Its dying child had seen me first, pointed at the doorway, and in its determination to cling to the child, it had come after me, tearing the blade where it hung from the bamboo post. In its grief, it could finally see me, although I had always been there. Each swing of the knife was accurate and would have pierced one of them. The other people watched from a safe distance, murmured among themselves. When the one bearing the knife finally collapsed to the dirt, they rushed to disarm it, carry it back into the house to its child. To that human I was death. And so I watched, with it and the others, the last moments of the child. I have seen death over and over and over.

To my seafarers, I was often *Sumanga*, the spirit who resided within the timber and guarded their vessels. I have witnessed some dive and never surface, and others lost in the lashing waves of a storm or pierced with blades and arrows.

In those days, they spoke to me, even if I did not speak back, even if they could not see me. I watched them dance, enter their trance states, and speak to me as a spirit, an ancestor, a god. We rarely replied, but those people did not expect replies. Together, we resided with our people on the ocean for generations, fishing, traveling from island to island, abiding each other's existence.

I have dwelled among those in the ocean and on land in Limasawa, Bohol, Panay, the Sibuyan Sea, the places that have changed their names but remained over time. Full-grown people, fishers, hunters, *babaylan*, have recoiled in fear of me. In Bohol, an old one wielded a *barong* against me, almost heavier than it was. In Mactan, the *kampilan* sword, which the person said was used to fell Magellan.

Those weapons, well-honed, used for years to cut rice and banana stalks, slit the throats of chickens and pigs, slicing the air uselessly. I am death, a *manananggal*, an *engkanto*. They see in me what they fear and do not understand. Over the years, they have forgotten how to speak to me.

Only the *babaylan* still try. They enlist their spirit guides—their *abyan*—drink their prepared herbs, drink liquor, anything to enter that state of awareness beyond their shells, their bodies. Often the *babaylan* ask of me: a healing, a rich harvest, protection for their animals, nets brimming with fish, fierceness in battle, the bestowal of a blessing. Like most people, they believe we give favor to them, control their fates, visit evil upon them. Few understand we do none of that.

"Oh great one, please give us," begin most sentences. "Please forgive us," is another. "Tell us what to do to earn your favor." Rarely do they listen.

"Who are you?" asked one of the *babaylan*. It was young then, its long dark hair pulled into a braid down its back. The older *babaylan* had left us after making the customary chants and requests. I, as usual, had promised nothing. In the darkness, it was just me and this young one, who had continued staring into the darkness beyond the fire. Usually, I, we, did not get asked such questions. They simply ascribed to us the stories they wished.

"Who are you?" the young one persisted.

"I am myself."

It seemed to still be listening, even after I replied. Seated, it swayed slightly and stifled a yawn. The transcendent state tires them. "You are . . ." it began. "I cannot really see what you are. You are like a shadow blurred." The young one reached a hand out, palm toward me, and moved it in a circular motion, as if wiping, blurring the air before it. "I see you and I don't see you." It yawned again, larger this time, drew a covering around its shoulders. "I must go now," it said. And it put out the fire, went inside to sleep on its mat.

The next time it spoke to me, it called me itself. The older *babaylan* had gone to sleep. The younger one started the fire and sat for hours until entering the trance. When it noticed my presence, its eyes widened in spite of exhaustion. The mouth also widened, in what I had come to recognize in them as delight.

First, it followed the ancient ways, welcoming me and sharing coconut water, coconut liquor, fruits and fish laid on a banana leaf. Its sharing harkened back to the old seafarers, who had always set aside fish for me, although I could not partake.

The young one did not rush. It told stories of those who had recovered from sickness, of those who had died, of the large catch days ago. "But I know these are not your doing," it said. "I do not know whose doing it is. Perhaps gods I cannot see, perhaps ancestors, or maybe our own." I saw its hair move in the breeze coming from the ocean. They grew cold in the dark and used their hair for warmth along with their coverings.

"What is your purpose?" it asked me.

"I have none."

"Does that not bother you? A purposeless existence?" It peered at me above the flames of the fire.

"I am not bothered by anything."

"Why do the others not speak?" It saw the two hovering with me.

"You addressed *me*."

"You do not speak unless addressed?"

"We do not speak if we have nothing to say."

It paused, tilted its head, closed its eyes. "You're not really speaking," it finally said. "You're buzzing." Its hands went to its ears. "Here. But I understand what you're saying or thinking. Your reply." It opened its eyes. "I think yours would be a . . . difficult existence."

I did not reply.

"Difficult for one of us," it continued. "We are unlike you. Our lives are inextricable from our feelings. You have seen that, yes?"

"I do not understand it."

Its eyes began to close. Communing was again tiring it. "You do not give to us . . ." it began to slip forward toward the fire, but caught itself, opened its eyes wide, ". . . or take from us. I understand that." It yawned and rose to move inside, to its sleeping mat. I followed. "What," it murmured as it lay down, pulled the cloth over itself, "have you learned about us?"

I watched it sleep, the breath gently rustling the cloth pulled close to its nose. This one had many questions. Rarely do we get such questions. It was too late to answer, but I stayed nearby. I stayed near as it prepared the drinks for healing fevers, the salves for wounds and rashes, the teas for pain. I do not understand what they call time. I know only that they arrive and depart, they change in size, move differently, and sometimes understand we are part of their world. This one grew to become one of the older ones.

I stayed near as it took over from the older *babaylan*, who was lowered into the ground. Some evenings it would talk to that old *babaylan*'s spirit. I saw that spirit, different from us, seemingly unaware of our existence. It communed only with the new *babaylan*, the protégé.

"I have learned you are better than most at seeing and listening to what is around you," I told it one night when it was in a trance. Its mouth widened in delight.

I stayed near as it took a partner, one of those who fished, as it tended the garden of food and healing herbs, as it improved upon teas and herbs and salves. I watched the partner bring home fish, salting and drying large batches. I watched as the garden grew, the plants strong.

"I have learned you rely on each other and must look ahead."

It looked at me with the expression I had come to associate with its questions. "Did we create you? Did we will you into being? Or have you always existed?"

"I do not know. I only know my existence, the existence of others like me."

The *babaylan* and its partner, the one who fished, never

had children. They trained a new *babaylan*, who came to live with them as a child, chosen by the community. The younger *babaylan* only saw me once and turned away. So it never looked again. "She's afraid of you," the old one said. "A pity."

They took in yet another child whose parents had died. This one also learned the ways of the *babaylan*. When it saw me, it did not turn away. "You may speak to it," the older one instructed, "when you are in your trance. But it may choose not to reply to you."

"Does it reply to you?" the youngest *babaylan* asked.

"Sometimes."

The one who fished grew old and so did its partner, the *babaylan*. The two younger ones cared for them. The one who had turned from me cleaned the house and cooked the food. It bartered the fish and food plants for the things they did not make themselves: mats, pots, more food. It took a partner and bore children. It left the path of the *babaylan* but remained loyal to the old ones. The youngest made the healing drinks and salves for the community. It visited the homes of the sick, learned the chants, spoke to me at night over the fire. It was now the young *babaylan*.

I saw the old *babaylan* grieve for its partner, who left one morning on a boat and never returned. The seas had not been rougher than usual, the night no darker. For a time, I do not know how long, I watched the horizon with the old *babaylan* early in the morning, late at night, waiting for the sail. "I understand," I told it as we waited together, "there is something in your people that does not let go. It is . . . beyond your existence, a tie to something beyond yourselves."

"Like my tie to you, and yours to me." It kept its eyes on the horizon as dawn broke. "It is our hope."

I stayed near as the old *babaylan* grew weaker, although

its back was still straight, and it still helped the young one make medicines for the people. One day, it lay down, as was the custom of the humans. They spoke of "heat," which tired them. It called to me. "I think I will be leaving soon. Perhaps today." It closed its eyes. For three days, it was between waking and sleeping and leaving. I had seen death before, but I had never stayed to watch the process. The body at times grew slack, almost empty, and then at other times was still fleshy, still filled with air, taking in air. It spoke to me, on and off, and the one who took care of the house peered fearfully at the corner where the old one looked when speaking to me.

And then the old one was gone. I watched the spirit leave its body, although the spirit did not notice me. It rose from the body and left the house, and I did not follow. Instead, I stayed and watched as they prepared it for the ground, the one who had spoken to me.

Others have spoken to me since. But no one has been like that old one. Only a few have understood me as I am: formless, attached to my people for eternity. I do not know why. Perhaps they *did* create us. Perhaps out of their questions and emotions, those things we do not understand, we were called into being. They sense us and continue to make us into what they will, a way to make sense of their own existence.

We do not question. We do not feel. We watch. We exist. Our people have new beliefs, a new god, something they call "saints." When they notice us, they still ask for healing, a better life, forgiveness. We travel with them where they go.

And so I am here, in new islands among others who have followed their people. Here the people also complain of "heat." Here the plants are similar.

Their activities now are different from those before. I have followed some into buildings, some with many, many rooms, which they clean again and again. They say the rooms are cool. When they step outside into the heat to arrange the outdoor seats, they sometimes look out at the ocean and the people below, who are unlike them and stay only briefly. Some labor among many rooms where those who are ill are cared for by healers, including my people. Some teach the younger ones and others sit on their own in small rooms, look at large screens for hours. I have been with those whose labor takes them outdoors, where they attend to the plants or create the buildings in which they live or labor. Sometimes one will pause while planting. Or they will pause after putting in the large glass, look through it to the outdoors and at the mountains. They have new names for these places: Koko Head, Diamond Head, the Pali.

Sometimes they gather by the ocean under the trees to eat and talk. Some of my people still get in boats to fish or to race each other. They sometimes travel upon the ocean in groups but usually return by nightfall. They venture into the depths of the islands. They congregate. Here I have heard new chants and encountered new spirits. They are much like me.

I continue to watch my people and perhaps that is my role: to witness. That old one has led me to wonder. I have shared my wonderings with the others, who are indifferent, as I once was. I wonder if another one will arrive like that one *babaylan*, will ask questions. I wonder if that is my purpose: to exist alongside one person for a time, for us to witness each other's existence.

ABOUT THE CONTRIBUTORS

Paulette Claus

ALAN BRENNERT is the author of the best-selling historical novels *Moloka'i* and *Honolulu*. *Moloka'i* was a 2012 "One Book, One San Diego" selection and *Honolulu* was named one of the best novels of 2009 by the *Washington Post*. His work on the television series *L.A. Law* earned him an Emmy Award in 1991 and his short story "Ma Qui" was honored with a Nebula Award in 1992.

KIANA DAVENPORT is descended from a full-blooded Native Hawaiian mother and a Caucasian father from Talladega, Alabama. She is the author of the internationally best-selling novels *The Power Eaters, Shark Dialogues, Song of the Exile, House of Many Gods, The Spy Lover*, and most recently *The Soul Ajar*. *Shark Dialogues* and its sequel, *Snows of Mauna Kea*, have both been optioned for film or TV series by ABC.

TOM GAMMARINO is author of the novels *King of the Worlds* and *Big in Japan*, and the novella *Jellyfish Dreams*. Shorter works have appeared in *American Short Fiction*, the *Writer, Entropy*, the *New York Review of Science Fiction*, the *Tahoma Literary Review*, the *New York Tyrant, Bamboo Ridge*, the *Hawai'i Pacific Review*, and the *Hawai'i Review*, among others. Originally from Philadelphia, Gammarino lives in Kaneohe, Hawaii, with his wife and kids.

Kate Chang

STEPHANIE HAN is the award-winning author of *Swimming in Hong Kong*, editor of the monthly *Woman. Warrior. Writer.* newsletter, contributing editor for the *Hawai'i Review of Books*, and founder of drstephaniehan.com—an online platform for women's writing workshops. She lives on Oahu, home of her family since 1904, and is at work on a memoir.

SCOTT KIKKAWA is the author of *Kona Winds* and *Red Dirt*, noir detective novels set in postwar Honolulu. He is a columnist and an associate editor for the *Hawai'i Review of Books*. Currently a federal law enforcement officer, the New York University alumnus lives with his family in Honolulu. *Char Siu* is his third full-length novel featuring Francis "Sheik" Yoshikawa.

B.A. KOBAYASHI is just another hapa haole from Manoa trying to stand out. He's currently studying creative writing at the University of Iowa. In his off time, he likes to take care of his bonsai tree and contemplate the world's end.

CHRIS MCKINNEY is a Korean, Japanese, Scottish American writer born in Honolulu. He is the author of the Water City Trilogy. Book one was named a Best Mystery of 2021 by *Publishers Weekly* and a Best Speculative Mystery of 2021 by *CrimeReads*. He has written six other novels: *The Tattoo, The Queen of Tears, Bolohead Row, Mililani Mauka, Boi No Good,* and *Yakudoshi: Age of Calamity*. McKinney currently resides in Honolulu with his wife and two daughters.

MORGAN MIRYUNG MCKINNEY is a nineteen-year-old writer from Honolulu. She is majoring in creative writing at Bryn Mawr College in Pennsylvania and hopes to publish her first novel soon.

CHRISTY PASSION is a Native Hawaiian poet and the author of *Still Out of Place*. The recipient of awards from the Academy of American Poets and the Hawai'i Literary Arts Council, she is a critical care nurse in Honolulu, where she lives.

MINDY EUN SOO PENNYBACKER is a surfing columnist at the *Honolulu Star-Advertiser*, and author of *Surfing Sisterhood Hawai'i: Wahine Reclaiming the Waves* and *Do One Green Thing: Saving the Earth Through Simple, Everyday Choices*. Her stories and articles have appeared in the *Atlantic*, the *New York Times*, the *Wall Street Journal*, the *Nation, Sierra Magazine*, the *Surfer's Journal, Stanford Magazine, Self, Martha Stewart's Whole Living, Fiction Magazine*, and elsewhere.

Craig T. Kojima

MICHELLE CRUZ SKINNER is the author of the short story collections *In the Company of Strangers, Balikbayan,* and *Mango Seasons,* which was nominated for the 1996 Philippine National Book Award. She was born in Manila and raised primarily in Olongapo, Philippines. She lives in Hawaii with her husband and two children and teaches at the Punahou School.

LONO WAIWAIʻOLE was born in San Francisco and spent his childhood moving up and down the West Coast, attending fifteen different schools before graduating from high school in Portland, Oregon. Waiwaiʻole is half Hawaiian, a quarter Italian, and a quarter something his family refers to as Pennsylvania Dutch. His debut novel, *Wiley's Lament,* was a finalist for an Oregon Book Award and an Anthony Award.

DON WALLACE is the editor of the *Hawaiʻi Review of Books.* He has won the Loretta Petrie Award for outstanding service to Hawaiian literature and a Michener Award from the Copernicus Society. He has published in *Harper's, Bamboo Ridge,* the *Surfer's Journal,* the *Wall Street Journal,* the *New York Times, Hana Hou!,* and elsewhere. The author of *The French House, One Great Game,* and *Hot Water,* he was born and raised in Long Beach, California.

Also available from the Akashic Noir Series

LOS ANGELES NOIR
edited by Denise Hamilton
318 pages, trade paperback original, $16.95

BRAND-NEW STORIES BY: Michael Connelly, Janet Fitch, Susan Straight, Héctor Tobar, Patt Morrison, Emory Holmes II, Robert Ferrigno, Gary Phillips, Christopher Rice, Naomi Hirahara, Jim Pascoe, Neal Pollack, Scott Phillips, Diana Wagman, Lienna Silver, Brian Ascalon Roley, and Denise Hamilton.

> A *Los Angeles Times* bestseller, SCIBA bestseller, and
> SCIBA Award winner; includes Edgar Award–winning
> story "The Golden Gopher" by Susan Straight

"Noir lives, and will go on living, as this fine . . . anthology proves."   —*Los Angeles Times*

SAN FRANCISCO NOIR
edited by Peter Maravelis
272 pages, trade paperback original, $18.95

BRAND-NEW STORIES BY: Barry Gifford, Robert Mailer Anderson, Michelle Tea, Peter Plate, Kate Braverman, Domenic Stansberry, David Corbett, Eddie Muller, Alejandro Murguía, Sin Soracco, Alvin Lu, Jon Longhi, Will Christopher Baer, Jim Nisbet, and David Henry Sterry.

"An entertaining anthology of overheated short stories by local writers . . . Here the city becomes the central character, the strongest on the page."   —*San Francisco Chronicle*

SAN DIEGO NOIR
edited by Maryelizabeth Hart
288 pages, trade paperback original, $15.95

BRAND-NEW STORIES BY: T. Jefferson Parker, Don Winslow, Luis Alberto Urrea, Gar Anthony Haywood, Gabriel R. Barillas, Maria Lima, Debra Ginsberg, Diane Clark & Astrid Bear, Ken Kuhlken, Lisa Brackmann, Cameron Pierce Hughes, Morgan Hunt, Jeffrey J. Mariotte, Martha C. Lawrence, and Taffy Cannon.

> Selected by *San Diego Union-Tribune* as one of the five best books
> of 2011, by *January Magazine* as one of the best crime fiction
> books of 2011, and by *Zoom Street Magazine* as the best anthology
> of the year.

"When it's done right, noir is a darkly delicious thrill: smart, sharp-tongued, surprising. The knife goes in at the end with a twist. *San Diego Noir*, a new fifteen-story collection by some of the region's best writers, has all that going for it, and the steady supply of hometown references makes it even more fun."   —*San Diego Union-Tribune*

OAKLAND NOIR
edited by Eddie Muller and Jerry Thompson
272 pages, trade paperback original, $19.95

BRAND-NEW STORIES BY: Nick Petrulakis, Kim Addonizio, Keenan Norris, Keri Miki-Lani Schroeder, Katie Gilmartin, Dorothy Lazard, Harry Louis Williams II, Carolyn Alexander, Phil Canalin, Judy Juanita, Jamie DeWolf, Nayomi Munaweera, Mahmud Rahman, Tom McElravey, Joe Loya, and Eddie Muller.

"Wonderfully, in Akashic's *Oakland Noir*, the stereotypes about the city suffer the fate of your average noir character — they die brutally. Kudos to the editors, Jerry Thompson and Eddie Muller, for getting Oakland right." —*San Francisco Chronicle*

SEATTLE NOIR
edited by Curt Colbert
276 pages, trade paperback original, $19.95

BRAND-NEW STORIES BY: G.M. Ford, Skye Moody, R. Barri Flowers, Thomas P. Hopp, Patricia Harrington, Bharti Kirchner, Kathleen Alcalá, Simon Wood, Brian Thornton, Lou Kemp, Curt Colbert, Robert Lopresti, Paul S. Piper, and Stephan Magcosta.

"The protagonists of *Seattle Noir* are all running scared in Seattle. But beyond that, there are as many layers of class and race as there are stories in the collection." —*Seattle Times*

PORTLAND NOIR
edited by Kevin Sampsell
280 pages, trade paperback original, $15.95

BRAND-NEW STORIES BY: Gigi Little, Justin Hocking, Chris A. Bolton, Jess Walter, Monica Drake, Jamie S. Rich & Joëlle Jones, Dan DeWeese, Zoe Trope, Luciana Lopez, Karen Karbo, Bill Cameron, Ariel Gore, Floyd Skloot, Megan Kruse, Kimberly Warner-Cohen, and Jonathan Selwood.

"The home of Chuck Palahniuk, Powell's City of Books—and the place with more strip clubs per capita than any other city in America—gets its due in this splendid entry in Akashic's noir series . . . The sixteen stories in this anthology demonstrate that a little rain is never a deterrent to murder." —*Publishers Weekly*